Santos' pulse drummed furiously and he panted for air. Good Lord but he wanted to take her, right here, on the counter, on the floor, wherever he could. But it wouldn't be right. "We must stop. This isn't the time, or the place."

"It is. It is." Abigail's hands moved restlessly over his body, leaving a lava-like trail of need.

"No, *minha querida*." He caught her hands, clamped them at her sides, and waited. The hectic pace of his blood cooled agonizingly slowly. Abigail's breathing steadied, and her tense muscles gradually relaxed. He loosened his grip. He couldn't see much in the dim light sneaking in the narrow window, but he thought he might have bruised her alabaster skin.

"I hurt you." He skimmed a fingertip delicately along her inner thigh. "I'm sorry."

"I won't break." An oddly triumphant note in her voice drew his eyes to her face. She slouched languorously against the wall of the hut, her dress about her waist, her torso and breasts bared to his gaze. "I don't want you to treat me gently. You make me feel fierce, wild, uncontrolled." She licked her lips, swollen from his kisses. "I like it."

No Life But This

Brenda Margriet

NO LIFE BUT THIS

This edition published November 2016.
Copyright © 2016 Brenda Margriet Clotildes
Cover Art by **Steven Cote**
Editing services provided by Story Perfect Editing

ISBN 978-0-9950008-7-2

**With thanks to the poem
"High Flight"
by John Gillespie Magee, Jr.**

DEDICATION

To my in-laws –
for welcoming me into your family,
and introducing me to your Azorean heritage,
including the deliciousness of
sopa verde, couve, chouriço, bacalhau, and *massa.*

DEPARTURE

Her fingers bumped gently across the globe. The surface was irregular, as if it truly was a miniature world—Everest shrunk to the height of a fingernail, the waves of the oceans smoothed to an infinitesimal roughness. Its high gloss finish glared where the light from the floor lamp struck it.

"Abigail?" Martin's shoes clicked briskly across the hardwood floor. "Your guests are wondering where you are."

She kept her gaze on the globe. Guests? It was her mother's funeral, for God's sake, not a party. She wondered vaguely who had thought to put a globe in the serenity room of a funeral parlour.

"We're already behind schedule." His voice was firm, no-nonsense. Usually his confident control made her feel safe. Today, it grated down her spine like claws on a granite cliff. "It's time you took your seat."

She gripped the globe with the tips of her fingers and gave it a whirl. She couldn't blame her dizziness on the blurring world before her. The last few days she'd been lightheaded, disconnected, out of touch. Not that anyone would have noticed. She'd been careful to act her normal sedate, organized, earnest self.

But inside she was screaming. Screaming so hard she couldn't hear herself think.

"Abigail." Impatience coloured Martin's voice.

She turned her head. He stood at her shoulder, his well-cut, dark grey suit masking a desk-job belly, appropriately sober tie, his thinning blond hair brushed straight back from a high forehead.

"In a minute. I need another minute." What a lie. She needed more than a minute. She needed…she wasn't sure. But she knew she had to figure it out. And soon.

"I've always wanted to travel. Just once, somewhere exotic, unusual." She swallowed a sob, guilt and grief rolling together. "But I couldn't leave Mom. She hated being alone." It had been more than a simple preference. It had been an illness, one her mother had struggled with for years.

Abigail closed her eyes and stopped the globe with a finger. Squinting through her lashes, she was disappointed to see her finger well below the tip of Greenland, lost in the nothingness of the Atlantic. She spun the globe again.

"Tobias is out there alone. He needs you."

She hunched her shoulders, the stiff taffeta collar of her black dress scratching her neck. Martin knew her weakness. She'd do anything for her younger brother.

"Tell him I'm coming." The coloured sphere revolved on its tilted axis, too fast for her eyes to follow. "In one minute."

"Fine." Martin's disapproving huff fanned her cheek. "One minute, Abigail, and that's all." His footsteps faded away.

The globe circled, slower and slower. She closed her eyes once more, held out her finger. Taking a deep breath, she pushed forward, and stopped it. When she opened her eyes, her shoulders slumped in despair. Again she'd stopped the spin in the middle of the Atlantic. She'd been looking for a sign, and she had it. She was going nowhere.

Tiny printing on the shiny surface caught her eye and she leaned forward. There, right next to her neatly rounded fingernail with its modest clear coat of polish, was the word "Azores" surrounded by small black blobs.

She paused, considering the nine tiny specs in the vast blueness, then straightened her shoulders and headed for the door.

There'd be time to think in the weeks ahead. Too much time. Right now, she had to go to her mother's funeral.

ARRIVAL

Santos Carregado pulled the twelve-passenger van into the taxi loading zone and set the parking brake. Grabbing the cardboard sign and crumpled sheets of paper his sister had testily thrust into his hand before he'd rushed out the door, he strode into Arrivals. A scattering of people milled about, no one going anywhere fast. To his right the building stretched, long and narrow, toward the Departure area. Muted sunshine fell through the glass ceiling two stories above. A sparrow, seemingly at home in the echoing space, swooped and swept, landing on a precarious edge along the outer wall. Santos took a seat on a log hollowed out into a bench.

He'd barely begun reviewing the list of names he held when a young woman interrupted him with a cheerful greeting.

"*Bom dia*," said Jacinta Fabre. She joined him on the bench, stretching her legs out, ankles crossed. "Picking up new tourists?"

"*Bom dia*, Jacinta. *Sim*." He smiled. "Lina booked you for a couple of days with us, right?"

She nodded in reply. Sturdy and athletic, Jacinta was one of the expert guides Santos contracted to help with his tour activities.

"What about you?" Santos asked. "What are you doing here?"

"My brother is on the Toronto flight." She rubbed her hands together, as if the anticipation was too much to allow her to sit still. "He's bringing his fiancée home to meet the family."

"I didn't know Louis was engaged." He was surprised his mother hadn't mentioned it. Usually she never hesitated to point out that sort of news. And sigh heavily over her own lack of daughter-in-law. "Your parents must be thrilled."

Jacinta laughed, a single dimple flashing. "Not exactly." She leaned forward and whispered in mock despair, "She's not Portuguese."

"Ah, I see." And he did see. Family, heritage, community—it was an important part of Azorean culture. "Catholic?"

"As far as I know. That's the only thing that's resigned them to the engagement." Jacinta's face glowed with slightly wicked excitement. "I can't wait to meet her. We've Skyped, but it's not the same."

"I'm sure it will all work out for the best." He felt a tug of sympathy for Louis. The next few days were not going to be comfortable. Thank God it wasn't his problem.

A motley collection of passengers started straggling through the set of doors leading from the baggage claim carousels.

"There they are." Jacinta jumped to her feet. Santos saw Louis, accompanied by a young woman with curly golden hair near the front of the crowd. "See you in a couple days." She raced off to greet them.

The trickle of people thickened to a flow. A young man wearing shorts, hiking sandals and carrying a large backpack

11

with a multitude of straps strode out. A family of four followed, the father dragging a baggage trolley piled impossibly high with suitcases, a child's car seat and a stroller, the mother carrying her red-eyed, weeping son and holding the hand of a little girl who skipped along gaily. Santos rose and moved toward the stream. He held the cardboard sign, green with yellow letters spelling out Ilha Verde Aventuras, at chest height, and waited. Before long, a couple approached, hesitant smiles on their faces.

"Mr. and Mrs. Thornton?" he said. They nodded. "Santos Carregado. It's a pleasure to meet you."

The Thorntons were robust and healthy-looking, in their mid-forties, with the air of seasoned travellers. Each carried a small shoulder bag and dragged a compact wheeled suitcase. First appearances indicated the Thorntons were the type of clients he liked best—organized, efficient and competent.

"It's lovely to be here." Tricia Thornton was petite, with close-cropped honey blond hair. "We've been looking forward to this trip for months."

"I'll do my best to make sure the wait was worth it." Santos looked over her head, scanning the crowd. Where was Abigail Garsson? "I'm expecting one other person from your flight, and then six more on another flight that should have landed directly after yours."

"No worries." Richard Thornton scrubbed his fingers through thick dark hair going grey at the temples. "Do you mind if we wait outside? We'd love some fresh island air."

"Of course." Santos pointed. "If you head out those doors, you'll see the Ilha Verde Aventuras van right there."

The couple wandered off, and Santos turned back to the parade of people, just as a young woman backed her way through the doors.

She wore a long flowered skirt and a white t-shirt, with a

sweater tied about her waist. A floppy straw hat hid her face as she struggled to pull an enormous wheeled suitcase. A small backpack with zippers and pockets and flaps and ties fell off her shoulder into the crook of her elbow, and the suitcase overbalanced, thudding to the ground. She crouched down to retrieve the handle and dropped the backpack.

Santos sighed. If this was Abigail Garsson, his week just got more complicated. Inexperience he didn't mind. Ineptness was always trouble.

He strode toward her, tucking the sign and papers under his arm. "Ms. Garsson?" he said, half-hoping she'd deny the name.

She straightened and peeped up at him from under the limp brim of her ridiculous hat. Wide eyes, the same light blue as the sweater knotted around her narrow waist, stared out at him from a pale, pointed face.

"Abigail Garsson?" he repeated.

She blinked and the tip of her tongue ran along her lower lip. She nodded.

"I'm Santos Carregado, from Ilha Verde Aventuras. Can I get that for you?"

Without waiting for an answer, he took the handle. His fingers brushed hers and she jerked away. He smiled, hoping to reassure her, but she flushed and stepped back, reaching into her pocket and dragging out an asthma inhaler. Her cheeks hollowed out as she sucked the medication into her lungs.

He smothered another sigh. Unlike the Thorntons, this woman looked lost, bewildered and muddled. If she couldn't get out of the airport without help, how was she going to handle the adventures during the next week?

****

The German father and son, married British couple, and Dutch sisters arrived shortly after, as expected. The sisters had almost twice the amount of luggage as everyone else. Santos grinned as he carefully wedged the last suitcase into the back of the van, forgiving them the inconvenience. The pair were sexy, fit and beautiful—his second favourite type of client.

He climbed into the driver's seat and twisted around for a quick check of his passengers. They'd kept to their family groups, with each pair taking up one row of seats, leaving Ms. Garsson the single seat next to him.

"Everyone ready?" he asked, receiving nods and smiles in return. He put the van in gear and negotiated his way out of the airport.

Every tour group had different dynamics, and Santos was always fascinated to see how each trip would develop. Some gelled almost immediately, others never did. As he drove the familiar route, he eavesdropped shamelessly, trying to get a sense of his newest explorers.

English was second nature to him, after having spent five years in Boston in his early twenties, so he had no trouble following the crisp but rolling accent of the British couple and the charming sing-song intonation of the Canadians sitting close behind him. He wasn't as fluent in German and Dutch, but he understood a phrase or two as the teenager did his best to strike up a conversation with the stunning blondes from Holland. His lips twitched at the boy's attempt to sound suave and sophisticated.

She was sitting so quietly he'd almost forgotten she was there. But Abigail Garsson's low, softly accented voice captured his attention. "It's so green. Such a deep, dark green," she said. Her voice was throaty, husky—a sensuous contrast to her pale appearance. She'd taken off her hat, revealing shiny, silky platinum hair too silvery to be called blond.

"It is called 'The Green Island' for a reason," he agreed, glancing over.

She blushed and dipped her chin, the long fall of her hair swinging forward to hide her face. The delicate line of her neck led to fragile collarbones and her breasts barely disturbed the fabric of her t-shirt.

Most of the people who signed up for the adventure tours he provided were outgoing, gregarious and audacious. Ms. Garsson didn't fit that description at all, but she'd paid her money, so it was up to him to make sure she enjoyed her trip. He set himself to putting her at ease. "Is this your first visit to São Miguel?"

"Yes." Her fingers fidgeted with the brim of her hat. "I mean, *sim*."

Pleased at her attempt at Portuguese, he determined to draw her out. "What made you choose the Azores?"

"Chance."

Santos slid a look from the corner of his eye in time to see her smile. The curve of her lips was as dainty as the rest of her, yet it held a glimmer of wickedness, a hint of mischievousness. This time he decided to wait her out—and was rewarded when she continued without prodding.

"I spun a globe. At first I thought I was pointing at nothing, just the middle of the Atlantic. And then I saw nine tiny dots."

He manoeuvred through a roundabout, attention on the traffic yet listening intently.

"I should probably apologize. I knew very little about your islands before then. The more I learned, the more they intrigued me. Things had...changed...in my life, and I needed to get away." He caught the motion of her shrug in his peripheral vision. "So here I am."

"There's no need to apologize, Ms. Garsson. Many people have never heard of the Azores."

"Abigail is fine."

"Call me Santos." He indicated the rest of the passengers with a backward tilt of his head. "When we get to the farm, I will introduce everyone."

She smiled again, that small, provocative smile, and turned to look out the side window.

****

Abigail focused on the scenery flashing by her window. Grassy fields divided by rock walls bordered the wide highway, while modern glass and steel towers clustered closer to the shoreline, boasting of the modernization of the Azorean capital, Ponta Delgada. She tried to lose herself in the view but found it difficult to ignore the confident masculine presence beside her.

She blamed fatigue for her reaction to Santos Carregado. She'd been travelling for eighteen hours straight, crossed a continent and most of an ocean, and her body clock was telling her she should be stretched out in bed. That was why, when she'd looked up from struggling with her stupid suitcase, she'd frozen in shock at the sight of him. That was why her breath had caught in her lungs and her brain had stuttered.

It had nothing to do with inky-black hair falling casually over a clear forehead, she assured herself guiltily. Nothing to do with wide shoulders and muscled forearms, skin bronzed by genetics and sun. With a light accent that was deliciously foreign. Or the air of competence and confidence he exuded.

She'd fallen back on her usual delaying tactic, taking an unnecessary hit from her asthma inhaler in a fumbling attempt to cover her shock. Thank goodness she'd recovered enough to string a few sensible sentences together when he spoke to her just now.

She felt stupid and lonely and completely off-balance. Had she really only left home yesterday morning? In some ways it felt like half an hour ago, and in others it felt like last week. It made her dizzy thinking about it. She pictured Tobias and Martin as she'd last seen them, just before she was swept through airport security. Her brother had waved cheerfully, but she'd seen the worry in his young, not quite yet adult face. Martin had stood, arms crossed, dark suit buttoned up, frowning. He would never cause her to make a fool of herself, never overwhelm her so that she couldn't speak. He was safe and steady and bor—

She cut her off her disloyal thoughts. Martin cared for her, wanted what was best for her. He'd been worried about her, travelling internationally for the very first time. Holding her own against his concern had exhausted her, stretched muscles of independence long unused.

But she had. And now she was here, 7000 kilometres away from all she had ever known.

The expressway circling Ponta Delgada was very impressive, much more modern than she'd been led to expect by her research. Soon Santos exited the wider roadway and began winding his way through twisting streets, walled with houses. The road grew narrower and narrower, until barely a lane. Doorways on either side opened directly onto the pavement—no lawns, no fences, no sidewalks, even, separated the houses from the traffic. It was fascinating, unfamiliar and so different from her home in Prince George, in Northern British Columbia.

It was exactly what she'd hoped for.

Abigail gripped her hat as Santos squeezed the van through an impossibly tight space between buildings on the left and a parked car on the right. Finally the road widened again, and they were travelling through farmland, black and white cows munching peacefully in steep-sloped fields lined with huge hydrangea bushes, blue, ball-shaped blooms swaying in the breeze.

A few minutes later Santos drove between grey stone walls and parked next to a compact two-story building with whitewashed walls and stone corners.

"Welcome to Quinta Carregado," he announced.

QUINTA CARREGADO

Abigail stepped out onto meticulously raked pea gravel and took a deep breath. The other passengers climbed out the side door, and they gathered in a loose group as Santos began unloading suitcases from the back of the van.

A late middle-aged lady, dressed in a boldly printed blouse and dark blue skirt, and a young woman in jeans and a green t-shirt, stepped out of the farmhouse. "Ah, *Mãe*, Lina," Santos greeted them. "Come meet our new guests." To the group, he said, "My mother, Senhora Serafina Carregado, and my sister, Laudelina."

He introduced the tourists one by one. Abigail tried to keep track, but her head was muzzy. With cloudy detachment she noted two stunning blondes, and one young man who reminded her of Tobias. A bolt of homesickness jolted through her.

Santos' sister spread her arms wide. "For the next few days, our home is your home." Her accent was thicker than Santos', but easy enough to follow. "If there is anything you need, please, ask. Activities will start tomorrow morning, so today you are free to do as you wish. Get settled in your rooms, perhaps have a short rest." She included everyone in her smile. "From our farm, it is easy to walk to the village, where you'll find small but excellent shops and restaurants. For now, if you will follow me..." She stepped off the low stone porch and headed around the corner of the farmhouse. Senhora Corregado nodded and smiled and disappeared inside.

Abigail crunched across the gravel to the back of the van and regarded her enormous suitcase with loathing.

"Would you like help with your luggage?" Santos' voice came from behind her left shoulder.

Flustered once again by his nearness, her skin heated and she blurted the first thing that came to mind. "This is my first international trip. I may have over packed. The troubles I had, dragging this stupid thing between gates, through customs..."

"Let me get it for you." Amusement shaded his tone.

He stepped past, his shoulder brushing hers, and all the hairs on her arm stood up. Instead of dragging the case by its strap, he lifted it easily by the handle, corded muscles in his forearm flexing.

"Come with me." The short sleeve of his shirt rode up and the edge of a tattoo circling his bicep showed briefly.

She closed her eyes, gathering her composure, then followed him to the back of the farmhouse.

"Oh." She stopped short as they rounded the corner. "It's perfect," she breathed.

A long, low building of dark stone crazily patterned with whitewashed mortar waited quietly in the sunshine. Six dark green doors, paired with white framed windows, broke up the facade, and hydrangea bushes bloomed busily all along the facade. Dull orange tiles, shaped like pipes cut in half length-wise, covered the roof.

"Would you like it more or less if I told you it used to be

the cow barn?" Humour glinted in his eye.

"Really? It's so pretty."

"Carregados—my family—farmed this land for more than two hundred years. Cows, pigs, chickens—they all lived there."

"Why did you decide to stop farming?" she said, so enthralled with the view she forgot to be nervous.

Santos lifted his shoulder in a deprecating gesture. "My father passed away. Neither my sister nor I wanted to be farmers."

"Oh." She felt a small tug of kinship at the knowledge they both knew what it was to lose a parent. "Well, it's lovely."

"Lina has put you in Quarto Violeta." Santos led her down a narrow path to the last door on the right. He swung the dark green panel open and motioned her in. An iron bed, covered in a crisp ivory counterpane and fortified with a multitude of pillows in various shades of purple, stood in the corner. Also tucked into the tiny space was a four-drawer dresser and an armchair upholstered in lavender flowered fabric. The floor was finished with large, square, terracotta tiles and the ceiling with bright white plaster. The wall adjoining the next room was made of rough horizontal timbers, while the exterior walls were the same random pattern on the inside as the outside. Light streamed in through two windows, the one by the door and another over the bed.

Santos slipped by her to place her suitcase next to the dresser. "Each room is unique. Our idea was, if you want to stay in an anonymous hotel, you'll stay in Ponta Delgada. Here, you know you are in the Azores."

"It's exactly what I was looking for." She investigated a small nook at the back of the room and discovered a tiny closet. Beside it a door led to a minuscule bathroom with a sink, toilet, and shower head. The entire room was tiled, and she realized it *was* the shower.

"Well, I'll leave you to get settled." Santos moved to the door. "If you need anything, just come to the farmhouse. The door right there"—he pointed across the yard—"leads to the dining room where breakfast will be served every day. My mother or sister can be found in the kitchen or office next to it most of the time as well. They will help you with anything you need." Still, he didn't leave, but regarded her steadily with those deep-set eyes.

"Thank you." She twisted her hands together. What was the protocol? Should she tip him? He had carried her bags, but he was the owner, or manager, or whatever. A wave of dizziness swept through her and she wavered.

"Are you all right?" His eyes narrowed but he did not approach her.

"Yes, I'm fine." She smiled, a bit unsteadily. "I'm going to unpack, and rest up for a bit. Thanks for carrying my suitcase."

"You're welcome. *Bom dia,* Abigail."

"*Bom dia*"—she hesitated, then added—"Santos." The name felt alien on her tongue, like the taste of an unfamiliar fruit, delicious and daring.

SETE CIDADES

The next morning, Santos hooked a green utility trailer emblazoned with Ilha Verde Aventuras in yellow to the van and loaded it with bikes and gear. He was just finishing when the blond Dutch sisters, Neve and Sabine Ottman, appeared from behind the house. He watched in appreciation as they strode toward him, elegantly long-legged, athletic yet curvy exactly where he liked curves to be. Despite their similar appearances, they weren't too difficult to tell apart. Neve's sultry grin rarely left her face, while he'd yet to see more than a polite smile from the staid Sabine.

"*Bom dia*, ladies. Are you ready for your mountain bike tour of Sete Cidades?"

Neve's face brightened even more. "We certainly are. Although we hope the route we take won't be too difficult. There are not many big hills in Holland." A dimple popped up at the corner of her mouth.

"I'm sure you will do fine. And the views will more than make up for the work required to reach them."

She grinned flirtatiously at him while Sabine looked on calmly. "Is it true it is an active volcano?" Neve asked.

"It is considered active," said a voice at his elbow. "But

there hasn't been an eruption since the fifteenth century."

He hadn't noticed Abigail approaching. She stood next to him, a tentative half-smile on her lips. Next to the vibrant Dutch women she appeared even more fragile than the day before. Her hair was almost white, her limbs delicate. He wondered again how she would withstand the adrenalin fuelled adventures planned for the week ahead, especially with her asthma.

"That's correct," he said approvingly. "You have done your homework. It has been so long since the last eruption that there is a village, also called Sete Cidades, right inside the crater, set on the shores of two lakes."

Abigail nodded. "Lagoa Verde and Lagoa Azul."

He held back a grin. Her throaty voice was alive, warm and rich, but her accent was atrocious. At least she was trying. "Maybe you should lead the tour," he joked.

She coloured slightly. "I knew so little, I wanted to learn as much as I could before I came."

Neve put a hand on his arm and drew his attention away with another question about the day ahead, and Santos forgot all about Abigail in the scramble of herding nine tourists into the van.

As he drove, he stole quick glances in the rear view mirror, gauging the mood. Their first breakfast together had helped break the ice, and the group was slowly beginning to gel. He could hear the Canadian couple comparing travel experiences with the husband and wife from England, while the German teenager was still doing his best to sweet-talk Neve and Sabine, his father sitting by with an odd expression on his face, half proud, half put out. Abigail had taken the seat directly behind Santos, and every time he caught a glimpse of her she was gazing raptly out the window, ignoring the chattering going on around her.

After half an hour on a winding, narrow road that climbed higher and higher, he pulled into a small parking lot. Everyone piled out, the group growing silent as they stood on the edge of a gigantic crater and caught their first glimpses of the two lakes, one blue, one green, far below. A tiny cluster of red-roofed buildings stretched along the far shore.

"Let me tell you the legend of Sete Cidades," Santos said, lifting his voice over the steady breeze. "A king had a beautiful daughter, Antilia. He refused to allow anyone to see her, keeping her safe within his castle. As Antilia grew, she fretted at her confinement, and finally convinced her nurse help her escape. She roamed the hills and valleys happily, careful always to return before her father discovered her absence. One afternoon she came upon a young shepherd boy. He fell in love with the beautiful princess, as she did with him.

"The shepherd boy asked the king for his daughter's hand in marriage. The king refused, flying into a rage. He banished the young man from the castle, and forbid his daughter to ever see him again. Despite her love, she agreed to follow her father's orders. The young couple met secretly one last time, and they cried, cried so many tears that two lakes formed—one blue, for the shepherd boy's eyes were blue, and one green, for the princess's eyes were green."

"How romantic," Tricia Thornton sighed, leaning her head against her husband's shoulder. There were nods and smiles of agreement.

"We'll spend a few more minutes here before we head down to the lakes," Santos said, "so feel free to explore on your own for a bit."

The group scattered, except for Abigail, still staring out over the wide crater. He approached her, ready to cajole her into joining the others.

Her quiet voice barely carried through the breeze sweeping over the ridge. "It's not romantic," she said. "It's awful."

He didn't think she'd meant anyone to hear, but he couldn't help responding. "Didn't you like the story?" Most tourists thought it a lovely fable.

She hunched her shoulders and shot him an embarrassed glance. "I shouldn't have said anything."

"I agree, it is a sad story," he said calmly, as if speaking to a wary kitten, "but do you really think it is terrible?"

She scuffed the dirt with her toe, then burst out, "How could the king be so cruel? First he traps his daughter in the castle, when all she ever wanted to do was live a little. And then when she finds happiness, he forces her to reject her lover."

Santos raised an eyebrow at her passion. "Perhaps she was too young to know what was best. Maybe her father saved her from a life of poverty and toil. The story doesn't tell us what happened after the princess and the shepherd were separated."

"No one has the right to tell anyone else how they should live their life, to force their will on another. Especially a daughter, someone they are supposed to love and cherish." The tip of her nose was pink and her slight breasts heaved under the light windbreaker she wore. She stepped back. "I'm sorry, that was rude. It's just a story." Another step back. "I'm sorry," she repeated, then turned away and scurried to the van.

He watched her go, unwillingly intrigued by her reaction. Maybe there was more to mousy Miss Abigail than he'd first thought.

****

Abigail sank into her seat, little quivers of anger shuddering through her. She took deep, deliberate breaths and gazed out the window, focusing on nothing. She couldn't believe she'd come unglued over a simple, old-fashioned legend. She really had to get a grip.

At first she'd been enchanted by Santos' story, not only by the words but by the deep, softly accented voice. She could see a slender, dark-haired girl, a muscular, ruggedly dressed boy, walking hand in hand over pastures knee deep in emerald grass and past hedges buttoned in blue hydrangeas. But the ending had spoiled everything. Antilia or whatever her name was should have had the guts to fight for her shepherd boy, not tamely accept her father's decrees.

She snorted at her own hypocrisy. As if she knew anything about stand up to others.

Santos gathered the rest of the group together and ushered them into the van. Why was she always making a fool of herself in front of him? She scrunched down in her seat and avoided making eye contact with anyone.

They pulled back onto the road and began winding down the steep, narrow lane leading into the basin of the crater. Cheerful chatter washed over her, and she tried to shrug off a feeling of loneliness. She was the only one not partnered up with family. That was her own doing, but it was harder than she'd thought it would be, to be completely on her own.

The van slowed to a stop as a lumbering herd of cattle crossed the road. A young boy, maybe thirteen or fourteen, directed the bored, black and white beasts with pokes from a long, thin stick. One of the cows broke away from the drove, huge udder swinging from side to side as she awkwardly trotted back the way they had come. The boy pursued her, forcing her to rejoin the herd.

She sympathized with the cow. She knew exactly what it felt like to be driven single-mindedly in a direction you didn't want to go.

She was twenty-nine years old, and coming to the Azores was the first major decision she'd ever made in her life. Until now, her mother's mental health had dictated everything, from how Abigail exercised and what she ate to what university she attended and what jobs she applied for.

Abigail loved her mother, wanted to please her, make her happy. But the lack of control in her own life had also made her want to scream with resentment.

She shook off her melancholic mood. The past was the past. Living on her own terms was the present.

****

They crossed the narrow strip of land between the two lakes and pulled to a stop in a small parking lot along the edge of Lagoa Azul. Santos unloaded bikes and helmets from the trailer, and she stepped forward diffidently to take hers.

"Here you go." He smiled, lines crinkling attractively at the corner of his eyes. His white t-shirt emphasized the darkness of his skin, wiry, dark hair visible in the V'd neckline.

"Th-thank you," she stuttered, then cursed herself. If she didn't get a grip, he was going to think she was attracted to him. Well, maybe she was. But it wasn't like she was going to act on it. After all, she had Martin waiting for her at home.

Homesickness tugged at her. Despite Martin's disapproval of this entire scheme, she wished he was here. He had been a haven for her during difficult times with her mother, and his steadiness was what had attracted her in the first place. She should really stop wishing he could offer her more than security. Hopefully after this holiday she'd be ready to settle into his life, accept the proposal she was sure he would make. They'd been together two years. It was time for a more permanent commitment.

She pushed her bike away from the group—away from Santos—and leaned it against a wooden post. She'd researched the best gear for mountain biking before she left, and was wearing tight black shorts and a bright pink tank top in stretchy, breathable fabric. The morning was lightly overcast, so she'd added a thin shell jacket, black with pink stripes. Around her waist she'd strapped a zippered pouch with essentials—passport, wallet, tiny camera, inhaler.

She dug the medicine out and sucked in a dose. The air was clear and moist, but her symptoms were almost always triggered by exercise, and she wasn't taking any chances. She waited a few minutes, shifting from foot to foot, took the second dose and tucked the inhaler away.

As everyone began clicking on helmets and checking seat heights, Santos gave a rundown of what the day would hold. "The route is about fourteen kilometres, round trip. The first part is the climb out of the crater, which may be quite a challenge."

He met Abigail's eyes and raised an eyebrow. Was he questioning her ability to keep up? She bristled, but didn't say anything.

"As we climb we'll share the road with local traffic. There are very few pull outs along the way, so if you need a breather please be careful. Once we get to the rim, we'll ride along a trail, and you'll have plenty of chances to take in the view."

He swung one leg over his bike and straddled it, calf muscles flexing. Abigail popped the top on her water bottle and took a quick slug. She really had to control her responses. She'd never been so viscerally attracted to a man before and it was disturbing. More than disturbing. It was disloyal to Martin.

"Everyone ready?" At the chorus of 'yeses', Santos kicked off and headed down the road.

****

Half way to the top of the crater, Santos stopped on the narrow shoulder at the side of the road. He wasn't surprised to see Richard and Tricia Thornton pull up only seconds later. From the beginning, the couple had struck him as knowledgeable, experienced travellers, and both had the lean, toned look of seasoned athletes.

He waved them on. "Keep going, if you're up for it. You can't get lost. Just follow the road to the very top. We'll meet there."

The couple slowed to a stop. "This is quite the climb," Tricia said. "Are you sure everyone can manage?"

"The little blond girl—Abigail?" Richard's voice rose questioningly. "She looked a bit daunted when we passed her."

The three of them glanced back down the road. The hill was so steep the road switched back and forth on itself, and from this vantage point Santos could see the German father and son—Eric and Victor Urbach—with the Dutch sisters not far behind. The British couple and Abigail had yet to round the lowest corner. "I'm going to wait here for everyone, make sure they're doing all right." He smiled confidently. "We won't leave anyone behind."

Richard nodded and the couple started up again. The Urbachs and Neve and Sabine approached, and he called to them to continue on. As they passed, he turned to face down the hill, wondering how long he'd have to wait for the three stragglers.

Not that he minded. It was a gorgeous day, and the view was one of his favourites. They were expected back at the recreational area for a late picnic lunch, but he'd allowed plenty of time. Or rather, Lina had. One of the things he liked best about his business was that the people he met were on holidays, and most weren't overly concerned about timetables. If they were a few minutes late, it was no big deal, and that suited Santos just fine. Lina was the schedule freak in the family, and his slower pace infuriated her. Often he was deliberately late, just to drive her *louca*.

Three bikes made the turn below and climbed slowly toward him. Abigail trailed a few feet behind Cedric and Cordelia Birtwhistle, and all three pumped and puffed their way toward him.

The couple stopped next to him with groans of relief.

"My word." Cordelia Birtwhistle was a short, stocky woman, not plump, but heavily muscular. She and her husband lived on a small farm in Yorkshire, and she'd confided to Santos she'd had to badger her husband into taking a holiday. "This is a climb, isn't it? I'm afraid I'm much more used to tossing bales of hay than pedalling up a mountain."

"We've got big hills in the Dales." Sweat dripped off Cedric's rather prominent nose. "But generally we drive up them."

Santos laughed. Cedric said something else, but Santos didn't catch it. He was too busy watching Abigail.

Gravel shushed as she braked next to him. Her pale skin was flushed with effort. Wisps of hair escaped from her long, sleek ponytail and clung to her neck. Her chest heaved with her laboured breaths, material dark with moisture clinging to the shallow valley between her breasts.

The moment she stopped, she reached for the water bottle clamped to the bike's frame and tilted her head to drink. A sheen of sweat glistened in the hollow of her throat and Santos had the disconcerting urge to lick it off her skin.

"Are you doing okay?" he asked, his voice slightly hoarse. He took a sip of his own water to clear it. "If you are finding the climb too much of a challenge, I can arrange to have someone pick you up here."

She glared at him. "I am *not* waiting here to be rescued." She took another long swallow and wiped her mouth with the back of her wrist. "It's just that I've done all my riding on a stationary bike. And it's not quite the same thing."

Her cheeks were still unnaturally ruddy and her hand trembled as it rested on the handlebars. "The rest of the group is meeting us at the top," he said to Cedric and Cordelia. "Why don't you go on, too. Take your time, there's no hurry. Abigail and I will follow in a minute."

****

With a determined grin from Cordelia and a morose sigh from Cedric, the couple set off, disappearing around yet another bend in the road.

Santos turned back to Abigail. She shook her water bottle with an expression of dismay. He slung off the pack he carried and dug out another bottle.

She accepted with a grateful look. "Thank you."

"You've probably had enough for now. But just in case, there's also a spring at the top where you can refill your own."

"Okay." She hitched her slim rear onto the seat, one foot on the pedal, one on the ground. "I'm ready."

32

"We can take a minute more. Like I said, there's no hurry." He searched for something to distract her until he was certain she was ready to tackle the next part of the climb. "When you said you'd only ridden a stationary bike, were you serious? You've never ridden on a real road?"

She frowned and settled both feet on the ground with a small sigh. "My father taught me to ride on the street in front of our house. But my mother was a little...protective."

"Couldn't your father convince her it was safe?"

Her face blanked. "He died when I was twelve."

"I'm sorry." He felt like a jerk, but how could he have known?

She shrugged. "He was killed in a plane crash. After that, my mom worried more. A lot more. It was simpler to give in. It made her feel better if I stayed in the gym."

"Mothers." He remembered the glow on Abigail's face when she'd seen the converted cow barn, and felt oddly anxious to bring that look back to her face. "Mine is sure I'll catch pneumonia if my feet get cold. Even now she chases me around the house trying to force me to wear slippers." Her eyes brightened and an unexpected sense of shared experiences rippled through him. "What about your asthma? Did she worry more because of that?"

"Oh." She bit her lip with small, white teeth. "Yes, I guess that was part of it." She looked up the now empty road. "Should we get going? I don't want anyone to have to wait too long for me."

"Maybe we should push our bikes for a bit."

Her eyebrows drew together. "That's not necessary. I can make it."

He studied her once more. Her colour was better and her breath no longer rasped in her throat. "All right. You lead."

They set off single file, and Santos found his eyes drawn

to her trim hips, snug in her black shorts. She was the exact opposite of the bold, curvaceous, confident women he normally flirted with, but the way she attacked the hill with grit and determination struck a chord in him. And he was fascinated with her voice, the rasp of it, the way it seeped into his blood.

She raised herself on the pedals for more leverage. Santos swallowed a groan at the tight, wiggly little ass directly in his line of vision. A bike was not the most comfortable place to have an erection. He swung to the outside and pulled up next to her, away from the distraction.

"Are you sure you don't want to walk for a bit?"

"I can do this." She leaned over the handlebars, wobbling slightly with each determined push on the pedals, but kept her balance. "I'm going to do this."

He dropped back again, keeping his eyes scrupulously on the road.

A few moments later she careened to the left, well into the lane of traffic, over corrected, and teetered back to the right. Before he could react, her handlebars caught on the high earthen berm through which the road ran and she stumbled to a stop, almost tumbling to the ground. He braked behind her.

She panted with effort, head bent, chest heaving, and he watched with rising frustration. Stubborn woman. "That's enough." He swung his leg over his seat. "We're walking."

She dismounted slowly and he could see the tremors in the muscles of her thighs. "Damn it," she rasped as she pushed the bike up the hill. "Damn it, I wanted to ride it, ride it all the way."

She was silent except for the hiss of her breath, and defeat dragged at her shoulders, but her eyes were dry. "Get back on," he said abruptly. She looked at him in surprise and he softened his tone. "Get back on, and I'll help you."

She settled back in the saddle and he placed his hand in the small of her back. Moist heat seeped through the thin material of her shirt into his palm. "One, two, three, go." They pushed off together and he could feel her muscles flexing with effort. "That's it, keep going." Her foot bobbled off the pedal but she quickly recovered. He concentrated grimly on pushing her up the hill. The sooner they reached the top, the sooner he could stop touching her, and the sooner he could forget his odd, irritating reaction to this wisp of a woman.

QUINTA CARREGADO - NEXT DAY

Abigail woke to the sound of a rooster crowing.

She stretched under the crisp linen sheets, muscles in her calves and thighs twinging and groaning, and creaked to a sitting position. The ride the day before had been intense, and she'd known she'd feel it in the morning. It would have been worth it, if only she'd managed to conquer the climb on her own.

Instead, she'd had to rely on Santos' goodwill to help her lurch painfully to the top.

Remembered embarrassment heated her cheeks and she crushed the bedsheets in a fist. She'd set out on this trip to prove she could do anything she put her mind to—and had stumbled at the first obstacle. It only strengthened her resolve to meet the challenges still ahead.

At least Santos had had the good grace to leave her alone once they reached the summit. In fact, he barely spoke to her the rest of the day. Not that she expected him to. He was the guide, after all, and had to make sure everyone was having a good time. And he did an excellent job of it, even cajoling a smile from Cedric, who only came on this trip because of his wife. He chatted with the Thorntons about various types of mountain bikes as though he designed them, and was similarly attentive to everyone else. Abigail wished she could be as outgoing, as comfortable with strangers.

The ride around the edge of the crater and back down to the lakes was a snap in comparison to the first part of the trek. After, everyone had been treated to a delicious picnic lunch. The Canadian couple, the Thorntons, invited her to sit with them. They were open and friendly, their shared nationality soothingly familiar, and she'd slowly relaxed.

At the table next to them, Victor sat with Neve and Sabine, the gorgeous Dutch sisters. The young German was about Tobias' age, and he and his father had come on this trip before Victor headed off to university in the fall. It was sweet to watch him flirt with the older women. Neve flirted back with a friendly air, enough to give him faint hope, enough to give him something to brag about to friends back home.

Through the window above her bed, low, misty clouds swirled over the ridges and peaks of the nearby hills. Her research had warned her of the changeable Azorean weather, so she held out hope the sun would put in an appearance later in the day.

She swung her legs to the floor. A few muscles complained from her exertions, but she wasn't too sore. Her gym workouts were paying off.

A quick but hot shower in the tiny bathroom left her loose and limber. She blow-dried her fine hair and tied it back in her usual ponytail. Their itinerary today was a hike into a tiny coastal village that could only be reached on foot, so she pulled on canvas shorts and a light t-shirt, heavy socks and clunky hiking boots. She crossed the small yard and entered the large, bright dining room.

Windows with foot-deep ledges were set in thick walls plastered and painted white and the floor was tiled in uneven, charcoal coloured slabs of stone. A heavy wooden door to Abigail's right swung open and Lina backed out of the kitchen carrying a tray piled high. The tantalizing scent of fresh bread, coffee and pineapple made Abigail's nose twitch.

Lina spotted her. "*Bom dia,*" she called over her shoulder.

"*Bom dia,*" Abigail repeated, doing her best to match the accent.

Lina carefully lowered her load onto the buffet, a long, heavy, battered table snugged up against the far wall. She tucked her glossy deep brown hair, a couple of shades lighter than Santos', behind her ear and smiled politely at Abigail. "You are our first guest today," she continued in English. "Are you—what is it you say?—a morning person?"

Abigail couldn't help but smile back. "I've never minded getting up early. But this is my first big trip. I don't want to waste it sleeping."

"Good for you." Lina gestured at the buffet. "Help yourself. If you need anything, just come to the kitchen." She disappeared through the doorway.

Abigail poured herself a cup of coffee and filled a plate with cheese, fruit and bread. Tables draped with mathematical precision in pristine white cloths with intricate red stitching along the edges were spaced about the room. Choosing a sturdy wooden chair at a table near a window, she spread the soft white cheese on a thick slice of bread. She chewed slowly, appreciatively. The crust was crisp and thick, the bread itself so light it melted on her tongue. The cheese, heavier than yogurt but with a similar sharp tang, was like nothing she'd ever eaten before.

Muted and muffled sounds seeped from the kitchen, and she luxuriated in having the dining room to herself. Being alone was still a novelty. Anna Garsson's paranoia had crept up gradually, beginning with mild panic attacks starting soon after her husband's death. Throughout Abigail's teenage years her worries and fears had grown until a simple trip to the grocery store was no longer possible. She was only completely comfortable when Abigail and Tobias were both in sight.

Abigail sipped her coffee. She was determined to learn from her mother's experiences. She wasn't going to let fear or weakness or timidity hold her back. Yesterday might have been a disappointment, but today held new adventures.

She was ready to meet them all.

****

Santos heard the rumble and clatter of guests in the dining room below and rolled out of bed with a muffled groan. Stumbling to the bathroom down the hall, he showered and shaved before making his way, eyes still half-closed, down the stairs.

Centuries of Carregado feet had worn the wooden treads, and wide depressions dipped deep in the centre of each step. Santos manoeuvred over them without thought, head ducked to avoid the low ceiling, and followed the route he'd taken every morning of his childhood. The life-giving scent of coffee greeted him as he pushed open the kitchen door.

"*Bom dia.*" He dropped a quick kiss on his mother's offered cheek. Serafina was arranging slices of bread in a woven basket lined with a red cloth and he stole a piece before she could whisk it out of his reach.

"This is for our guests," she scolded automatically, without heat. "Your breakfast is over there, as you very well know." She nodded to a small table tucked behind the door to the dining room.

He dropped into his seat and practically inhaled his first cup of coffee, then settled in to demolish the plate of eggs, bacon, fruit, bread and cheese his mother had prepared for him. No matter how many times he insisted he could get his own breakfast—after all, he'd managed every day for almost five years when he'd lived in Boston—she always had it waiting for him by the time he came downstairs. When he'd first returned home it had given him a twinge of guilt, but he'd finally decided to enjoy it. The only way to stop her would be to get up before her, and he wasn't doing that. He'd seen enough dawns as a boy, when he and his father had tended the stock before Santos went off to school.

Lina and Serafina served breakfast with unending food and traditional hospitality. At least Lina did when she was in the common area. In the kitchen her smile faded.

"Are you sure you don't want me along for the hike this morning?" she asked as she placed another soft cheese on a plate. "It's a bit bigger group than usual."

"You know you're needed in the office." It was an old argument. When he'd first broached the idea of a guest house, they'd decided he would handle the outdoor activities and Lina would do the administration, booking new travellers, ordering supplies, making all the arrangements. "You're so good at all that stuff," he added, placating. "And besides, *Mãe* probably needs help with the laundry."

With a disgruntled sniff, Lina headed back to the dining room, shooting him a dirty glance that he ignored with the habit of long practice.

Relaxing in his chair, sipping his second cup of coffee, he watched *Mãe* and Lina whip in and out, loaded trays to the dining room, dirty dishes back to the kitchen. After he left with the guests for the day, they would tidy everything up, Lina would do whatever she did in the tiny office tucked behind the kitchen, and his mother would set the guest rooms to rights.

All in all, it was a smoothly run, efficient operation, and more successful than he had dared hope.

Lina hauled a precariously loaded tray into the kitchen and eased it onto the plank board table in the centre of the room. When the family had finally made the decision to go ahead with the adventure tour/bed and breakfast idea, they had gutted the old kitchen, expanding it and replacing everything with modern appliances and fittings. Everything but the big table now enthroned in the middle of the room. It had been in the family for generations, and none of them could bear to see it discarded. Time moved on, Santos thought, but tradition was to be respected.

"We've got a healthy bunch of appetites this time round. Mom's in heaven, feeding them." Lina wiped her forehead with the back of her hand. "But they're all yours, now."

"I'll head on in, give them the itinerary for today." He drained his mug and placed it in the sink. Soiled plates, cups, cutlery and more spread out over the counter. Thank God they'd installed two dishwashers.

He pushed open the door and stepped into the dining room. His eyes swept over the room, settling almost immediately on Abigail.

She sat with the other Canadians in the seat farthest from the kitchen door. Sun slanting in the window beside her bleached her hair almost white. No, not white. That was too cold a word. The strands held the warm lustre of a golden pearl. She wore a light blue cotton t-shirt with short sleeves, and despite spending most of yesterday outdoors the skin of her arms and neck was still milky pale. Yet it, too, had an underlying glow of health and vitality.

Had she changed so much in one day? The morning

before he hadn't noticed her standing at his elbow until she spoke. Now she drew his attention without even trying.

"Good morning, Santos," Neve called from across the room, waving.

"Good morning." He moved deeper into the room, smiling greetings. "*Bom dia*, everyone."

A chorus of hellos in various accents greeted him. Most of the faces were eager and good-natured, although he noticed Sabine and Cedric appeared more resigned than excited. Maybe he'd ask Lina to set up something a little more sedate for them in a couple of days.

"In about one hour, we'll be heading to Fajã do São Paul. This village is accessible only on foot or by boat. We will be hiking in. Going down will only take us an hour, but be prepared for at least twice that, and probably more, for the return journey. The path is clean and well maintained, although it is very steep, so be sure to wear appropriate foot gear."

"What is so special about this village?" Neve asked. "Other than we have to hike to get there, of course."

"For one thing, it is not on the power grid. The few families there live as if electricity or indoor plumbing do not exist." Neve gave a delicate shudder and a few of the others laughed. "But what makes it truly special is its location, on one of our *fajãs*." He expected blank looks at this statement, yet was only faintly surprised to see Abigail nodding. "You may have noticed that São Miguel doesn't have too many beaches. In most cases, our land rises straight out of the ocean. A *fajã* is a shelf of land, formed by erosion and volcanic activities, that juts out like a ledge at the base of a sea cliff. It is very fertile land, and in some cases it can form a small lagoon. They are one of the unique features of our islands." He checked his watch. "The van will be departing at ten. If everyone could gather in front of the house shortly before, that would be great."

Guests began to wander out of the dining room. Santos needed to finish preparing for the day, yet found himself drifting to Abigail's side.

He'd managed to convince himself his reaction to her while helping her climb the hill in Sete Cidades had simply been plain old male hormones. Lying in bed last night he'd realized it had been more than three months since his last relationship—a short-term adventure with a raven-haired Spanish beauty with lush red lips and an enthusiasm for sex in the open air. The hiatus explained why the sight of Abigail's scrawny little *nádegas* bouncing up and down in front of him had turned him on.

She rose from her chair as he approached. "*Bom dia,* Santos."

His gut tightened at the way her husky voice pronounced his name. Her pale blue eyes smiled at him, her joy in the new day evident in their sparkle. He dragged his gaze away from her face, only to roam lower, over her slender torso, past her hips, down to her slim ankles. Her feet were encased in new-looking hiking boots. "I hope those are broken in," he said gruffly, determined to push aside this improbable fascination with her body. "I still expect you to keep up with the group, even if you get blisters."

Her chin lifted, her lips narrowed. "I'll keep up."

"Like you did yesterday?" He didn't know why he was poking at her. It wasn't like she was the weakest client he'd ever had.

"You're the one who insisted on helping. I didn't ask for it, and I didn't need it. I would have made it on my own." She fisted her hands on her hips and stared him down. "I refuse to be coddled and fussed over. Stay out of my way and quit worrying about me." She pushed past him and strode out the door.

Through the window he saw her stalk past Neve and Sabine and disappear into her room. The sisters were sitting on a bench on the patch of lawn between the main building and the converted barn. Now *there* were two women he could see himself with. Either one suited his tastes perfectly. So why did the thought leave him cold?

"That's a new technique for handling a guest." Lina's mocking voice came from behind his left shoulder.

He sighed and turned to face her. "I only expressed a slight concern that she may hold up the group. It was a valid comment."

She watched him with lifted eyebrows and head tilted to one side. "And what happened yesterday? Doesn't sound like she was pleased with whatever you did."

Irritation rippled through him. "She was the last one to the top of the crater. If I hadn't helped we'd still be waiting for her."

"Really?"

Lina's drawl set his teeth on edge. She might be three years younger, but he'd never been able to put anything by her.

"She has asthma, she looks like a strong wind could blow her off a cliff, and she struggled with the climb. I repeat—valid comment."

"You'll just have to keep your eye on her, won't you?" Lina gathered up the last of the used dishes and headed for the kitchen. She propped the door open with her elbow and fired one last shot before she disappeared. "I'm guessing you won't find that too much of a hardship."

****

Through the years of her mother's mental illness, Abigail had suppressed strong emotions. Raised voices or angry gestures could tip her mother's fragile balance, triggering violent panic attacks. Seeing her gasping for breath, shuddering and trembling, frightened Abigail so much she soon learned to hide her frustration and resentment behind a patient facade.

It was lucky she had the practice, though, because Santos' interfering sniping made her want to slam doors and throw things.

Her room was too small for pacing. She flopped down in the lavender chair and glared at the boots that so offended him. Sure, they were new. But she'd done her best to break them in before leaving home. She wasn't an idiot. Just because she'd never ridden a bike up the side of a volcano or hiked into a remote village didn't mean she wasn't capable.

A little blue light flashing on her tablet drew her scowling attention. She snagged it from the top of the dresser. Quinta Carregado was quaint, but acknowledged modern interconnectivity by offering Wi-Fi in all the rooms. She'd already sent a number of emails home, and now unread replies from Tobias and Martin waited in her inbox. She tapped the screen and opened her brother's message.

Glad you're having a good time. I miss you, but don't let it go to your head. I'll get over it.

She grinned, some of her fury dissipating.
Then she opened Martin's message.

Dear Abigail,

I know I should say that I hope you are enjoying your holiday, but I'm sorry, I can't. From what I read in your emails, I think you, too, have realized that this was a mistake, and if you had listened to my advice, you wouldn't now find yourself in this situation.

She bit the underside of her lip. In her messages, one sent the day she arrived and the other yesterday after the mountain bike trip, she'd tried to hide her homesickness and disappointment, but obviously hadn't managed as well as she had hoped.

We miss you here at the office. I suppose if anything good comes of this experience it will be that we have discovered what a valuable employee you are. I have a few questions about the McIntosh file. Perhaps you could call me so we could discuss it? It would be too difficult to do so via email.

She gaped at the screen. She couldn't count the number of hours she'd put in at the company, and only now they were realizing how good she was at her job? Martin was one of the senior accountants at her firm and while he wasn't technically her boss, it made for some tricky situations. Like this one. No way she was calling him, especially after that comment. She was on vacation, for crying out loud, and besides, whose afternoon? Hers or his? The time difference was seven hours. It would serve him right if she called him in the wee hours of the morning.

I hope you are taking care of yourself. You know I worry because of your delicate health. Are you taking your inhaler as you should? And eating properly? You must keep up your strength. I hope the food is palatable. In those foreign countries...

There was more, but she closed the email, clenching her jaw against the urge to scream. With the restricted life she had lived, the only men she met were through work. She shuddered when she remembered how grateful she'd been when Martin asked her out. At first his protectiveness had been a balm, but she could now admit the novelty had worn off long ago. She was a grown woman, for God's sake. Martin might think he was showing how much he cared, when instead all he'd done was prove he didn't trust her to be a responsible adult.

She was still seething when she climbed into the van as the group set out for Fajã do São Pedro.

FAJÃ DO SÃO PEDRO

The view was dizzying.

Abigail dug her fingers into the gritty top of the rock fence before her and carefully peered over the edge. The cliff dropped off, straight and fierce. For a moment the sensation of falling was so real she could feel herself tumbling, the slap of spiky branches tearing into her skin as she plummeted past trees and shrubs. She shuddered, the rush of adrenalin making her nauseated.

Thank God the first part of the trail ran along the top of the ridge. It would give her some time to prepare for the descent.

Santos swung open a simple gate made of barbed wire strung on twigs and gestured the group forward. He had a smile and a word for everyone. Except Abigail. For her, he reserved a curt nod.

She sailed past with her chin in the air. Between his overbearing, insulting comment about her boots and Martin's condescending email she'd had enough of men for the day. She dug her camera out of her pack, determined to lose herself in this new experience.

The path was narrow and winding, beaten smooth by the

tread of many boots and numerous hooves. She dodged a suspiciously fresh looking pile of manure. More than once during the last couple of days, she'd thrilled at the sight of men—old and not so old–ambling along, riding donkeys laden with immaculately shining metal milk cans hanging almost to the animals' knees. She'd had to remind herself she'd only travelled across the globe, not back in time.

As they trudged along, Santos kept up a running commentary on the abundant plant life and geographical features. The trail only allowed them to travel single file, but the silence was so pervasive that Abigail, once again at the back of the pack, had no trouble hearing. No traffic, no planes, no hum of electric wires. She heard the cheeping of sparrows and the buzz of cicadas. Otherwise, only Santos' deep voice with its hint of an accent—not that she was into accents—drifted to her ears.

The group halted for a short break where the trail began its descent to sea level. The ever-present hydrangea bushes, plump with blue blossoms, and some other plant with long, blade-like leaves and a single large purple flower at the end of a long stem, circled around a landing wide enough for everyone to gather.

As she sipped from her water bottle, Abigail surveyed the route below. The drop wasn't as severe as where they had begun their walk, but it was still steep enough for caution. The path, a greyish brown line, sliced steeply in a wide zig-zag, passed through deep green fields dotted with black and white cows and bisected by low, dark walls, then disappeared behind a rugged bluff. She couldn't see the *fajã* or the village. Azure water tipped with white tumbled silently far, far— far!—below.

"If everyone's ready, we can get going again."

Santos' voice came from close by. She hadn't noticed

49

him approach. He stood next to her, their right shoulders almost touching, as she faced out over the vista and he looked inward to the group. She sidled sideways a bare inch.

He turned his head and watched her with slightly narrowed eyes. "How are you doing?"

Damn it, enough of this. "What?" she snapped. "I'm not holding up the group, am I? I'm right here. What's your problem?"

Victor, the young German, was just stepping through the gate leading down the slope. He stopped at her sharp words, his eyes flickering from her face to the back of Santos' head. She could almost see his thoughts forming.

"Is something the matter?" He moved to her side.

She shook her head, embarrassed at her outburst. "No, no. Everything's fine."

Santos mouth quirked at the corner. "I was simply asking if Abigail was feeling fit enough for the rest of the journey."

"For God's sake," she couldn't help retorting, "stop being such a worry wart."

His sexy—damn it, not sexy, it was aggravating, that's what it was—half-smile vanished. Good. She'd rather annoy him than amuse him.

Victor studied her with concern, and she was once again forcibly reminded of Tobias. Trust a seventeen-year-old boy to make her feel like an old crone.

"Would you like me to walk with you?" He turned to Santos without waiting for her reply. "I will keep an eye on her, if you like."

The man-to-man tone should have infuriated Abigail further, especially since amusement had returned to Santos' lips, seeped into his eyes. Instead the absurdity of the situation hit her, and she swallowed a giggle. "Thank you, Victor," she said formally. She even took his arm and let him lead her through the gate.

She couldn't resist a glance over her shoulder. Santos stood on the landing, waiting for the last of the group, a wide, white grin splitting his dark face.

****

Abigail sat on a low stone wall in front of a squat white cottage and took off her heavy hiking boots and thick socks. Maybe it wasn't a good idea, as she still had the return climb to do, but her feet were sweaty and the dark blue water of the lagoon looked *soooo* inviting.

"Want to come wading with me?" she asked Victor. The young man had kept her company all through the descent and continued to hover over her.

"Why not?" He shucked his boots and tucked them next to Abigail's beside the wall. They padded across the dark, coarse sand to the edge of the lagoon.

"There aren't any sea shells." Abigail scanned the water. Flat, black rocks pocked with sand-filled basins were visible through the clear, clean depths. But no shells.

"That's odd." Victor waded in and began to cast about, searching. "You're right. I wonder why."

"And the sand is almost black." Abigail thought back to the travel shows she'd devoured when a trip like this had been only a dream. "Not golden, or white, like the videos I've seen of the Caribbean or Hawaii." Abigail wandered through the cool shallows, gentle waves lapping just below her knees.

"Or Costa Rica. There are beautiful beaches there."

"You've been?"

He nodded. "Last year." He kicked through the water, fists sunk in the pockets of his shorts. "My parents consider travelling part of our education. They make my brother and sister and I study where we're going, learn a bit of the language. I've been to Greece, Spain, Costa Rica. And now the Azores."

Envy cramped her chest. Did he realize how lucky he was, to have the chance to see so much of the world? To be able to step out of the humdrum of every day?

They reached the far end of the lagoon. She clambered onto the reef that protected the peaceful pool from the violent depths of the Atlantic and began to circle back, the rocks cool and gritty under her feet. Victor followed behind her on the narrow ledge.

"How about you?"

She blinked and shot a quick glance over her shoulder. "Me?"

"Where have you been?"

"Nowhere." That sounded pitiful. She kept her eyes down, concentrating on her footing, trying not to feel inferior to this globetrotting teenager. "Well, here. I mean, this is the first time I've travelled away from home."

"Really?" The incredulity was easy to hear in in voice. "What about school? Didn't you go to university?"

"There's one in my town. I went there, took business classes."

"My parents wanted me to go to the university close to home, too, but I've been accepted at one about a day's drive away. They're making me live on campus for the first year, but after that I'm going to get my own place. I can't wait to get out on my own."

She knew he wasn't criticizing her, but couldn't resist defending herself. She stopped in her tracks and faced him. "My mother was ill. She needed me. I couldn't leave her." She tried to hide her bitterness, but the silence that followed seemed to indicate he'd caught at least a hint of her turmoil.

They settled onto the rocks and dangled their feet in the water. Maybe it was because Victor reminded her of Tobias, maybe it was simply time to share her story. Regardless, Abigail found herself talking about her mother.

"She didn't leave our house. I mean, for years. When I was a teenager she would force herself to go out once in a while, but after I got my driver's license she relied more and more on me." Silver flickers in the water revealed a school of small, slender fish. She held still and they came closer, nibbling on the algae coating the rocks near her feet. "I have a brother, about your age. It was really hard on him."

"Wasn't there anyone else who could look after her?"

"No. My father died when I was twelve. He was killed in a plane crash while on a business trip." She lifted her foot from the water, watched droplets slip off her heels, landing with small ripples in the calm water of the lagoon.

"But she let you come here, right?"

"She died, too." It was easier to say it quickly, baldly. "About two months ago. The doctor said it was an aneurysm. There were no symptoms, no warning. One moment she was there...the next...not."

The ruffled water in front of her stayed completely in focus. No tears blurred her sight. Maybe she'd finally cried herself out.

"Oh." Victor patted her hand as it rested on the rock between them. "I don't know what to say."

Her lips curved at the awkwardly given comfort. "You don't have to say anything." How she wished Tobias could be as carefree, as innocent. "It's okay. It's getting easier." Which was the truth. Except for certain unexpected moments like now, when grief clawed at her throat, tore at her lungs, as fresh as the first day.

In a way, Abigail was glad for those times of wrenching

emotions. She deserved the pain.

Because after the shock of her mother's death had worn thin, a horrifying, terrifying feeling had surfaced in Abigail's conscience.

Relief.

****

Santos sat cross-legged on a rock at the base of the cliff. The *fajã* and its village was so tiny he could survey the entire place from here. He'd set the group free, told them to explore on their own. The villagers were used to the invasion—in fact, they welcomed it. Santos paid a small fee to the headman every time he brought a group down.

Victor was still taking his duties seriously, and hadn't left Abigail's side. Undaunted by Neve and Sabine's lack of interest, he'd obviously decided Abigail might be a more willing participant in his teenage dreams.

Santos frowned. He remembered those days of hormones and horniness fondly, and Victor's preoccupation with Neve and Sabine, only a few years older than him, was certainly expected. But Abigail? No way would she dally with such a young man. She'd be looking for someone more mature, confident. Someone dynamic to balance out her natural deference.

Someone like himself.

He shook off the thought. Abigail was not the kind of woman he naturally sought out for companionship. All his instincts warned him away from her.

Neve and Sabine came into view, strolling out from between low-roofed, white-washed cottages. Neve sighted him and waved, smiling brilliantly.

Now there was someone who would understand the

rules. Who would enjoy a fling when the time was right and not expect anything after. Abigail was too cautious, too sober, to simply let loose and enjoy the moment. She was the type to look for permanence, for commitment. No way was he getting tangled up in that. Some day he supposed he'd end up married, but that day could wait. And so could his mother. She'd expect him to bring home a nice Portuguese girl— which was why he rarely dated one.

Sabine wandered off to join Victor and Abigail. Neve approached Santos on his rock.

"Give me a hand?" She reached up and he grasped her wrist. She took a firm grip and scrambled next to him, folding her long legs and hugging her knees. The ceaseless ocean breeze had whipped away the overcast skies of the morning. This close to the shore there was a briskness to the wind that tugged and pulled at the light windbreaker she wore, giving tantalizing hints of a lushly curved breast and contoured waist.

A strand of sunshine hair caught at the corner of her mouth and she brushed it away. "So, what do you do when you're not guiding groups of tourists?"

He leaned back on his palms and stretched his legs, letting them dangle over the edge of the boulder. "A little of this, a little of that. There's always something to do around the *quinta*."

"I mean for fun. With friends—maybe a girlfriend?"

Okay, so subtlety wasn't one of Neve's attributes. That was fine with him. He preferred to have things clear, out in the open. "No girlfriend."

"Ah."

He didn't know how she did it, but with that one syllable Neve signalled her availability, her willingness. She didn't move an inch from where she sat, yet she seemed to melt closer to him, her body pliable, alluringly sensual.

It was an offer he'd rarely refused. He liked women, women liked him. And if one of them invited him on a private tour...he rarely disappointed. With clients, he insisted on waiting until they were no longer guests at Quinta Carregado. But for a man with no intention of settling down, beautiful foreign women were the perfect partners.

Which is why he surprised himself by sliding from the rock. "It's almost time to head back. I should let the others know. I'll see you at the gathering point in a few minutes."

Confusion flashed in her deep blue eyes. He smiled to take the sting out of his desertion, and wondered if anyone had ever walked away from her before once she'd let that potent sexuality loose.

Wondered why *he* was walking away. And yet he kept on going.

****

Abigail managed to shake off Victor before they started their return journey. It wasn't easy. She had to guilt him into it by pointing out he was ignoring his father shamefully.

"You're supposed to be spending this last holiday before university together," she scolded. "You're neglecting him, and he has no one else to keep him company." She crossed her fingers behind her back at the tiny white lie. Eric appeared happy enough in the company of the Thorntons and Birtwhistles, although she was certain his son didn't know that. He had barely spared his father a glance during the last few hours.

She tilted her head back and studied the trail as it climbed away from the tiny *fajã*. Wandering through the hamlet next to the lagoon had definitely been worth the precarious trip down. She hoped it would be worth the challenge the return journey promised, and dosed herself from her inhaler.

Santos' condescension still rankled, pin-pricks of aggravation heating her throat whenever she thought of it. Fifteen minutes later, as he led them away from the village, she settled into the middle of the pack, determined to prove him wrong.

The path was thickly edged with tall, red-barked cedar, heavy, richly green fronds swaying high above, the spicy, medicinal scent tickling her nose. She breathed deeply and stepped out with strong strides, sticking close to Richard Thornton's heels.

He looked over his shoulder. "You doing okay, Abigail?" he inquired, his smile crinkling the lightly weathered skin around his eyes.

"Yes, thank you." For some reason, his question didn't bother her. Maybe because he asked it so casually, without any hidden overtones. "I hope I say the same once we're at the top," she confessed.

"You'll do fine."

His calm acceptance lifted her spirits and she moved forward with more confidence. The track wound and dipped, zigged and zagged, climbing relentlessly upward. Soon her heart thudded and pulse points at her neck and wrist throbbed. She forced herself to inhale and exhale evenly and regularly.

Ten minutes into the hike, she thought she'd have to swallow her pride and admit Santos was right. She couldn't handle it. Then she sighted him, leading the straggling group with no sign of breathlessness or strain, and it pissed her off. She bore down on trembling legs muscles, heaving one foot in front of the other.

Damned if she would give him the satisfaction.

Ten minutes further along, she was astonished to realize the exertion no longer pushed her to her limit. She slipped into a mechanical, energy-efficient rhythm, and for a while simply enjoyed the wonders of heart and muscle, blood and bone, working smoothly together.

She glimpsed hard blue water through the luxuriant foliage. Giant ferns spread out their enormous fans in the dappled shade, and the path dove into a tunnel of greenery. The dimness dulled not only the light, but the sounds of feet crunching on the red gravel. Past the Thorntons and Santos, the end of the archway was a wide beacon, glowing with radiance. One by one they slipped out of the darkness and into the day.

Rounding a rocky outcropping covered in a rioting purple morning glory vine, the rush and chatter of water greeted her. It grew louder and louder as they approached an old stone bridge. She wished she'd paid more attention in physics class so she could remember the force that held the dark stones braced against each other over the tumbling creek. Maybe then she would trust the rickety looking structure. It was no wider than it had to be, and the parapet was barely a foot high. A faint sense of vertigo swirled through her as she peered over the edge, and she looked away, concentrating fiercely on the opposite bank until she reached the safety of the other side. Ladder-like steps cut into the stone led up and over a narrow ridge, and she clambered until she reached a small plateau, where Santos called for a short rest.

****

Damned if Abigail wasn't keeping up just fine, Santos

noted. Her face, flushed with effort, gave her pearly, satin skin the blush of health. She climbed the last steps to the ledge freely, without a hint of distress, her breathing calm and even. He smiled as she reached level ground. She glared at him. He smiled even wider.

Neve stepped into his line of sight. "Sabine has a blister on the back of her heel. Can you come take a look?"

Kneeling in front of Sabine, he examined the puffy, fluid-filled pocket. "You should have said something sooner," he said with a hint of reproof. "I'll do what I can, but you'll be very uncomfortable the rest of the hike." He dug gauze out of the small first aid kit he carried on all outings.

Sabine bit her lip as he taped a pad over the swelling. "I thought I could make it."

He glanced up from his bandaging and noticed Abigail watching him minister to Sabine, a smug look on her face. He dipped his head, acknowledging her right to a little gloating, but she spun away, striding to the edge of the landing.

He wandered around the group, making sure no one else needed attention, and accidentally on purpose wound up next to Abigail.

"Go on." He nudged her with his elbow. "Say it."

She sniffed. "Say what?"

"You're dying to say 'I told you so.' You were right. I shouldn't have assumed you weren't capable."

"Damn right. Between you and..." She hesitated. "Let's just say I'm tired of people meddling in my life."

He knew his tourists didn't materialize out of nothing onto his island. He knew they had friends and families, experienced troubles and joys, all before he met them. Yet he never bothered to think about them other than as clients. Where they came from, where they returned to after—none of that ever mattered to him.

Which was why his sudden wish to learn more about Abigail was so unsettling, unwelcome. He snapped his mouth shut before he could delve deeper into her unfinished sentence and retreated to the safety of his tried and true formula for dealing with guests.

"Are you enjoying your trip so far?"

"It's a beautiful country." She lifted a shoulder. "I'm just a little...disappointed...I guess. I signed up for an adventure. So far all we've done is ride a bike and take a walk."

He was sure her casual disparagement of his tour was simply a little revenge for his earlier comments, but it still put his back up. Despite the prick to his pride he kept his tone smooth and friendly. "Hopefully tomorrow will sate the appetite you seem to have for thrills."

She narrowed her eyes. "What's tomorrow?"

He leaned forward, forcing those pale blue eyes to meet his, daring her to look away.

"Ready to jump off a cliff with me, Abigail?"

PARAGLIDING

Abigail trudged through the sparse, golden grass, past low, scrubby brush, dread tingling in her chilled fingertips. The moist breeze yanked strands of hair out of her ponytail and whipped them against her cheeks. She crossed her arms tightly over her stomach and hunched her shoulders, forcing herself toward the edge.

She was standing on the peak overlooking Lagoa do Fogo, a beautiful blue-green lake curled into yet another volcanic crater. Toward the west, Sete Cidades was hidden by misty clouds, but amazingly she could see across the entire width of the island, from Ponta Delgada on the south coast to Ribeira Grande on the north. It really was a tiny, tiny island.

She only hoped that stunning view wouldn't be her last.

Santos' taunt yesterday hadn't been theoretical. In a few minutes, she would be jumping off this mountain, supported only by billowing fabric and slender lines.

She was going para-freakin'-gliding.

When she signed up for this tour, one of the attractions was the unknown elements. All the other programs had every day—practically every hour—meticulously plotted. Ilha

Verde Aventuras simply provided a list of possible activities, and noted that each tour would be customized based on the people who signed up. After a life that had been controlled and scheduled with complete safety in mind, the randomness of such a week had held immeasurable appeal.

At least it had when she'd been safe at home. Right now it was a different story.

The evening before, everyone had been given the choice between paragliding with Santos, a picnic with Lina in the back fields of *Quinta Carregado*, or free time to explore Ponta Delgada on their own. After Santos' jeering remarks, Abigail had had no choice. Which was why she, Neve, Victor, and Victor's father Eric were now gathered in this high meadow, waiting for the experienced paragliders to ready the tandem equipment.

She'd barely slept, tossing from side to side, front to back. Her body was exhausted from the hike to Fajã do São Pedro but her mind kept slipping and sliding on terror. She simply couldn't shut down the slide show flickering in her mind's eye, one disastrous scenario after another after another. About three in the morning, she decided she couldn't do it. She would tell Santos no sane person would voluntarily go paragliding, and ignore any ribbing he might dish out. She wasn't risking her life to prove a point—to herself or anyone else. Letting out a huge sigh of relief, her body melted into the mattress, and she slept.

But the decision made in the darkest hours couldn't stand the bright light of day. She'd come on this trip to test herself, to stretch her limits. Her mother had spent the last years of her life locked in a world of fear and worry, trapped in her own home. Death had found her anyway.

Abigail had vowed to be different. If she was truly determined to shake free of her mother's grip, what better way to do so than jump off a cliff? It would be a grand gesture, one that would prove to herself and others that she was free—free to live her life her way.

A small blue car crawled along the zig-zagging road below her feet. The shriek of a seagull echoed in the wind. Her heart pattered so rapidly in her chest she felt dizzy.

Martin would never allow her to do this. He would be as horrified as her mother, would try to talk her out of it. Perhaps forbid her to go. So she'd neglected to mention it in her daily email to him.

She liked to think Tobias would have strapped on a harness with her.

Abigail turned away from the vertical view before her and surveyed the activity on the tundra-like field. Huge, fragile-looking swathes of crumpled fabric in bright colours were spread out on the dry brown grass, with a team of men and women organizing the lines leading from each wing. The very thin, threadlike lines.

She shivered, forcibly repressing the image of those flimsy fibres shredding, tearing, releasing, and went to join the others.

"Isn't this exciting?" Neve's eyes sparkled. "I can't wait."

"It's going to be amazing." Today Victor was bouncing between his self-imposed role as Abigail's guardian and gauche attempts at attracting Neve's attention. Abigail spared a thought for Tobias—would he be as enamoured of the Dutch blondes as Victor? Would he be as awkwardly confident?

Then the enormity of what she was about to do chased her brother from her mind. "Sure it'll be amazing," she muttered under her breath. "As long as we don't die." Eric, twitched one shoulder, clearly indicating he was of the same mind.

Santos worked alongside other experienced paragliders, their actions smooth and practiced as if choreographed, readying the tandem equipment. Abigail swallowed, her mouth gritty and dry. Every second brought her closer to the edge—literally. But she couldn't back down now. Wouldn't let herself.

After what seemed like eons of waiting, Santos waved them over. "All right, everyone, time to strap in." He handed out heavy, awkward harnesses, festooned with thick straps and muscular clips.

One of the women helped Abigail. "My name is Jacinta." Her accent was heavier than Santos'. "You will be gliding with me." She yanked a strap, snugging it tight, jerking Abigail's hips. Handing her a helmet, she pointed at one of the waiting wings, glowing from the ground in bold blue and yellow stripes. "That one is ours. I will be right with you." Abigail waddled over and stared at the delicate contraption. She clipped on the helmet with shaking fingers.

Her chest heaved. She knew she was breathing too fast, too shallow, but couldn't control it. Tiny spots jigged before her eyes, and she leaned over, hands on her knees, determined not to faint but unwilling to place a bet against it.

A large warm hand dropped gently onto her shoulder. "Are you okay? Do you need your inhaler?"

She straightened, willing away the light-headedness, and focused on the complicated clasp of the harness in the middle of Santos' chest. She dragged in a deep breath, released it slowly. "I've already taken it." She repeated the cautious in and out breathing and her panic eased. Her chest felt tight, but her lungs were clear.

Santos slipped his hand down her arm and grasped her fingers. "You're freezing." He reached for her other hand, rubbed them between his palms. His skin was pleasantly rough, dry and warm.

"It's the wind." What a lie. It was terror, plain and simple.

He chafed her fingers. "You don't have to do this, you know."

"Yes, I do."

"Why?"

She lifted her gaze from the glitter of metal and nylon strapping criss-crossing his solid torso. A huge pack—oh, God, the emergency parachute—hung on his shoulders. His helmet was dark blue and covered in stickers with unfamiliar logos. She met his eyes, a rich, mahogany brown, framed by short, thick lashes and heavy eyebrows.

"*Because* I'm scared." A longer explanation would betray feelings and emotions she wasn't ready to share. Admitting her fear was bad enough.

He nodded, the concern on his face lightening. Still studying her, he yelled something in rapid Portuguese over his shoulder. Jacinta answered. He released one of Abigail's hands, keeping the other in his strong clasp, and tugged her toward a different wing, this one solid red. Jacinta led a confused-looking Neve in the opposite direction. "I thought I was with Jacinta," Abigail said.

Santos squeezed her hand. "Now you're with me."

****

Before she had another moment to think, Abigail was standing in front of Santos, connected to him by the tandem harness. She stared blindly forward, gazing out over fields dotted with cows and marked by hydrangea hedges, over the large village of Ribeira Grande, all the way to the smooth, arching horizon and the end of the ocean. Maybe if she concentrated on that awe-inspiring view, she would forget that, in only a few seconds, she would be running purposefully toward a cliff edge and launching herself off.

Abigail felt Santos' movements through the straps joining them, the tugging and jerking energetic enough to make her stagger slightly. A strong hand gripped her elbow.

"Steady."

She could barely hear his voice through the blood thrashing in her ears. She closed her eyes and forced air through her nostrils.

"Ready?"

She shook her head, eyes still squeezed shut. A bead of sweat trickled down her temple and she shuddered.

Santos dipped his head to hers. He wasn't touching her, yet she could feel the heat of his body at her back, through the many layers of clothing and equipment between them. His breath, warmer than the ocean breeze, curled against her neck.

"You can do this." He spoke quietly, firmly. "Nothing bad is going to happen. I've done this hundreds of times before. Remember, you need to do this."

She wondered at his understanding. It was there in his voice. He *knew* she had to do this. He *believed* she could.

She opened her eyes, drew in a quivering breath, held it for the count of ten, and let it out.

"Okay." Two syllables were all she could manage.

"Good girl." His approving tone went another step further in allaying her terror. "When I say go, start running. When the wing goes up it's going to pull on us. It may even pull us backward. Lean into it and keep going, even if you feel like you are running in place. Keep running until I tell you to stop. If something gets fouled up—"

Abigail moaned and closed her eyes again.

"—not that it will," he hurried on, "but if it does, we'll stop and try again. Now open your eyes."

She stood, frozen.

"I want you to open your eyes, Abigail." He seduced her, coaxed her, into obeying, his voice deep and sensual. "I want you to see yourself, see how brave you are."

She dragged her eyelids up.

"On my count. Three—two—one—go!"

Abigail raced forward, blanking her mind to the enormity of what she was doing. After only a couple of steps she was jerked to a stop, but Santos shouted for her to keep going. She dug in to the coarse, rocky soil, pushing back with her toes, and suddenly something released her with a gasp and she was sprinting forward, taking huge steps, the cliff getting closer, her heart pounding with exertion and fear, her panting breaths the only sound in her head, and the edge was right there—right there!—but her feet were no longer touching the ground even though she was still frantically running, running...

She was flying.

****

Abigail's legs flailed furiously.

"Stop running," Santos instructed. "Pull your arms in and slip yourself back in the sling."

She leaned back and brought her arms inside the straps, now taut with tension against the wind's lift. She wriggled backward into the canvas sling, and settled in against Santos' chest, his legs just below and outside of hers, her ass practically in his lap.

He may not have thought this through carefully enough.

Tremors rippled through her arms and legs, and she was

scarily silent. He stretched his neck and peered around to get a glimpse of her face.

Tears poured down her cheeks. His heart stopped.

"We'll go back," he said immediately. "It's not worth it. We'll go back." He manipulated the controls and the wing swung around.

"No." Her voice broke and she cleared her throat. "No," she repeated, stronger this time. Then, softly, reverently, "My God, it's so beautiful. I never imagined..."

Santos leaned back, determined to give her the experience of a lifetime.

He remembered the rush of adrenalin during his first launch, the stunning sensation of being carried by air, the mind-blowing view of his island from above. Flying in an airplane didn't come close. For one thing, there was the silence. A paraglider travelled with the wind, and while the suspension lines sang and whistled and the vents in the wing flapped, it was akin to a canoe on a lake. Tranquil, serene, no motorized engine tearing the calm.

After a minute or two, Abigail's body went lax, the last of her tension seeping away. He caught a thermal and they swooped higher. She gasped.

And laughed.

The sound rang out, clear and joyous. No hint of hysteria, no tinge of terror, coloured it. Only simple, utter, exultation.

By now everyone was in the air. Santos and Abigail soared above the others, gazed down on the bright colours of the other wings highlighted against the rich greens and browns of the island cliffs and the royal blue of the ocean.

"It's so peaceful. I never imagined it would be so quiet." Abigail's voice was soft and dreamy, the huskiness even more pronounced, as if she'd just woken from sleep.

Thank goodness for the thick layers of canvas between them. Santos shifted slightly and they swung and swayed under the red wing. "Was it worth it?"

"Oh, yes."

"I'm glad. And proud of you. Not everyone fights through their fears."

She was silent for a long time. Then—"Thank you."

"For what?"

"For understanding. For helping me do this."

"It wasn't me, Abigail. It was you. Your courage, your heart." He guided the wing through another thermal and they sailed even higher, dancing through the sky, free of the surly bonds of earth.

****

Abigail didn't want to come down.

Ever.

Maybe it was the elation coursing through her system, maybe it was the sensation of being apart from the ordinary. She wanted to stay like this forever, suspended in a forget-me-not sky on silvered threads under a poppy red kite.

Cradled against Santos' body.

It didn't matter that they were hundreds of feet above solid ground, hanging from a frail and fragile wing. She felt more alive than ever before.

Deep, emerald chasms slashed the side of the mountain, only to be broken up by lighter green pastures. Odd sounds drifted up—the lowing of cattle, the rush of vehicles on the express way. A seagull flew alongside, only a dozen metres away, its beady yellow eyes regarding them suspiciously before uttering its raucous screech and veering away.

Far too soon she saw the wings below them circle the

landing meadow. One after the other, the taut material crumpled as the magic ended, the ride finished.

"It's our turn. Time to go back." Santos' voice was calm and contained, but did she catch a hint of the same wistfulness she was feeling?

She sighed. "I know."

He manoeuvred the controls. The vents in the wing above flapped energetically and they spiralled down, down, down. It took much less time than she thought, than she wished. Santos instructed her to slip out of the comfortable sling and let her legs dangle. She lifted her arms to the outside of her chest harness and watched the pasture rush toward her.

"Start running."

She bicycled her legs, but wasn't ready for the speed at which they reached the ground. She took two stumbling steps before collapsing, landing hard on her shoulder and twisting onto her back. Her momentum pulled Santos with her and he sprawled beside her. The silky wing draped them like a tent, sunlight washing the red from the material glowing about them.

Abigail lay stunned, staring at Santos. He held himself on one elbow, half covering her, so close each panting breath pressed her breasts against his chest. One of his legs lay over hers, his groin nestling her hip.

Joy pounded through her veins. Every nerve was sensitized, her eyesight sharper, her hearing so acute she was aware of blades of grass rubbing together. The heady scent of crushed grass, rich earth surrounded her.

The primal, undeniable urge to share life, to share wonder, surged through her. Desire whispered, then shouted, told her to lift her mouth the scant inches necessary, and brush his lips with hers.

So she did. She wrapped her arms around his neck, pulled herself to him and kissed him.

****

Every muscle in Santos' body locked. Abigail's lips were soft and supple, eager and enticing. She held herself off the ground, suspended by her arms around his neck. She adjusted the angle of her kiss and their helmets clacked together. He reared away, breaking the embrace.

Her body thudded down. She stared at him, eyes clouded, face stricken, and a small, desperate sound escaped her. A faraway part of his brain registered the laughter and shouts of the team as they struggled to lift the encompassing wing off them. He had only seconds.

He swept his lips over hers, insistently, gently. She gasped and he took advantage of her opened mouth, running his tongue along the soft underside of her upper lip.

Desire thrummed through him and he fought the urge to bear down on her body so she could feel how much he wanted her. A voice in his head scolded him for kissing a client, chided him for kissing a woman so innocent.

He drew away. Her face was flushed, her eyes closed. The lids drifted up, revealing pale, pale blue eyes, fringed with almost white lashes.

And she frowned.

He opened his mouth to ask her—what? He wasn't entirely sure. But at that moment the fabric surrounding them whipped away. Instantly he rolled off Abigail, rising to his knees.

"Everyone okay under there?" Jacinta shouted cheerfully. "That was quite a landing."

"All good." Santos fumbled with the buckles attaching

him to Abigail. She jumped to her feet as soon as they came undone.

"How was your flight?" Jacinta asked, helping her out of the harness.

"Unforgettable."

Santos lifted his eyes, unsurprised at the odd note in Abigail's voice. She avoided his look, unstrapping her helmet and shaking out her fine fair hair. He could still taste her on his tongue, feel the strength of her arms around his neck. He pinched his finger in one of the clasps on his own harness and let out a sharp oath.

Jacinta gave him a sideways glance yet spoke to Abigail. "I'm so glad you enjoyed it. Maybe you'll have a chance to do it again before you leave our island."

Abigail stepped out of the harness and straightened her shoulders. This time, she looked Santos square in the face. "Yes," she said defiantly. "Maybe I will."

QUINTA CARREGADO – SAME DAY

Neve claimed the front passenger seat, Victor and Eric the first bench. Abigail slipped behind the men, sliding next to the window. She listened with half an ear to their excited conversation but didn't take part in the exultations.

She'd never done anything so bold, so uninhibited, in all her life. Never mind flying unfettered through an exotic sky—she couldn't believe she'd kissed Santos.

When he pulled away, her first sensation was shock, quickly followed by humiliation. She was sure she'd made a complete ass of herself. Of course he didn't want to kiss her. She was pale and thin and quiet. He'd be attracted to someone bold and confident and sexy. A vision of Neve popped into her head. And then Santos had leaned in and kissed her back, softly, sweetly.

Her bones melted and her blood thickened. No kiss had ever made her feel that way. Not even Martin's.

She swallowed a lump of guilt. She'd barely thought of Martin all day, and certainly hadn't been thinking of him when she kissed Santos. She hunched her shoulders and shrunk down in the seat, regret tainting the thrill of memory.

She knew Santos didn't mean anything by the kiss. He

probably felt sorry for her, wanted to give the mousy little Canadian a sexy memory she could giggle over with her girlfriends back home. She didn't care. Those few seconds, enveloped under the silky red wing, marked a turning point in her life. A turning point she wasn't quite ready to examine.

She watched through the window as Santos helped the crew pack away the last of the gear in the truck that had been driven down from the launch site to the landing area. He smiled at Jacinta, slapped one of the men on the back and waved at the others as he headed to the van. He moved easily, with a physicality she associated with athletes. She remembered the press of his hips against hers, the heat of his body, the soft rubbing of his lips.

Her belly tingled.

"Everyone aboard?" He slammed the door shut and reached for the seatbelt shoulder strap.

"Aye, aye, Captain." Neve gave him a playful salute.

He turned to grin at her and Abigail caught his profile, silhouetted against the sun lowering out over the ocean. It was a strong face, with a proud nose and aggressive jaw. It was the face of an adventurer, a man who met life head on and relished it.

It was *not* the face of a man who would be interested in a wan little accountant from British Columbia.

And yet he'd kissed her. She hugged that fact tight.

The van bumped over the hillocky meadow to the gravel track leading out of the field. They reached the smoothly paved main road and began the return journey, Santos answering Victor's eager questions about how to get a paragliding license.

Whether it was Santos' kiss or the paragliding, she'd never felt so empowered, so invigorated. Battling back her fears, forcing past her mind's limitations, stepping out beyond her reservations had changed her, in ways she wasn't sure she could describe.

She couldn't wait to tell Tobias. About the flight, not the kiss. She knew she should call Martin, too, but wasn't sure she could speak with him without revealing how different she felt. About herself. About him.

She shoved those thoughts deep into a corner of her mind, unwilling to study them too closely. Not now. Not yet.

****

The van crunched onto the neat gravel drive at Quinta Carregado. Abigail followed Eric and Victor out and hurried around the farmhouse to the door in the back that the guests used. She found Lina in the small office off the kitchen.

"How was your day?" Santos' sister resembled him physically, but there was an attitude of reserve about her Abigail found perplexing. The young woman was perfectly polite, and yet there was a sense of aloofness surrounding her.

"I can't begin to explain. It was..." A grin she simply couldn't hold back split her face. "It was fan-freaking-tastic. I was absolutely petrified, and then—I wasn't. I flew with Santos, and it was awesome."

"You flew with Santos?" Lina's dark eyebrows rose. "When we spoke this morning, he'd partnered you with Jacinta."

Abigail didn't want to admit to her near panic attack. She shrugged as nonchalantly as she could. "I guess he changed his mind."

Lina looked as if she was going to say more, but only nodded. Was she surprised Santos has passed on a chance to fly with Neve, Abigail wondered? If so, what would she say if she knew Abigail had kissed her brother?

Abigail rushed to fill what was becoming an awkward silence. "I'd love to call home, tell my brother all about it, but I didn't bring my own phone with me." Knowing she'd have access to Wi-Fi, she hadn't wanted to go to the trouble and expense of getting a short term international plan. She had also wanted off from the leash for a while, to break away from being constantly available, especially to Martin. She was beginning to realize she may have subconsciously made some decisions before she'd even left Prince George. "Can I use yours? I was hoping you could just add it to my bill."

"Of course." Lina stood up and made room for Abigail. A computer took up most of the desk space, the rest of the surface strewn with papers. "I'll get some fresh air. Even on the mornings when it's pouring rain and Santos' breath is making clouds in the damp, and he still has to take a group of tourists out for a bike ride or a hike, I envy him. At least he doesn't spend hours in front of a screen." She disappeared into the kitchen.

Abigail dialled Tobias' cell phone.

"Hello."

The breath snagged in her throat, his familiar tone slicing an unexpected stab of homesickness through her heart. She pictured him, pale blue eyes hiding behind blonde bangs, arms and legs still gangly despite the fact his twentieth birthday was only a couple of months away.

"Hello? Anyone there?"

She found her voice. "Tobias, it's me."

"Abigail!"

He said her name with such joy she laughed out loud. "How are you?"

"I'm doing okay."

It was what she wanted to hear, but she heard a quality in

the words that pricked at her. "Are you sure?"

"No, I'm awful." The sarcasm transmitted through the ether did more to ease her nascent concern than another denial. "How are you? Why are you calling?"

"I guess I just wanted to hear your voice." She paused. "And to tell you I went paragliding today."

Silence.

"You did not," he said in disbelief.

Her cheeks ached she was smiling so hard. "Did too."

Another pause. "Spill. I want deets."

Her words were mere ghosts compared to the sensations she was trying to share, but she did her best. In the end, she had to cut off Tobias' eager questions. "Look, I'm running up a huge bill here. I've got to go."

"I'm glad you called." He sounded wistful. "It's weird, being here without you. The apartment seems so empty. I know we've only been here a month, but still." After their mother's death, neither Tobias nor Abigail had wanted to stay a moment longer than necessary in the house that had seemed a prison for so many years. They'd put it up for sale after the funeral and moved out immediately.

Abigail's familiar foe, guilt, latched onto her gut. "I knew I shouldn't have left you. I should have waited. It was too soon after Mom—"

Tobias cut her off. "Stop it. Do not feel sorry. Sure, I'm lonely, but it's only for a week or so. This is good, for both of us. If things had been different, with Mom, I probably would have left home a year ago, right after graduation, and gone to university somewhere away from Prince George. Now I'm nineteen years old, and this is the first time I've ever been completely alone. We needed this. *You* needed this."

Her nose tingled with the threat of tears. "I didn't need to come this far. I could have chosen somewhere closer to home. In case you needed me."

"You're only a day's flight away. And I'll always need you. You're my big sister."

She swallowed. "Tobias—"

His voice was deep and resonant, yet she could hear the remnants of the little boy she loved and cared for. "You deserve this holiday. I know what you did."

She frowned. "What are you talking about?"

"I didn't, at first. But as I got older, I realized what you were doing. I would never have had the chance to do some of the things I did, if you hadn't bullied Mom into agreeing. And if you hadn't promised to stay with her, keep her company, I don't think she would have let me leave her sight."

"I had a normal childhood, a good childhood, until I was twelve. You were so young, just a toddler, when Dad died. I couldn't let Mom's troubles give you anything less than what I'd had."

"Well, thank you," he said. "I just wanted you to know I know so we can all know together."

She smiled, appreciating his attempt to lighten the mood. "I miss you."

"I know."

This time she laughed. Tobias' revelations had lifted a weight from her. She did deserve a treat, a chance to enjoy herself, free of responsibilities, free of duty.

"I love you. I'll be home soon, and we'll be together then. You're my main man, after all."

****

Santos finished tidying up the van, locked the doors and headed to the farmhouse. His guests were on their own for the rest of the day, and he was free to relax for a few hours. If he *could* relax. He still hadn't recovered from the shock of Abigail's kiss. Her mouth innocent yet wanton, her body fragile yet supple. Every time he allowed himself to remember, arousal flooded his veins.

His body had zeroed in on this woman, despite the warnings his brain kept shouting. Those warnings, however, grew weaker and weaker the longer he thought about her, the more he learned about her.

He stamped off his dusty feet on the mat outside the front door. She wore no wedding band, he mused, and she was the one who had initiated the kiss. With any other woman, he would take that as an invitation to spend a few days together after the tour was over. He'd done it before, and would do it again. It was a simple, unencumbered way to enjoy sex and seduction without long-term hassles.

Warning bells sounded again. Instinctively he knew that wasn't a solution for his problems with Abigail. She promised to be anything but simple. The air around her vibrated with complications.

He headed for the kitchen, ready for a cold bottle of Sagres. When he designed the changes to the farm, he'd closed off a corner of the garden as a private retreat for the family. At this time of day, it would be warm from the sun, sheltered from the wind. The perfect place for beer and a nap.

He stepped into the kitchen and instantly recognized Abigail's voice coming from Lina's office. That throaty tone was unmistakable.

"I miss you."

Pause.

"I love you. I'll be home soon, and we'll be together then. You're my main man, after all."

Followed by the soft click of the receiver being lowered into the cradle. The little witch. Looking so sweet and shy, kissing him like she'd never been kissed before, and all the while she had a lover at home. His half-formed plans crumbled about him. If he had one rule, it was never get involved with a woman already in a relationship.

He leaned a hip against the battered old table and waited.

She came out of the office, lips curved in a gentle smile, and jolted when she saw him. "Oh my goodness." She pressed a hand to her chest. "You scared me."

He gestured with the bottle he held. "Came to get a beer." The glass was cold, moisture beading on the sides. Rage, out of all proportion to her crime, burned in his chest, all but flamed off his skin. He was surprised the liquid wasn't steaming out of the neck.

"I see."

Her eyes darted, looking for the quickest way past him to reach the dining room. He straightened slowly, put the bottle down with a sharp thunk.

She studied him nervously. "I should probably get going. You're off duty, aren't you? I'm taking up your private time. I should get out of your space." Her mouth closed so quickly he heard her teeth snap together.

"You didn't mind being in my space earlier."

Her gaze drifted to his mouth, then jerked back to his eyes. She braced her hands on the office door jamb. He stepped closer, so close he could feel her breath in little pants on his throat.

He lifted one hand, still damp from the beer bottle, and cupped her chin. She shuddered, once, then held herself perfectly still. He let his thumb rub the hard edge of her jaw—solid bone under silky, soft skin—then trailed it along her bottom lip. Her mouth was a soft, rosy pink, unpainted, unglossed. He realized he'd never seen her wearing even a hint of cosmetics.

His body stirred, stiffened in response.

She stared at him, eyes wide, the golden colour she'd started to acquire standing out on her opalescent skin like a layer of that make up she didn't wear.

He couldn't believe she had tricked him. Not with words, but with actions, attitude.

Damn if that didn't piss him off.

If she wanted a bit on the side while she was on holidays, who was he to stop her? He wasn't her conscience. In just over a week she'd be going home, back to another man.

So why didn't he give her something to remember him by?

****

Sliding his hand to the nape of her neck, he wrapped one arm around her waist, and pulled her to him. He almost groaned at the sensation of her breasts against his chest, her pelvis pressed to his hips, the firm length of her legs tangled with his own.

She didn't struggle, but tucked her chin down, hiding her face. He tugged on her ponytail, perhaps a shade harder than necessary, and she gasped, letting her head tilt back. Before he could lose himself in her brilliant eyes, he seared his mouth to hers.

Lying under the silky red wind of the paraglider, he hadn't dreamed such an astounding mix of sensations. Desire and confusion rushed back, a dizzying combination. He wanted to brand her with his mouth—her lips, her neck, her breasts, her body. He wanted to caress her with the softest of touches. The frustration was there, but so was the wish to cherish, to protect.

He had no idea what it meant. And right now, he simply didn't care.

Abigail sagged against him, clutching his shirt with her fists. Her tongue met his, hesitantly exploring. He reached down to grab her ass, the ass that had been taunting him in his dreams ever since that fated bike trip.

Suddenly she twisted her face away, pushed at him with her palms flat, leaned against his grip on her hips. "No," she said. "I shouldn't be doing this."

He'd actually forgotten about the boyfriend. He let her go instantly and stepped back. "No, you shouldn't be." He scrubbed the back of his hand against his mouth, wiping her taste away. "I heard you talking to him."

Her forehead wrinkled. "You did?"

"On the phone. You said you loved him. What the hell are you doing, kissing me when you've got a boyfriend at home?"

He didn't think she could go any paler, but somehow she managed. He saw the muscles in her neck move as she swallowed. "How did you—oh! No, that wasn't...I mean...that was Tobias. I was talking to my brother."

His heart raced, pounded in his temples. "Your brother?"

"Yes." She wrung her hands together. "My younger brother."

His blood cooled. God, he must look like an idiot. Yet— "Then why did you say you shouldn't be kissing me? Why did you push me away? Especially since you're the one that started all this." He motioned between them.

"I didn't...it wasn't..." She paused, tried again. "I'm not the type of woman who does this sort of thing." She clenched her fingers so hard the knuckles showed through her thin skin. "Not with a man like you."

His eyes narrowed. "What do you mean, a man like me?"

She laughed shakily. "You're good-looking." He snorted and she hurried on. "You must know that, of course you do. And you're outgoing and charming and can talk to people. What would you see in a woman like me?"

He didn't have an answer, despite the fact he'd asked himself the exact same thing only a few minutes ago. His mouth open and closed, and he felt like a fool.

Abigail, on the other hand, was nodding. He thought he saw relief in her eyes. "Exactly. Nothing. This was just an"—she flapped a slender hand—"an aberration. An accident."

He found his voice. "An accident."

She nodded more vigorously. "Yes. I'm sorry I kissed you. I didn't mean to, you know, start anything." She sidled past him and scuttled to the dining room door. "Thanks, for the paragliding. And everything."

He was left staring at the empty doorway.

****

Abigail closed the door of her room behind her. She walked, carefully and precisely, to the lavender chair and lowered herself onto it.

Her legs shook. Her heart thudded. Her lungs struggled to pull in enough air. Her brain fogged with confusion and need, chagrin and desire.

She groped for her inhaler, lying on top of the dresser, but didn't take a dose. The tightness in her chest had nothing to do with her asthma. She raised a trembling hand to her mouth and brushed her fingertips along her lips.

She hadn't lied to Santos—after all, she hadn't been talking to Martin. But he'd given her the perfect opportunity to explain, to tell him she did have someone waiting for her at home, and she hadn't.

Because even though she was never going to allow a repeat of the kisses she and Santos had shared today, she hadn't wanted to completely destroy the dream—the oh, so impossible dream that Santos wanted her—by telling him she was practically engaged.

What kind of horrible person was she?

She untied her boots and tugged them off, then headed for the bathroom, shedding clothing like falling leaves. The water warmed and she stepped under the fine spray.

One fact stood out after today. She couldn't marry Martin.

Not when one kiss from Santos made her forget her own name.

She couldn't tell Martin when she was seven thousand kilometres away. Breaking off a two-year relationship wasn't something you did over the phone or via email. No matter how much your cowardly heart wished you could.

She rinsed off shampoo and soap and turned off the water, reaching for a fluffy ivory towel that smelled of fresh air. Wrapping her long hair turban style in one and another around her body, she stepped in front of the mirror and studied herself.

Her skin, normally milky pale, was golden now on her neck and arms. Still not tanned, Abigail judged critically, but definitely healthier-looking. One of the many worries her mother struggled with was a fear of skin cancer. Abigail, as usual, had taken the easy way out and simply avoided the sun, in order to placate those fears. She picked up her SPF 30 sunscreen and began smoothing it on her shoulders, a wry smile twisting her mouth. Her defiance only went so far.

The deeper tone of her skin made her hair look less washed out, too. Some days Abigail felt like a blond Morticia Addams. But the sun-washed glow on her face added vibrancy to her long, pale strands.

It was as if her appearance was reflecting the stronger, richer person growing inside her. She closed her eyes and tried to recapture the sensation of slipping through the air, the whistling of the wind in the suspension lines, the satiny red curve of the wing above.

Santos' strong body at her back.

She opened her eyes and glared at her reflection. No more daydreaming about Santos. No more flirting. No more fantasizing. She owed that much to Martin.

She could never tell Santos how much he had changed her life, simply by desiring her. And she could never act on her own wants. But she would thank him forever for breaking through her barriers.

For showing her she didn't have to settle.

****

"Have more chicken." Santos' mother, Serafina, held out a platter bearing the remains of a succulent roast chicken.

"*Não, obrigado, Senhora.*" Santos waved it off with a smile. At least, he hoped it was a smile. It didn't feel right on his face.

He forked up a mouthful of potato, chicken and dark, leafy *couve*. Normally his appetite satisfied his mother, who worried he would waste away to nothing if he didn't have at least two helpings of everything. Tonight he was too pissed off, confused and horny to eat.

He believed Abigail when she said she was talking with her brother. But there'd been something in her face, something he couldn't quite read, that niggled at him.

"Are you not feeling well?" Serafina reached across the corner of the table and laid her wrist on his forehead, as if he were three, not thirty.

"I'm fine, *Mãe*." He scowled, more for form than anything else.

"Everything went well today, didn't it?" Lina sipped her wine.

"*Sim*, fine." He stabbed another piece of chicken.

The three of them were in the garden, dining together as they did most evenings, while the guests fended for themselves. He wondered where Abigail was eating. And who she was eating with. Not that it mattered, of course.

"Abigail certainly seemed to enjoy herself."

He froze for an instant, fork halfway to his mouth, then continued the motion. It wasn't unusual for Lina to comment on one of the guests, although he didn't appreciate feeling as if she had plucked his own thoughts out of the air. Her face was placid and innocent—which was when he most suspected her of mischief. He glared at her suspiciously. "You talked to her?"

"She borrowed the phone in the office. I never thought of her as good-looking before, but when she was telling me about her paragliding flight with you, all excited and flushed, she was almost pretty." Lina helped herself to another potato. "I thought you'd planned to partner Neve." It wasn't quite a question. Santos clamped his lips shut, holding back the urge to defend Abigail. She was more than 'almost pretty', damn it, although he wasn't sure how to describe her. He didn't dare react to Lina's comment, though, for fear of revealing more than he wanted to. Lina often tweaked him about his 'tourist groupies' as she called them, and normally he laughed it off with ease. Abigail, however, was no laughing matter.

Which only made his scowl deeper. "I talked to Jacinta, too." Lina dabbed her mouth with a napkin.

That in itself wasn't unusual. Jacinta Fabre and Lina had

gone to school together. So why did trepidation tickle the back of his neck like a cool breeze?

"She says that you and Abigail had a bit of a...rough...landing." Innuendo spiced the bland words.

Damn Jacinta and her sharp, knowing eyes.

He stifled the urge to strangle his beloved sister and concentrated on his plate. "Abigail fell, pulled me down after her. It was no big deal."

"Are you okay?" Serafina asked anxiously, unaware of the subtext. "No one tells me anything. You know I worry when you go paragliding. It can't be safe."

He slitted a look at Lina. "It was nothing. We stumbled a bit, that's all. I've flown hundreds of times, *Mãe*. You must stop worrying."

Serafina's gaze switched between her offspring, a small wrinkle of worry on her brow.

"It took a little while to untangle them from the wing." Lina's eyes sparkled, enjoying his torment. "Jacinta says you were under there for almost a minute. It must have been quite the tumble to muddle you up that bad."

"It was nothing," he repeated through gritted teeth.

And from now on it would be nothing. Abigail was off limits. She'd said it herself, they weren't right for each other, and he agreed with her.

Now if he could only convince his libido.

LAGOA DAS FURNAS

A babble of laughter and languages filled the dining room the next morning. Ilha Verde Aventuras offered beds, breakfast and exciting expeditions, and every tour was also treated to a *cozido*—the traditional Azorean stew cooked in the steaming vents of a volcano. According to the Carregado family, it was an experience not to be missed. And part of the experience was preparing the meal.

Everyone was gathered around the tables and put to work cutting up enormous quantities of vegetables and meat. Abigail chopped carrots into large chunks, directed by Senhora Carregado in a flurry of incomprehensible Portuguese and broken English. Neve and Sabine peeled potatoes and cleaned cabbage. Victor valiantly dismembered a chicken. Lina dashed about the room, instructing, guiding. Santos was nowhere to be seen.

Today wouldn't be dangerous or over-the-top adventurous, which was fine by Abigail. She'd had enough of that yesterday. A break from anything that raised her pulse— whether it was paragliding or Santos—was just what she needed.

Yesterday was a mistake, a one-off. She'd surprised

Santos by kissing him, so of course he'd kissed her back. It was only natural for a sexy, healthy male to react to a come on like that, no matter what kind of woman was issuing the invitation. And his second kiss—well, she wasn't naive enough to believe it had been anything more than a...than a...well, she didn't know what, but it hadn't meant anything important. She knew that, as clearly as if Santos had printed it on a billboard.

Santos appeared as soon as they finished packing the food in a large, heavy pot according to the exacting standards of Senhora Carregado.

"Oh, sure, now you show up, once the hard work is done," Neve teased.

"What kind of host would I be, if I didn't allow you the opportunity to enjoy each and every step of the process," he bantered back. The rest of the group joined in ribbing him, and he shrugged and nodded, eyes twinkling.

He didn't spare Abigail a glance. She wondered wistfully if he was as disturbed by their kisses as she, but dismissed the thought with a sigh.

Careful to keep out of Santos' way, she trailed along at the back as the group headed for the van.

****

Santos chauffeured his flock to the shores of Lagoa das Furnas. Together they buried the *cozido* in the hot steamy sand near the bubbling hot springs. Then he shepherded them into the nearby village to explore Terra Nostra Park, a magnificent botanical garden, while they waited for their meal to slowly cook.

Now he wandered, one beautiful blonde to his right, another to his left. Sabine was quiet and sedate, while Neve flirted with casual expertise. As they strolled around the thermal pond with its iron-orange water she chattered on, telling a supposedly amusing story about people he didn't know. He must have nodded and smiled at appropriate times, as she seemed pleased enough with his attention.

He should be in heaven. Which just showed what a fraud he was, because he was more engrossed in searching for Abigail than in either of the women next to him. She and Victor had disappeared behind the manor overlooking the pool a few minutes ago and had yet to reappear.

Normally he would have enjoyed taking part in preparing the *cozido* with the group, but this morning he'd spent the time repairing a leaking faucet in one of the guest rooms instead. He told himself it had nothing to do with avoiding Abigail, but he was self-aware enough to know he was lying. His brain may have decided she was off limits, but his body had yet to get the message. He could still feel the warmth of her in his arms, the suppleness of her body, the fire in her kiss.

No hint of that woman had been in evidence today. Instead the self-effacing, retiring woman from her first day on the island had returned. All the glorious confidence, all the sexy allure she'd exuded yesterday after paragliding— gone.

He felt as if he'd lost something precious.

"I never would have guessed such an enormous garden was hidden in the middle of this tiny village." Neve's comment broke into his thoughts.

He had to shake off this obsession with Abigail. "It is amazing, isn't it?" he said, determinedly cheerful. "The house was originally built as the summer home of the American consul in the 1700's, and the gardens were private."

He did his best to keep the conversation going as they followed the lower path around the slight rise on which the grand old house stood. Black swans floated with haughty grace in the creek next to them, their gaggle of grey-fuzzed offspring following close behind. A flash of moonshine caught his eye, and he turned in time to see Abigail, silvery hair swinging in its usual ponytail, and Victor disappear through the heavy, leaded glass doors leading to the restaurant.

Neve squeezed his arm and he refocused on her. "What's through there?"

He followed her pointing finger. A shadowy arch marked the end of the path. "Nothing. It's just a small grotto."

"A cave? Let's go see." She tugged him toward it.

"You go ahead," Sabine said. "I would like a drink. I'll meet up with you later."

Santos stifled the sudden urge to encourage her to stay. Since when did he shy away from being alone with a sexy, sensual woman? Neve wound her arm through his and they strolled through the arch, leaving the sultry heat of the afternoon behind for the still, damp coolness of the rock chamber.

Water shushed and lipped against the stones. The voices of tourists and chittering of birds outside the arch grew muffled. As soon as they were hidden from view, Neve pulled him to a stop. She placed both hands on his shoulders, slid them up the back of his neck and curled them into his hair. They were much of a height, and she only had to lean upward slightly to lay her mouth on his.

She obviously hadn't taken his subtle rejection at Fajã do São Pedro to heart. Her lips moved over his with expertise, teasing, sucking. He rested his hands on her hips, drew her closer, and waited for the surge of heat, rush of desire.

It wasn't that he didn't feel it. What man wouldn't, with an armful of beautiful, willing woman?

It was simply that it wasn't enough. Her kiss was pleasant, nothing more.

Gently he lifted away from her questing mouth. She settled back on her heels and studied him, head tilted to one side. Her eyes glittered in the faint rays of light that struggled this far into the dim. "It's not there, is it?"

He shook his head. "I'm sorry."

"Well, at least I tried." She shrugged and stepped back. "Too bad. I think we could have had a good time together."

"You're beautiful, sexy. It's just..." He wasn't sure what it was. What had changed—in him, with him?

"Don't worry. I don't hold it against you." Her mouth quirked. "Or Abigail."

He frowned. "This has nothing to do with Abigail."

It was Neve's turn to shake her head. "I've seen how you look at her."

"There is nothing between us. She's a client, that's all." And even if there was, it would only be a temporary, fleeting thing. She wasn't of the islands, wasn't of his world. She had a life to return to. Jealousy at that unknown life reared up and bit him with surprising force.

Neve patted his arm as they retraced their steps out of the grotto, back to the path. "You keep telling yourself that."

QUINTA CARREGADO – THAT EVENING

The *cozido* was a tremendous success, with everyone eating their fill of the tender chicken and perfectly cooked vegetables, complemented by glasses of dry red Portuguese wine. They returned to Quinta Carregado replete and sated, and after thanking Santos for the wonderful day, scattered to their own pursuits.

Too restless to close herself in for the night, too weary to head into the village as others were doing, Abigail retrieved her book from her room and wandered into the garden between the guest rooms and the farmhouse. She chose a bench tucked next to the stone wall and tried to lose herself in Jack Reacher's latest dangerous exploits, but soon found it too dark to read as the brilliance of day faded quickly into the velvet of night.

Yet still she sat, luxuriating in the simplicity of breathing the soft, dusky air.

"Do you mind if I join you?"

Santos' low voice nudged her out of her dreamy contemplation. He stood silhouetted against the charcoal sky. The light from the kitchen window limned the sharp-edge of his nose, the arch of his cheekbone. The scent of soap teased her nose. She scrambled to answer.

"No, of course not." At least she didn't stutter. She'd pledged she would treat him calmly and politely. Stammering like a school girl with a crush wouldn't exactly display the level of sophistication she was hoping to achieve.

He settled onto the wooden bench, leaving several inches between them. Despite the gap, awareness ruffled her skin.

"What did you think of the *cozido*?" Santos sank lower, shoving his hands in the pockets of his well-worn jeans. He'd changed out of the green golf shirt he wore while fulfilling his tour guide duties and into a t-shirt. The tattoo decorating his right bicep was a dark shadow on his dusky skin, and Abigail curled her fingernails into her palms, restraining the urge to push up his sleeve, study it more closely.

She shifted on the seat, surreptitiously moving away from him. "It was delicious."

He crossed one ankle over the other knee and studied the sole of his running shoe. The lowing of unseen cattle drifting across the field toward them only emphasized the silence between them.

He cleared his throat. "Are you staying long on the island, after your time with us? Or do you go home right away?"

She glared at an innocent hydrangea blossom, colour leeched to grey in the evening light. Why did she let him throw her system into disarray so easily? He was only being polite, as usual. "I am staying one more week. I have a room booked in Ponta Delgada."

"I see." Silence descended once more.

Normally his conversation flowed effortlessly, filling awkward silences, exhorting and encouraging everyone cheerfully. She must make him very uncomfortable if he couldn't hold a simple dialogue with her.

The tension grew unbearable. She jumped to her feet, clutching her book to her chest. "I think I'll go to my room. Goodnight."

Her abrupt retreat was halted by a warm hand on her elbow.

****

"Abigail." He loved the feel of her name on his lips, his tongue.

His hand encircled her arm. Her skin was warm and silky under his fingers and a fine tremor shivered through her.

When he'd seen her through the kitchen window, his decision to keep her at arm's length had fled his mind as if it had never existed. The last of the sunlight stealing over the roof of the farmhouse had lit her platinum hair with liquid gold, draped her shoulders, pooled at her feet. His breath had lodged in his throat. He hadn't been able to look away.

"Abigail," he repeated, simply for the pleasure of tasting her name.

Her eyes widened, irises silver in the starlight. White teeth worried her pale bottom lip and desire shot through his groin. One quick tug and he could have his arms around her, his mouth on hers. He could feed the fire in his veins with the sweetness of her kisses.

She trembled again and her eyelids lowered. Before he could give in to temptation he released her, fisting his hands in his pockets. The denim tightened, pressing uncomfortably on his cock.

"Don't go yet. Stay with me a while." Heightened awareness roughened his voice. He sucked in a breath and tried to regain his usual composure. "We can talk." He felt like a dolt, almost begging for her time, but he wasn't ready to let her leave.

She met his gaze steadily. "About what?"

"Anything. What you think of my island. Where you are from. Your favourite colour."

"Why?"

For a moment he was stumped. *Because I'm fascinated by you against my will* didn't have a good ring. *Because you're not the type of woman I'm normally attracted to and I want to get you out of my head* sounded worse.

His plan to ignore her wasn't working. Obviously he needed to take a different tack. As a boy, his favourite dessert had been his mother's homemade custard—until he'd eaten an entire bowl of it and made himself sick.

Maybe he needed to do the same with Abigail. Needed to gorge himself in order to cure this unlikely fascination.

Abigail huffed out a breath. "Oh, never mind. I didn't realize that would be so difficult to answer." She threw her hands in the air, the paperback book she held almost clipping him on the chin. "I'm going to my room."

Before she took two steps, he whirled her around and pulled her to his chest. The book dropped to the ground. She gave a short cry. He took advantage of her open lips, covering them with his own.

The rush of sensation was more blinding than the first time, more devastating than the second. So much for hoping he'd exaggerated the depth of his attraction. That wish was blown away by the frantic lust crashing through his nerves, skittering over his skin.

Lost in the lushness of her mouth, he walked her backward and pressed her against the rough stone wall. He cradled her face in his palms, leaning into her, feeling her softness mold to his chest, his groin, his thighs.

He couldn't hold back a deep, rumbling groan as her fingers danced down his spine and up again. He slipped a hand under the hem of her t-shirt and caressed the smooth warmth of her ribcage. His thumb brushed the underside of her breast, then higher, to circle around her nipple, already hard and wanting.

She moaned low in her throat, a dizzying siren's call. He cupped her breast, soft and heavy behind the smooth material of her bra, and she arched, pressing into his palm.

He dragged his lips from hers, nibbling and lipping his way along her jawbone to the unpierced lobe of her ear. Her breath rasped against his cheek, ragged and irregular, as he tickled with the tip of his tongue, suckled the delicate skin.

Her hands clutched his shoulders. He reached for her ass and lifted her, her legs automatically locking around his hips.

"*Mãe de Deus*," he gasped. His cock, trapped behind his fly, nestled firmly between her thighs and he thrust toward her, eager, mindless, lost in an animalistic fog.

Suddenly she was writhing in his arms. "No. Wait." Her fists pounded his shoulders and her legs dropped from his hips, stretching for the ground. "Let me go. Let me go!"

He released her and she stumbled. He grasped her elbows to steady her. "*Querida, amor,* what's wrong?" Her chest heaved, matching the pounding of his pulse. "I'm sorry, I didn't mean to scare you." Although he could have sworn he hadn't, was certain her responses were born in passion.

Abigail rested her head against the wall and closed her eyes, fair lashes almost invisible against the paleness of her cheek. "How could you?" she whispered.

Awareness of their surroundings returned in a rush. With Abigail in his arms he'd completely forgotten where they were, forgotten his mother was home, forgotten other guests could have wandered from their rooms at any time. He dropped her arms and stepped away.

He willed his heart to stop racing and concentrated on her words. "Kiss you? Very easily it turns out."

She opened her eyes and shoved him with the flat of her hand against his chest. He fell back another step. "Too easily, if you can spend all day flirting with another woman and then kiss me the moment her back is turned."

His mind, fogged with lust, was slow to grasp her meaning. "You mean Neve?" He sent a quick, silent prayer of thanks that she had kissed him out of sight, in the grotto. "*She* was flirting with *me*."

"And you were enjoying every minute." She lifted her chin, defying him to deny it.

He couldn't help a small surge of smugness at her criticism. He moved forward, placing his hands on either side of her head, bracketing her against the wall. "Of course I enjoyed it. What man wouldn't?"

With satisfaction, he watched colour flood her cheeks, her eyes snap with fury. She shoved him again. This time he refused to move.

"I want to go to my room," she said through clenched teeth, staring past his shoulder.

"Sometimes we can't have what we want."

She swallowed audibly and closed her eyes briefly.

He ducked his head, allowed his lips to brush her ear. "For example," he murmured, "I want you, right now." He inhaled, revelling in the fresh scent of her hair, the intoxicating perfume of her heated skin. "*Quero transar com você*, here, now, up against the wall. I want to take you hard."

****

Abigail's knees weakened and she pressed her palms against the stones behind her, reassuringly solid in a world increasingly nebulous. She fought the urge to fist her hands in his hair and drag his mouth back to hers. His voice, dark and devilish, conjured up a shockingly detailed vision of herself, hoisted in his arms, her naked legs wrapped around his bare, lean hips, the clench of his buttocks as he thrust into her, his face between her breasts, her head falling back in ecstasy.

"I want to take you hard," he repeated in a sinful purr. He raised his head and she stared, mesmerized, into his hot, dark eyes. "But I can't."

She shuddered, whether in dismay or relief she wasn't ready to decide. She ran a tongue over dry lips and his eyes darkened further. "You don't mean it. You can't want me."

"Ah, but I do, *meu amor*. And you want me."

Fear replaced the burn of desire. Not of Santos, but of her own screaming need to believe him. She forced the image of Martin into her mind—safe, secure Martin, who would never make her feel like she was about to go up in flames. Kind, well-meaning Martin, who deserved better than being cheated on, even if he would never find out about it.

She needed to get away from Santos. Needed space to think. Afraid to touch him again, she dipped under his arm and sidled away. He reached for her and she scurried backward a couple steps.

"No." She shook her head rapidly, bobbling like a puppet with a cut string. "You said it yourself, we can't always have what we want."

"You're not afraid, are you?" He stepped toward her and she backed away again. "Yesterday you threw yourself off a cliff. What else is there to be afraid of?"

"I'm not afraid." She wished she could recapture that

sense of accomplishment, the overwhelming confidence that had filled her. Instead she was guilt-ridden, and chilled from the inside out. She hugged her elbows tight to her sides.

"Then what is it, Abigail? We're adults, without commitments, without attachments. Why can't we have what we want, what we both want?"

She had to tell him. Had to. "Because I have a commitment," she whispered. "I have an...attachment."

His eyes narrowed, and the latent sexuality in his face hardened. "What?"

She gulped and forced the words out. "His name is Martin Belaney. We've been together two years. I think he's going to ask me to marry him when I get back."

Santos stood stock still.

"I'm sorry," she said. Then turned and fled on numb legs and bumbling feet to the safety of her room.

CANYONING

Santos stood at the edge of the ravine, watching Cordelia Birtwhistle rappelling carefully down. Jacinta Fabre, an experience climber as well as paraglider, had led the way and was watching from a rock ledge next to the narrow river below.

"Just a little bit further," he called over the rush of water. The rope anchored to the rock at his feet slackened as she reached solid ground. "Great job." He looked at the group beside to him. "Okay, who's next?"

He scanned the now familiar faces. Neve and Victor eager, Sabine, Eric and Cedric stoic, Richard and Tricia confident.

Abigail apprehensive.

He blanked out his immediate, instinctive reaction to offer her reassurance. After last night, he no longer trusted his responses to her.

He no longer trusted her.

"I'll go." Eric, Victor's father, stepped forward and Santos hooked him into the harness, reviewing the procedures yet again. As the older man lowered himself tentatively over the lip of rock, Santos offered quiet encouragement and guidance.

The route they were taking this morning was a relatively simple beginner's course he had done many, many times. Which was lucky, because no matter how he tried, he couldn't keep his mind on the job at hand. It kept circling back to the bomb Abigail had thrown at him last night.

He wasn't sure why he was so pissed off at her. It wasn't like they'd done anything more than heavy petting. And it certainly wasn't as if he'd thought there would be anything more between them than a holiday fling. If he was looking for something else, something more—he shuddered slightly at the thought—more permanent, he'd look closer to home. To someone who understood his heritage, would be accepted without question by his family.

The line wrapped around his waist tugged as Eric unhooked at the bottom of the climb, jerking him from his reverie. Jacinta shouted up an all clear.

"Next?" Santos said, scanning the group still with him.

"I'll go." Abigail moved forward, her movements jerky, her face pale and set.

"All right." His hands moved swiftly over her harness, checking the buckles, hooking in the rope. Try as he might he couldn't completely avoid touching her, his knuckles brushing against her. She twitched at every accidental contact.

"Damn it, relax," he said.

Her eyes widened at his abrupt tone.

"I'm not going to hurt you." He double-checked everything one last time and pointed to the ravine. "You're all set. Let's give it a go."

****

I'm not going to hurt you.

Santos might believe that, but Abigail knew it was too late for that. He had hurt her with the cold treatment he'd meted out since she'd first seen him that morning. She doubted any of the others noticed anything out of the ordinary—although Neve had given both Abigail and Santos a few considering looks—but she knew the difference.

She'd grown used to his smiling greetings, his casual encouragements. And while she knew she'd done the right thing telling him about Martin, she was bewildered by his bitter reaction.

He was acting as if he were angry they couldn't be together. Which was silly, since she wouldn't be too hard to replace. He only had to lift an eyebrow and Neve would come sashaying over. Abigail was sure of it.

"Just hold onto the rope and lean back. Release one clamp at a time and move down slowly." His voice was smooth and professional, devoid of his normal friendliness.

She needed a break from the tension tugging between them, even if it was only during the few minutes she'd be at the bottom of the cliff while he was still at the top. If she'd known how difficult being near him would be, she would have made an excuse to avoid today's activity.

Then again, maybe not. She hadn't done anything wrong. Who was he to ruin her longed for, very expensive holiday?

She followed his directions and backed off the side. If she hadn't been in such turmoil she was sure she would have been too petrified to move, but with her thoughts swirling around Santos she had little worry to spare for the descent.

She soon joined Jacinta, Eric and Cordelia at the bottom. They stood on a broad expanse of black rock, slippery with spray from the cascade to her right. A vigorous stream of water poured into the narrow gorge, tumbled past, then disappeared unceremoniously to her left. The cleft in the rock continued all the way to the sea, revealed as only a light grey patch far in the distance. Ferns and moss clung to the pocked stone walling the cleft, and the rich scent of damp vegetation filled her nostrils.

"I hope Cedric is next," Cordelia fussed in her thick Yorkshire accent. "If he doesn't come soon, I'm afraid he'll chicken out."

"He'll be fine." Jacinta pointed with her chin to the people silhouetted against the sky above them. "Santos will talk him into it."

Whatever Cedric's doubts may have been, Santos did indeed convince him to do the climb, and before long the entire group was gathered on the rough rocky ledge at the base of the cliff.

"Good work, everyone." Santos adjusted the strap on his helmet. They all wore similar safety gear, including heavy waterproof suits. "Now that you've practiced on a dry wall, we'll move on to a wet climb."

Abigail shuffled to the brink of the rocky platform and peered over. Water plummeted in a straight chute, bursting into a plume of spray about eight metres below. The chasm was so narrow at this point that the only way down was to follow the water. Vertigo whirled through her and she backed up quickly, pressing against the security of the rock wall, spongy with foliage.

Jacinta led the way, then one after the other the tourists followed. From Abigail's vantage at the back of the pack she saw each of them slip out of sight. Sabine was the last to disappear over the edge, leaving Abigail alone with Santos.

****

Santos was excruciatingly aware of Abigail hovering behind him as he directed Sabine on how to manoeuvre down the rock face. She lowered herself, water tumbling onto her head and shoulders and he watched carefully, making sure she found her footing.

Once Sabine reached the lower ledge, he could ignore Abigail no longer. "You're up," he said over his shoulder.

She stepped forward, chin held high, hands fisted at her sides.

"You're not facing a firing squad," he said gruffly.

"I know," she snapped back. "But you're acting like you wouldn't mind pulling the trigger."

He paused in attaching the rigging to her harness. "What are you talking about?"

"You've barely looked at me since I told you about Martin." She stuttered slightly on the name but met his gaze squarely. "It's as if you're angry with me for telling you."

A piercing whistle shrieked out of the depths. Santos leaned over and saw Jacinta gesturing, her arms wide, the others milling about her. He gave a thumbs up, motioning to indicate Abigail was on her way.

"I'm not angry with you." He tugged a tad forcefully on a strap, causing her to stagger forward.

She braced herself for an instant, her palms against his shoulders, then snatched her hands away. "Really? Because it sure seems that way to me."

"I'm disappointed." The words were out before he could think. "I was looking forward to getting to know you better." *In the most intimate way a man and woman could get to know each other.* But it was no use saying the last thought out loud. Sex was completely off the table, now that he knew about Martin.

"Oh." She seemed stunned at the idea. "You weren't just...amusing...yourself with me?"

"I might not be looking for a lifetime commitment, Abigail, but that doesn't mean I can't care about you." And wasn't that a shocker? He did care about her, which made a holiday fling even less likely. He didn't want her to do something she might regret when she returned to her boyfriend. "Look, we'd better get going. The others will be wondering what's holding us up."

She bit her lip and fidgeted with the rope tied at her waist. "I'm sorry. For leading you on," she added with a rush. "I know I kissed you first. None of this would have happened if I hadn't done that."

She looked so forlorn he felt the last of his blue funk fade. "Hey, don't worry about it." He chucked her under the chin. "I'll get over it. It's not like you broke my heart. Now, let's get you down this cliff."

QUINTA CARREGADO – A PROPOSAL

Abigail's sleep that night was disturbed by erotic, confusing dreams involving Santos, a wall and a talking hydrangea bush bigger than the farmhouse. Santos had been carrying her in his arms and attempting to lean her against the wall, but every time he did it moved away, and all the while the bush sneered, "He doesn't want you. How could he want you?"

She woke up feeling groggy. Moisture beaded the window over her head, diluting the struggling daylight. It reminded her of the gorge, where she'd struggled down cliffs slick with water, mist coating her skin with dampness.

Her dreams left her with a sense of frustrated humiliation. She'd been stunned when Santos admitted he cared for her. Who would have thought he would ever say such a thing? But it had made his next words more gut-wrenching.

It's not like you broke my heart.

She wished she was the type of woman who could break a man's heart. Someone bold and sexy and confident. Her forehead wrinkled in a scowl. Someone like Neve.

Shaking off the lassitude of her fractured night, she

made her way to the dining room and practically inhaled her first cup of coffee. Though she had little appetite, she forced herself to take a small helping of fresh island pineapple, one slice of Senhora Carregado's signature homemade bread and a dab of fresh white cheese. She nodded at the Thorntons and the Birtwhistles, seated together. Earlier in the week she'd naturally gravitated to the Canadian pair at meal times, but lately they had partnered with the only other married couple. Abigail's solitary state was still a novelty to her, so she took a place at an empty table in the corner without concern.

Victor and Eric arrived shortly after, with Neve and Sabine the last to appear. Neve smiled and waved. It would have been a lot easier to hate her if she wasn't so open and friendly. Abigail did her best to reply with a smile of her own, but green-tinged emotion made her attempt half-hearted. What she wouldn't give to have that effortless charm, that God-given allure.

Neve chose her breakfast and made a straight line for Abigail. She plopped gracefully into the seat opposite. "Good morning. Sleep well?"

She didn't get a chance to answer the innocuous question as Lina called across the morning babble. "Abigail! There's a call for you in the office. From someone named Martin."

****

It was after midnight in Canada. Why would Martin be calling so late? Had something happened to Tobias? Her fragile, newly found courage regarding her own safety was no match for the terror of losing her baby brother. She scurried through the dining room.

"He left messages during the night, as well," Lina told her as Abigail crossed the kitchen into the tiny office. "Let me shut the door for you. It will be quieter."

Abigail snatched up the receiver, scattering sheets of paper off the crowded desk and onto the tile floor. "Martin? Is everything okay?"

"I am the one that should be asking that question," he replied testily. "You didn't send an email today. Or yesterday, I should say. I've been worrying for hours."

She was still tangled in a vista of disaster. "Tobias? He's all right?"

"He's fine," Martin said. "But I'm not. When I didn't get your message, I tried to call, but only got the answering machine. You have no idea the thoughts that have been going through my head."

She eased her grip on the receiver and allowed her neck muscles to relax. Martin would never lie to her, especially about Tobias. As her anxiety faded, his peevish tone registered. "It's just past seven in the morning here. It was the middle of the night when you called."

"Which is one of the reasons we set up this schedule. If you send your email before you go to bed, I get it before leaving work. Then I can relax for the rest of my evening, knowing you are safely asleep."

"I'm sorry. I forgot." She pulled out the old-fashioned wooden-armed swivel chair tucked under the desk and sank into it. "I was so exhausted last night I dropped into bed without thinking of it."

"You know I only conceded to this plan because you promised to keep in touch every day."

The room shrank about her. Even though Martin was thousands of kilometres away, his disapproval was clear. She battled back her instinctive urge to apologize a second time. "You know what they say," she said with forced cheerfulness, "no news is good news."

"I don't understand why you are taking this so lightly. I spent the last several hours imagining you lying in hospital, injured and all alone."

She knew he meant well, that he cared for her. But she did not need him to take over her mother's role as neurotic over-protector in her life. "If anything drastic had happened, you would have been notified by the tour company. You are my emergency contact."

"This vacation was a ridiculous idea from the start. It was bad enough when you chose to go to such a little known location. Your refusal to let me go with you only made it worse."

The thought of Martin and Santos in the same room made her break out in a cold sweat.

"Maybe you should cut your trip short. The organized part of your tour ends in a couple of days, right?" He didn't wait for her answer. "I'm sure you'll be ready to come home then." His tone brisk, he continued. "Yes, that's what I think you should do. And once you're back, we can set a date for our wedding."

Abigail's chest tightened, squeezing her lungs, cutting into her breath. "Wedding? Martin, what are you talking about?" Instinctively she reached into her pocket for her inhaler, only to realize she'd left it in her room. She'd used it so rarely since arriving in the Azores she'd stopped carrying it.

"You know as well as I do our relationship is leading toward marriage. I was planning to propose in the next few months, once you'd recovered from your mother's death. But your absence has had one benefit—it has confirmed my feelings for you. I want to solidify our commitment to each other, and sooner rather than later."

A fine drizzle patterned the window overlooking the

back yard, turning the view of hedge, field and far-off ocean into an Impressionist painting. Abigail blinked, her head spinning. "Martin, I...I don't know what to say."

He was right. She had recognized marriage was the next logical step. Hadn't she told Santos so herself? But now, with the words finally out in the open, she felt trapped, cornered, at bay.

"I'm sorry, this isn't how I'd planned to propose. I'll make it up to you when you return, do it right, make it as romantic as you want. Now, how will you go about changing your ticket so you can return early?"

His complete conviction that she would bow to his command snapped her out of her daze. "I'm not changing my plans, Martin. I'm staying here as long as I intended."

"Now, Abigail." The friendly condescension in his tone raised the hackles on the back of her neck. "Can't you take my feelings into consideration? I've allowed you your little escapade. Now it's time to come home."

For years she'd bowed to her mother's whims, knowing they were the product of an illness she could not control. Habit had made it easy to allow Martin to direct their relationship—what they did, where they went, who they befriended. She'd actually welcomed his guidance, as the stress of caring for her mother left her with little energy to deal with the minutia of life.

But her few days on São Miguel had shown her how hollow such a life was. She'd never felt so deeply alive as in the seconds before the wing of the paraglider had lifted her off the earth. Or felt so powerfully feminine as when she'd been in Santos' arms.

Suddenly she knew what she had to do.

"I can't marry you," she blurted. She pressed her fingers to her lips, as if to stop more words from bursting out.

"What did you say?" Martin's tone was more irritated than shocked.

God, was she really going to do this? Break up with her boyfriend of two years, a man who wanted to marry her, over the phone? Was she really throwing away a steady, reliable man because of a few kisses from a stranger?

"I can't marry you," she repeated. "I'm sorry, Martin. This is a horrible way to tell you." She fiddled with a glass knob on the drawer of the desk.

"I don't understand." Now she could hear his bewilderment.

"Things have changed. *I've* changed. It started when Mom died, and it hasn't stopped yet." She wanted to tell him that sometimes she just wanted to scream and scream and scream until she had no voice left, but didn't think he would understand. "I don't think marriage is in my plans anymore."

A hollow hissing filled the line. She waited, not sure of what to do next.

Finally, Martin spoke. "This probably isn't something we should be discussing over the phone."

She wanted to point out that he had started it with the whole "set the date for our wedding" thing, but bit her tongue. "You're right. But I needed to tell you how I felt." It wouldn't have been fair to let him go on believing nothing had changed between them, when so much had. And not only because of her confusing, complex feelings for Santos. So much more was bubbling inside of her. Too much to deal with right now.

"We'll talk more when you get home."

"Of course. But don't expect me to change my mind." She was serious about making this break, and she was going to do it right. "And Martin? I think it will be best if we give each other some space right now. Please don't expect any more emails from me. I'll stay in touch with Tobias, so check with him if you want to know how I'm doing."

"You're going to cut me off, just like that?" His disbelief was clear. "I can't agree to that."

"You don't have to agree, Martin," she said gently. "It's simply what is." And she hung up the phone.

****

Santos took his place at the kitchen table and settled in for breakfast. He sipped his coffee, idly noticing the door to the office was closed.

Lina and his mother loaded trays with fresh supplies. "Keep an eye on Abigail, will you?" Lina tossed his way. She shouldered open the door to the dining room, holding it for Serafina to slip through. "She's on the phone. Someone was trying quite frantically to get a hold of her. I hope it's not bad news from home." She followed their mother, leaving Santos alone.

His mug thumped onto the table. Had something happened to her brother? Or was it Martin? He might be jealous of the man, but that didn't mean he wanted anything bad to happen to him.

His thoughts screeched to a halt. Jealous? Is that why he was so ticked off? He was jealous?

He envisioned Abigail as she'd looked in the garden—wide-eyed, fiery and fierce. Remembered how she'd felt in his arms—like quicksilver, molten and slick. Then he pictured her in the embrace of another man—an amorphous figure, dark, hazy, yet overwhelming her slight form.

It was only when the sharp edge of the table cut into his palm that he realized he was clenching the wood so tight his fingernails were white.

Damn. What the hell did he do now? He'd never been in this position before—the man on the outside, looking in, wanting someone else's woman.

The office door opened and Abigail stepped out. She placed a hand on the door jamb and leaned heavily against it, swaying slightly. Santos was on his feet and striding toward her before the conscious thought had formed.

"*Querida*, what's wrong?" He slipped an arm about her waist and led her to his breakfast chair. "Is it your brother?" He forced himself to ask, "Or Martin?"

She stared at him, white surrounding the hydrangea blue of her irises, but remained silent.

His stomach dropped. He crouched beside her and grasped her slack hands. "Tell me. I want to help, if I can."

She licked her lips, her mouth trembling. "I broke up with Martin."

The words didn't compute right away. "What?"

Her voice was stronger this time. "I broke up with Martin." She eased her hands from his grip and straightened her back.

His eyes searched her face. The colour was coming back to her cheeks and her eyes had lost their glassy stare. "I thought you were going to marry him."

"So did he." The corner of her mouth quirked. "I guess you were both wrong."

He rose to his feet, swung a chair around and straddled the seat, resting his arms on the back. If he didn't put some distance between them he was afraid he might do something disastrous.

Like sweep her into his arms and kiss her senseless.

"Maybe you'd better explain what's going on. In words of one syllable or less."

She laughed shortly, rubbing her forehead with her long,

slender fingers. "I'll try." She met his gaze briefly, then dropped her eyes, a faint blush blooming in her cheeks. "I told you my mother was over-protective, right?" He nodded. "Well, it was a bit more than that. It was an illness. She foresaw disaster at every turn. Even something as simple as going to the mailbox became traumatic. Before long, she couldn't leave the house, became horribly upset if Tobias or I were out of her sight for too long."

"How old were you?"

"It started in my teens, after my father died." She pulled her ponytail over her shoulder, draping it over her collarbone, revealed by the wide neck of her t-shirt. She looked too fragile to have carried such a burden.

"It must have been tough on you."

"It was. And I'm afraid I didn't always handle it as well as I should have. But I loved my mother, and I wanted to make her life as comfortable, as pleasant as possible." She fidgeted with her hair, toyed with the ends. "Any chance I could have a coffee? I left mine in the dining room."

"Of course." He pulled a thick white mug from a cupboard, filled it with steaming liquid and handed it to her. "Sugar? Milk?"

"No, thanks." She sipped carefully, hummed with pleasure. "Your mother makes the best coffee. Thanks."

He sat down again and prodded her to continue. "Where does Martin come into all this?"

"As you can imagine, it was tough to meet anyone when most of my time was spent with my mother. Martin is another accountant at my firm." She eyed him diffidently. "Did you know I was an accountant? Can't get much more boring than that, can you?"

"I'm sure it has its moments." He bit back his impatience and said gently, "So you started dating?"

"Yes. I don't think I realized until just a few minutes ago how much like my mother he was. Both of them controlled my life. For my own good, of course," she added with soft sarcasm, "but still. When my mother passed—"

"She died? When?"

"Two months ago. An aneurysm."

He took her hand again, and this time she clung to his. "I'm sorry." He rubbed his thumb across her knuckles, offering what comfort he could, wishing he could do more than make empty gestures, mouth clichéd phrases.

"I miss her every day." Her eyes glittered with tears, but they remained unshed. "I wish we could have travelled together, explored together. All too often I resented her illness, wished it would just go away. But when she died, all I wanted was to have her back."

He was beginning to see the core of strength hidden inside the frail exterior. "Martin must have helped you through it."

"He did. You mustn't think of him as cold, or unfeeling. He means well. But I can't live like that any longer. I need to make my own decisions, live my own life."

Finally he could ask the question he most wanted answered. Needed answered. "So why did you break up with him?"

For a breathless moment she stared at him, lips slightly parted, a pulse beating rapidly in her throat. She blinked and the spell was broken.

"He told me we were getting married. Didn't ask, simply told me. And I knew, right then, I couldn't. It would have been a huge mistake. So I said no. I told him it was over." She drew in a shaky breath. "I still can't believe I did it."

DANCING WITH DOLPHINS

Santos manoeuvred the van out of the courtyard of Quinta Carregado and began winding his way down the narrow, steep streets to the village on the shore below. The group behind him was loud, excited and rambunctious— every single one of them thrilled with today's activity, swimming with wild dolphins in the open Atlantic.

He stole a quick glance at Abigail in the rear view mirror. She was talking to Tricia Thornton with the calm reserve she showed most people. No one would guess she had just finished a traumatic phone call to her boyfriend.

Ex-boyfriend.

He slowed the van at an intersection and took the chance to rub his thumbs into his eye sockets, gravelly from lack of sleep. Normally his outdoor lifestyle had him dropping off as soon as his body relaxed between the sheets. For the last two nights, each time he drifted off, the memory of Abigail's slender body, rosy lips, fragile skin, leaped to mind. Every single one of his muscles would snap to attention, and there he'd be, staring at the ceiling, gritting his teeth, sleep snatched away once more.

This morning's events meant he was free to pursue

Abigail, and she was free to accept his attentions. An edgy thrill rolled through his belly. Abigail with a boyfriend was no more than a distraction. Abigail without one could be dangerous.

Ignoring the jitters lurking under his skin, he turned left toward the marina and considered his next step. Abigail had appeared shocked more than distraught this morning. While he didn't mind being her rebound lover—his body contracted at the images that thought raised—he wouldn't want to take advantage of her.

He'd give her a day or two, see if that courageous heart of hers would force her to make the first move.

If it didn't, he would.

****

Abigail felt a sense of relief and freedom she'd never experienced before. She was finally, completely on her own. No mother, no Martin. No one to tell her what to do, and only Tobias to worry about.

And what was she doing with that new found freedom?

Thinking about Santos.

She chatted with Tricia Thornton as the van rattled its way through the village's cobblestone streets to the marina, and the entire time her skin was super-sensitized to him, the hair rising on her arms and neck every time she felt his eyes on her.

And he was watching her. A couple of times when she'd glanced toward the front, she'd seen his eyes sliding away from hers in the rear view mirror.

By the time Santos pulled into a free space near a low, single story building at the water's edge she was fretting with nerves.

"Our guide is waiting for us," he announced. "Just head through those doors."

Abigail climbed out and followed the group inside. They were greeted by an athletic young woman, dark haired like most of the island's residents but with shockingly blue eyes.

She paid close attention to the instructions the woman provided as she handed out snorkels, masks, fins and wetsuits. The suits weren't the full body versions with hoods she'd seen on TV and in movies, but had short legs and sleeves and no head covering.

The men and women headed for their respective change rooms. Abigail entered a narrow stall between Cordelia and Sabine.

She changed into the one-piece swimsuit she'd brought with her. It had seemed rather revealing when she'd bought it in Prince George, with high cut legs and a plunging neckline, but she'd felt just reckless enough to purchase it. It was nowhere near as skimpy as the bikini she'd seen Neve sunbathing in a couple of days ago. That had been nothing but strings knotted in strategic places.

She began to wiggle into the wetsuit.

From the booth to her left she heard puffing and panting and Cordelia's north of England voice leaked through the thin wall. "I cannot be seen in this!" she whispered despairingly.

Abigail realized the comment hadn't been meant for her ears and said nothing. Yanking at the tight, rubbery material wrapped around her waist, she made little, jerking hops in an attempt to get it higher on her legs. She caught sight of herself in the mirror on the back of the door and snorted.

One arm was in its sleeve, but now it was trapped at her hip. Her reflection flailed helplessly. She muffled her giggles, but it was no use.

"Are you okay in there?" Sabine asked from her right in her cool, crisply accented English.

"Y-yes, fine," she replied between snickers. If she bent forward and twisted...like...that...she might be able to get her shoulder in.... A rolling laugh escaped.

"This is ridiculous," moaned the invisible Cordelia. "I look like an over-stuffed sausage."

"Mine's still stuck around my knees." Tears rolled down Abigail's cheeks. "If I can't winch it any higher I'll have to waddle like a penguin to the boat."

"Oh, thank God," called Tricia from the far end. "I'm not the only one that will look like an idiot."

Neve chimed in to the rising hilarity. "This is ridiculous. I need help." Abigail heard a cubicle lock snick as Neve opened her door. "Come on, ladies, everybody out!"

****

Santos changed into his wetsuit and waited for his guests in the front lobby of the tour office, a wide open space with durable carpet tiles on the floor and large windows overlooking a view of the harbour.

A sudden shriek, followed by muffled giggling, escaped from the women's change room. His eyebrows shot to his hairline as the ruckus continued. He couldn't decipher any words, but it was easy enough to distinguish most of the women's voices. Especially Abigail's husky tones.

Victor, Eric, Cedric and Richard joined him, now garbed in their short wetsuits and carrying the rest of their gear.

"What is going on in there?" Cedric stared at the door as a particularly shrill squeak reached their ears. The Yorkshire farmer had been good-natured although reluctant throughout most activities so far. Santos was surprised to see him looking unselfconsciously confident in the form-fitting outfit.

Richard grinned at Santos. "At least they're enjoying themselves."

A few minutes later, the changing room door opened and the women streamed out, eyes bright, cheeks flushed.

"Dare I ask what went on in there?" Santos asked.

Tricia Thornton wiped what looked suspiciously like tears off her face with a trembling hand, a wide smile splitting her face. "Nothing. We were just getting into our suits."

For some reason that set the women off again, all of them laughing so hard they had to lean against each other to stay upright. His gaze swept from one side to the other, landed on Abigail, and stalled.

He'd seen innumerable women wearing wetsuits. So why did the sight of this one affect him so deeply?

The rubbery material clung to every slight curve. He'd known she was slim, had felt her pressed against him enough times to know that. But the tight black suit revealed delicate dips and contours in sensual detail. The flare of her hip, the slenderness of her thighs, the subtle swell of her breasts.

Most erotic of all her was her abandoned laughter. Her arms wrapped around her middle as she giggled uncontrollably, shoulders shaking.

He shifted the stack of towels he was carrying and held them strategically in front of his groin. Today was going to be torture. And waiting for her to recover from breaking up with Martin well-nigh impossible.

Santos exchanged bemused looks with the other men, including Victor. They waited patiently for the women to curb their glee, then everyone spread out in a loose semi-circle before him, ready for their next instructions.

Manuel, the skipper of the boat designated to take them

out, approached. Gruff and surly, he had been a fisherman for years before a bad back forced him to find a new occupation. He knew the waters around São Miguel like few others, and could be trusted to navigate properly around the dolphin pods. It was too bad he disliked tourists, and couldn't hide it.

"The boat, she's ready. Bring them." He stomped out the door without waiting for Santos' answer.

"All right, everyone, time to head out." He ushered the group through the doors, down a clanking aluminum ramp and onto the cement pier. Tied to a metal ladder and bobbing on the gentle wash was a long, narrow inflatable boat, grey with yellow stripes and seating for ten.

Santos assiduously avoided watching Abigail climb into the watercraft. If he didn't look at her, maybe he wouldn't embarrass himself.

Manuel untied the rope and stepped onto the bouncing boat as easily as stepping out his own front door. He stood behind the steering column at the back of the boat and started the motor. At the same time, he fished a cigarette out of a pack tucked into his chest pocket and lit it. His face, dark and seamed from a lifetime on the water, relaxed as the nicotine hit his system.

"Where are we going?" Victor asked him, face aglow with excitement.

"Where the dolphins are," the skipper growled.

"Yes, I know, but..."

Santos made a shushing motion with his hand at the young man, lifting a shoulder in apology at Manuel's brusqueness. "There are *vigias*—lookouts—posted on the headlands. They radio in to Manuel"—he pointed to a shortwave radio clipped to the surly captain's belt—"and let us know when they sight a pod. But keep your eyes open. Sometimes we see them first from the boat."

He did his best to keep up the chatter he normally found so easy, but his attention constantly drifted to Abigail. She was sitting a few rows away, staring rigidly forward. He continued with his automatic spiel while watching her reach into a small bag and pull out her inhaler. He hoped her asthma wouldn't stop her from swimming. She returned the medication to the bag and twisted in her seat to face him, a slight frown creasing her forehead. Silver blond hair whipped in the breeze, as if invisible fingers were sliding through the silk. He remembered the feel of those strands against his cheek, their sweet, fresh scent, and stuttered over his spiel.

He cleared his suddenly dry throat and soldiered on.

****

Abigail breathed deeply, in through her nose, out through her mouth, and waited for the tide of fear to subside.

She hadn't been anxious on the way to the marina, distracted by her thoughts of Santos and Martin, and the laughter in the ladies room had relaxed her even further. But the moment she'd seen the boat, panic reared in her throat. The craft seemed much too fragile to survive the treacherous Atlantic—a blow up toy without roof or railing. She called up the memory of paragliding—her terror before, her confidence after—and forced herself aboard.

Her seat perched near the edge of the rounded rubber side, and she was certain any sudden movement—from either her or the boat—would pitch her into the water. She peered cautiously over. Sunlight streamed into the pale blue depths and she could see the flashes of fish flickering by the rocks several metres below. Her head spun and she clutched the seat desperately as the boat pulled away from the ladder.

A few minutes later she was still sitting securely in the

boat, despite the way it bounced over the water. The sea was calm, without the great, curling, white-tipped waves she had feared, and she relaxed enough to release her grip on her seat and clench her hands in her lap.

Compared to jumping off a cliff supported by only flimsy silk, this should be nothing. She was a strong swimmer, as her mother had insisted on lessons for both her and Tobias. It was the only time she had encouraged any potentially dangerous activity. Torn between two evils, her fear of her children accidentally drowning had overpowered her fear of letting them learn to swim.

Abigail stared into the opaque, faded denim depths. She'd never swum anywhere but a pool before. Her stomach churned at the knowledge of the thousands of metres of water between her and the ocean floor.

Never mind what was swimming in it.

Her chest tightened, her lungs compressed, and she dosed herself with her inhaler. She really had to stop using the medication as a nervous crutch. She knew it wasn't asthma making her breathe light and shallow, yet she still felt better for having taken it.

It was time to take control of her fright. She closed her eyes, concentrated on the crisp wind in her face, the taste of the salt spray on her lips, the growl of the engine. Once again she recalled her euphoria after paragliding, recaptured her sense of power and potential when she and Santos landed. Slowly her breathing smoothed out, her pulse quieted.

She opened her eyes. Actually getting into the water would take a determined act of will, but she was no longer worried she'd end up a quivering wreck on the floor of the boat.

Turning on her seat, she concentrated on Santos as he lectured with skill and knowledge about the dolphins they hoped to see. His calm confidence as he explained about habitats and feeding behaviour, responsible eco-tourism and environmental stewardship, soothed away the rest of her nerves.

He was in mid-sentence when Neve shouted out, "There!" Her blue eyes widened with delight and awe.

Abigail swung in her seat, and promptly forgot anything other than the amazing display before her.

Sleek bodies broke the surface of the water, racing the waves, so much a part of the ocean they seemed simply another rolling crest. She jolted as a grey torpedo exploded, launching itself out of the depths, and in joyous abandon twisted rapidly, spinning on its tail, before crashing back below the surface. Her breath clogged her throat and inexplicably tears pricked her eyes. It was too much beauty, too much grace, too much...simply too much.

"These are common dolphins." Santos' voice broke through the rush of wind, the slap of water. "You should be able to see a distinctive hour-glass pattern on their flanks." A group of ten or twelve of the creatures arched out of the water, playing leapfrog with the waves, keeping pace with the boat effortlessly. "This is a good sized pod, perhaps thirty to forty animals. Manuel will hold our position here, and we'll see if they approach."

Abigail waited, her hands clenched in her lap, no longer in fear but in delighted anticipation. She willed the animals to come near. The playful pod swept away, tantalizingly close but not close enough. And then, as smoothly as if the movement had been choreographed from the beginning, they made a graceful turn and began circling the boat.

Santos moved to the prow, manoeuvring with agility between the rows of seats, his steps adjusting easily to the rise and fall of the deck. "As we discussed, only two swimmers in the water at a time. To start with, we'll give each pair two minutes in the water. We have no guarantee how long the pod will stay with us, but that should give everyone a chance." He smiled, an easy, assured smile that sent shivers down Abigail's spine. "Neve and Sabine, why don't you go first?"

Abigail bit back a sharp stab of jealousy. What if the pod decided to leave? What if she never got into the water? She wriggled in her seat, all fear forgotten, anticipation sparking off her fingertips.

Neve and Sabine pulled on their masks and snorkels, and slipped smoothly into the water. They paddled away and waited, suspended in the buoyant saltiness. Moments later, a sinuous body slipped between them. Others circled round, backs cresting through the waves.

Abigail watched mutinously for long, breathless minutes. Finally, Santos motioned the women back to the boat. They dragged themselves over the side, helped less than courteously by their cranky captain.

Two by two, the rest of the group took their turns. Each returned to the boat giddy with excitement. Abigail bit her lip and watched the water worriedly, but the dolphins showed no signs of leaving.

Victor and Eric returned to the boat, and finally Santos looked at her and grinned. "Ready?"

She moved quickly, positioning her mask over her nose and mouth. She lifted an eyebrow when she saw Santos do the same.

"I'm coming with you," he replied to her unasked question. "No one goes in the ocean alone."

He sat next to her on the edge of the boat, his sun-warmed shoulder brushing against hers, the snug material of his wetsuit molding his muscular thighs. Her legs, dangling in the cool water next to his, looked unnaturally pale compared to his olive skin.

She slipped the rubber snorkel into her mouth and slid over the side. Santos did the same on her left.

Concentrating fiercely on breathing through her mouth, she flippered gently away from the boat. She stared straight down into nothingness—murky blue shot through with sunbeams that weakened and faded into midnight. Water splashed into her ears and over her head, but she ignored it.

Careful not to dip the end of her snorkel into the water, she peered from side to side. A flicker of movement below and to her right caught her attention.

Soon dolphins surrounded her. The agile creatures spun and twisted and danced, flowing silkily through the water. She could hear them talking—clicks and clacks, squeaks and whistles. One especially bold creature swam directly beneath her and turned on its side, regarding her intelligently from its black eye, the trademark grin eerily human. She gazed solemnly back, an odd sort of communication passing between them, until with a sinuous flick of its tail it disappeared into the depths below.

Santos' hand clasped her wrist, shockingly warm in contrast to the cool of the water. Surely it wasn't time to go back to the boat already? It had felt like only seconds. Instead of motioning her to the boat, however, his palm slid down and he wound his fingers between hers. His eyes, clear and bright behind the wide mask, crinkled in a grin.

Linked together, they floated gently in the satin of the Atlantic Ocean, and watched the dolphins' graceful ballet.

A DINNER INVITATION

"That...was...amazing." Neve squeezed water out of her hair with a towel.

"It was magical," Tricia agreed. "Spiritual, in a way."

The women were in the change room once more, the adventure over. Thrills still chased each other over Abigail's skin as she struggled out of the wetsuit and into dry clothes.

The pod had stayed with the boat for almost an hour, giving everyone plenty of chances to swim. Once the curious animals had seen their fill of the alien species visiting their world, they swept away, disappearing in moments. Abigail had battled a fierce longing, an overwhelming urge to follow them, to join with them, just one more time.

Manuel and Santos had a rapid discussion in Portuguese. The skipper set to ranging far and wide, and Santos explained they would try to sight either another dolphin pod or one of the many species of whale known to frequent the waters around the Azores. Unfortunately, they returned to the harbour more than an hour later without having seen anything else.

Abigail knew she should be disappointed, but couldn't summon up the emotion. She was still in a peaceful turmoil from her time with the dolphins. Each time she had entered the water, visited their world, she had felt a preternatural affinity with the creatures. It was an experience she would never, ever forget, and she clung to the sensations, already fading.

The drive back to Quinta Carregado was quiet and restful. Everyone in the group seemed as affected as Abigail, and spoke in soft tones or not at all, as if returning from a religious encounter.

Deciding what to do for dinner seemed utterly prosaic after the enchantment of the afternoon.

"I'm hungry," Victor complained as they milled about the courtyard after disembarking from the van.

"Of course you are," Abigail teased, but her gut gurgled in sympathy just as Santos stopped next to her. He raised an eyebrow, a corner of his mouth twitching. A blush warmed her cheeks.

"Me, too," agreed Neve, and everyone else joined in the chorus. Normally the group split up after the day's activity, but this afternoon everyone seemed unwilling to separate.

"Richard and I had an amazing meal at a restaurant right on the ocean our first night here. We've been meaning to go back." Tricia glanced at her husband and communicated wordlessly, in the way of long-time spouses. "Why don't we get cleaned up, meet back here in an hour or so, and all walk down together?"

A murmur of agreement swept through the others. Abigail hesitated. She'd spent most of her evenings alone since arriving in São Miguel. Solitude was something she cherished, after almost constant attendance on her mother for so many years.

But not tonight.

"I'd love to come along, if that's all right," she said

diffidently.

Tricia looked surprised but pleased. "That would be great."

Without pausing to think, Abigail turned to Santos, still standing at her elbow. "Why don't you come, too? Unless, of course"—she laughed, a tight, nervous laugh—"you've seen enough of us for today, or have something else to do, or whatever." She bit her lip to stop herself from warbling on.

His eyes narrowed as he studied her face. She did her best to meet his gaze boldly, but she'd used up her tiny cache of courage simply asking the question, and her eyelids dropped. Everyone else had wandered off, except for Tricia and Richard who stood to her left. She couldn't see their faces, but did see Richard take his wife's hand and draw her quietly away, out of sight.

Abigail stared at Santos' feet, clad in brown leather sandals with thick soles. His toes were long, dusted with dark hair, the nails neatly clipped. She imagined sucking them, swirling her tongue around them, and a flush sizzled through her.

Good God, what had got into her? She'd never had such shocking thoughts in her life.

Every experience, every adventure, every *day* in the Azores was peeling off layers of reserve, of fear, of constraint. She stood on the edge—whether of disaster or discovery she couldn't say. All she knew was, after tonight, everything would change.

If only he said yes.

A warm hand cupped her chin, lifted her face, but she kept her eyelids lowered. Santos' thumb brushed along her jaw and her belly heated, clenched. His fingers slipped from her chin, trailed down her neck and toyed with the end of the ponytail hanging over her shoulder. She held back a gasp, liquid longing heating between her legs. His hands grasped her shoulders, smoothing the skin in a slow circular motion. Her knees trembled.

"Look at me, Abigail."

She couldn't resist the command. Her lids drifted up and her gaze met his. His eyes were hot, knowing, confident. She swallowed, her mouth painfully dry in anticipation.

****

Abigail's eyes shone with the clear brilliance of blue diamonds, scintillating despite the wariness on her face.

"That's better," Santos said. God, she was beautiful, he thought with vague surprise. He'd admitted she was attractive, pretty in an unusual way. But he was wrong. She was stunning in her courage, her vulnerability.

He'd been unwillingly ready to wait days for her to gather enough daring to take this step. Instead she's shocked him once more with her determination to grasp life with all her might.

"Now, ask me again," he ordered gently.

She drew in a breath, lifted her chin. "Santos, would you like to join us for dinner?"

"*Sim*," he said, "yes, I would."

A vibration quivered through her. He felt it under his palms as they cupped the cool skin of her shoulders. She blinked slowly and her breath gasped out, puffing against his throat.

"Oh," she said. "Okay." With a visible effort, she gathered calm around her, and once again he was struck by the strength of her spirit. "I'll just"—she gestured with one hand in the general direction of her room in the converted barn—"go get ready."

"I'll meet you back here."

She took a cautious step backward. "Yes. Right." Another step. "In an hour."

He couldn't help the grin curling the corner of his mouth. "In an hour."

She turned and fled.

Santos strode into the farmhouse. Pride in Abigail outweighed any smugness he felt. She hadn't said anything directly, but he was certain at least part of her decision to break it off with Martin had to do with the kisses they'd shared. It would be a delight to watch her bloom and blossom now she was out from under that relationship.

He showered off the sea salt and changed into a crisp white shirt and neatly pressed, tan-coloured cotton pants, then made his way to the kitchen. His mother was stirring something on the stove. He greeted her with a kiss on the cheek. "*Te abençoe, Senhora.*"

"*Te abençoe, filho.*" She waved a wooden spoon, dangerously covered in a thick red sauce. "Sit, sit. Dinner will be ready soon."

"Will you excuse me?" He dipped his head in apology. "I've been invited to eat with the guests. We're going into the village."

"You don't do that very often." Serafina poked his breastbone, with a clean finger, thank goodness. "It's that Neve, isn't it? I've seen her look at you."

He rubbed his chest and smiled at her ferociousness. "It's not Neve."

"Her sister, then?"

He regarded her round, rosy face with exasperated affection. "Not Sabine, either."

Her eyes widened in horror. "Do not tell me you are having an affair with one of the married women."

"No! I'm not having an affair with any of them. If you must know, Abigail invited me to go along."

She looked blank, then frowned. "The little mousy one?"

"She's not mousy." She was lithe and limber with opalescent skin and a hidden well of bravery he found fascinating.

His mother studied him with twin creases slashing between her brows. "You're a grown man. I know you've been with women, don't think I don't."

"*Mãe*!" As his affairs occurred only after the guests had left Quinta Carregado, he'd hoped his mother had been oblivious. After all, it wasn't as if he'd brought any of those women back home to meet his family on a more personal level.

"And what you do with those women is between you, them, and God." She pinned him with a glare. "But this Abigail, she is…she is different. Than the others."

He suppressed the urge to squirm, a feeling he hadn't had since he was a teenager. "Maybe. But I like her."

"You like lots of girls. That Jacinta who helps us, you like her, don't you?" Serafina regarded him slyly from the corner of her eye. "A nice girl, good family. She would make you a good wife."

He shook his head firmly. "I am not marrying Jacinta."

"Because of this Abigail?" She planted her fists on her hips.

"*Mãe*! Abigail will be gone in little over a week. You have nothing to worry about." The attraction between he and Abigail was something neither one of them could ignore, but it had no future. He knew that, and he was sure she did, too.

"Are you certain?" Serafina asked softly. To his discomfort, a look of sorrow settled on her face. She reached up and patted him gently on the cheek. "Go to dinner," she said. "And when you come back, you tell me about this Abigail. You tell me about this one that is different."

****

Santos leaned in front of Abigail in order to answer a question put to him by Richard Thornton, seated on her right. The Ilha Verde Aventuras guests were grouped at a large rectangular table, laid with a simple white cloth and covered with the remains of succulent seafood meals.

At least Abigail assumed they'd been succulent. She'd eaten mechanically, far too aware of Santos sitting next to her to appreciate the delicacies placed before her.

The animated buzz and chatter washed hollowly over her, as if from a great distance. She didn't even hear what Santos was saying—the brush of his forearm against hers was an electric connection disrupting her senses. She sniffed surreptitiously, revelling in the scent of clean, hot male, and flushed when Santos slid her a smiling glance.

Richard turned away and Santos relaxed in his chair. He tilted his head and grinned lazily at her, thick, dark lashes framing eyes bright with an intensity that took her breath away.

Instead of shuffling her chair away—her first instinct— she purposefully shifted closer, her shoulder grazing his bicep. She held his gaze, watching the flare of awareness, the spark of anticipation grow. When she licked her lips, trying to ease their dryness, his focus dropped to her mouth. His body tensed, and she felt power surge through her as waves of desire vibrated off him, catching her in their wake.

"How about you, Abigail?"

She dragged her eyes away from Santos. Neve, sitting opposite, quirked an off-centre grin. Flustered, Abigail

134

stumbled to catch up. "Ah...uhm...I'm sorry, what did you say?"

"We were talking about how much we are looking forward to tomorrow. What about you?"

"Oh, yes, me, too." She cast her mind about, desperately trying to remember the itinerary for the next day. Her second to last day with the tour.

Her second to last day near Santos.

"Have you done much horseback riding? Aren't there cowboys in Canada?" Neve asked.

Horseback riding. Right. Abigail felt her conversational feet settle under her. "No, I've never been on horseback," she answered. "And there are plenty of cowboys in Canada, especially Western Canada."

"Is that where you are from? Western Canada?"

"My home town, Prince George, is in the middle of British Columbia. Alberta is better known for cowboys, but the area just south of my city is called the Cariboo, which has a lot of cattle ranches."

Tricia Thornton joined the conversation. "British Columbia is a beautiful province. It has everything—oceans and deserts and mountains. Richard and I love Victoria."

Santos offered the wine bottle to Tricia and at her nod, refilled her glass. "My cousin lives in Victoria," he said. "He tells me often what a beautiful city it is."

Abigail turned to him in astonishment. "Your cousin lives in Victoria?"

"For about ten years. Married, with a couple of children." Santos twisted the stem of his wineglass, the red liquid clinging seductively to the wide bowl.

She didn't know why she was so amazed. Portuguese immigrants, from both the Azores and the mainland, had flooded Canada after World War II, and there were vibrant communities in many cities, including Prince George. But knowing Santos had family—even if only a cousin—in her home province, added an unexpected link between them.

"Have you ever been?"

He shook his head. "Most of my relatives, the ones who left São Miguel, ended up in Fall River, Massachusetts. I lived there, and in Boston, for five years."

"That's why you speak English so well."

"Thanks." He grinned. "You wouldn't have said that if you'd met me shortly after I went to the U.S."

"How old were you?" She propped her elbow on the table, dropped her chin in her hand. Across the table, Neve gave a quiet sigh and struck up a conversation with Cordelia Birtwhistle.

"Twenty. My dad's sister and her husband had moved there a few years before, so I stayed with them at first. Then, once I had steady work, I found a place of my own."

Nostalgia warmed his voice. Abigail felt a twinge of familiar regret, but pushed it aside. Maybe she hadn't had the opportunity to travel when she was younger, but she was going to take full advantage of her chance, now that she had it. "Weren't you homesick? Living so far from home?"

"A bit. But the Portuguese traditions are pretty strong there, so it wasn't as much of a culture shock as it could have been." He rubbed a finger along the side of his nose absently. "Moving to Boston, living and working there, now *that* was a big change."

What would it be like, to simply pick up and leave, start fresh somewhere new? Would it be terrifying or exhilarating? A little of both? "Why did you come back? Didn't you like Boston?"

Santos shifted in his seat. "I loved Boston. I had to come home. My father died."

"Oh. You told me he'd passed. I didn't realize when." She laid her hand on his forearm. "I'm sorry. I know how difficult it is to lose a parent."

"Ah, *querida*." He laid his warm palm over hers. "You were so much younger. It was hard enough for me. I can't imagine what it would have been like to lose him as a child, as you did. And now you've lost your mother as well. I can't imagine being without mine."

She laced her fingers into his and studied their linked hands. He squeezed gently and the wordless sympathy relaxed muscles she hadn't known she'd tensed. "I wish I could have known my father as an adult. My memories are vague and childish, and I'm sure I've made a hero out of someone that was only human, like the rest of us." Santos' thumb caressed her palm, soothing her. It gave her the impetus to admit diffidently, "Sometimes I am angry with him. For dying. If he hadn't, maybe my mother would have been different. My life would have been different."

"I was angry with my father, too," Santos said. She looked at him sharply and he shrugged. "When he died, I had to come home. Lina was still in university, getting her business degree, and there was no way my mother could run the farm on her own. We have family, of course, but they have their own lives, own work. It was up to me."

A burst of laughter from Cecil and Richard interrupted Abigail's thoughts. She scanned the table, saw everyone chattering amiably, their faces bright with humour. She and Santos were a quiet island of gravity amid the good spirits, and she shook off the solemn pall draped over her.

"I can't picture you as a farmer." She gave him a half smile and nudged him with an elbow, reluctantly releasing his hand. "Getting up at the crack of dawn, milking cows, collecting eggs."

"Me, either." He puffed out a breath through his nose. "I'd been a tour guide in Boston, on a trolley, and enjoyed it enough that the idea of working in tourism kept niggling at the back of my mind. So I talked it over with my mother and Lina, and as soon as she was finished school we sold off the cows, renovated the barn, and took the plunge."

The server, a jolly older man whose belly plumped out his black shirt in a testament to his restaurant's delicious food, reached between them and started clearing plates, nattering to Santos. Abigail didn't know if it was his exuberant hand gestures as he dangerously waved soiled dishware over her head, or if she was actually soaking up some of the language, but she managed to grasp the gist of the conversation.

"Is he kicking us out?" she asked Santos.

He laughed, his eyebrows raised in surprise. "Did you pick up on that? We'll have you speaking Portuguese yet." A blush heated her neck at the approval in his voice. "It's not that he's forcing us to leave, but his daughter is having a birthday party for his grandson, and he wants to get to it before it's too late." He glanced around the table. Everyone seemed deep in conversation and not particularly eager to head out. "He said if we settle up our bills now, he'll leave me the key and I can lock up behind us."

"Really? That seems rather...trusting."

"He's married to my dad's cousin. Or maybe his second cousin." He paused to think, then waved it off. "Anyway, he's family."

"Ah." Both her parents had been only children, and after her father's death, her mother had lost touch with the few friends and family they had as she retreated into her world of worry. The idea of having links to such a large, sprawling family, to a close-knit community, set off a yearning inside her.

In the end, it wasn't necessary for Santos to close the restaurant. Once the bills were distributed, everyone paid up, and soon the group was out on the sidewalk.

"What a lovely night." Tricia Thornton tilted her head back and breathed deeply.

"A perfect night for a walk." Richard wrapped an arm about his wife's shoulders and smiled down at her, eyes liquid in the dim light glowing from the restaurant window. Then it snapped out and an even deeper darkness descended. "Which is lucky, given that's the way we have to get home."

Santos had suggested using the van, since the whole group was travelling together, but his offer had been refused.

"You're off duty, joining us for fun, not work," Cedric had said. "In fact, I intend to buy you a drink. I was a tad hesitant about this trip"—he ignored Cordelia's indelicate snort—"but it has been amazing, old chap." Thanks to Cedric, Santos hadn't even paid for his own meal, as the British man had organized a collection to which everyone contributed. It had given Abigail a private thrill to see Santos appreciated and recognized by the others. He was a good man, a likable man, and she was glad she wasn't the only one who noticed.

The group began making its way up the hill leading to Quinta Carregado. Only a few metres along, Santos' warm fingers wrapped around her upper arm, the backs brushing against the curve of her breast. He drew her to one side.

"Santos?" she asked, confused.

"I'm not ready to go back yet," he said softly. "Will you walk with me on the beach?"

The simple knowledge he wanted to spend time alone with her made her decision easy. "I'd love to," she said.

Richard noticed they'd stopped. He paused, his arm still

draped over his wife's shoulder. "Everything okay, Abigail?"

"Of course." She was more than okay. Santos wanted to be with her. A warm glow kindled in her belly and she felt her cheeks flush, glad of the dark.

"We're going to head home the long way," Santos said smoothly. "You go on and we'll see you back at the *quinta* later."

"Just the two of you?" Richard asked, a hint of disapproval in his voice.

"Richard." Tricia shook her head warningly, a wry grin lifting the corner of her mouth. "I'm sure Santos will take good care of Abigail."

Abigail opened her mouth to protest that she didn't need to be *taken care of*, but before she could speak, Richard said, "I know. It's none of my business." His gaze hardened on Santos. "One thing, though. She may be a young woman, alone in a strange country, but that doesn't mean she's without friends." He paused and waited until Santos nodded. "All right. See you tomorrow." The couple turned and faded into the night.

Victor and Eric had been close enough to hear the conversation. At the Thorntons' departure, Victor lowered his brows and opened his mouth. Eric spoke to him in German, and after a slight hesitation he moved along in his father's shadow. With one last fierce look at Santos, he disappeared around the corner.

Leaving Abigail and Santos alone on the quiet street.

ON THE BEACH

Santos turned to Abigail. In the dim light, her face was a pale oval, her hair streaming like moonbeams down her back. "It seems you've made a couple conquests."

Abigail gaped at him. "What? What do you mean?"

"You have Richard ready to defend your virtue"—which he had to reluctantly admire, knowing his own thoughts when it came to Abigail's slender, delectable body—"and didn't you notice the venom in Victor's glare when he looked at me just now?"

"Victor?" Her voice cracked with incredulity. "He's just a boy."

"He wouldn't thank you for calling him that. When I was his age, I...never mind." He wasn't about to tell her any of his teenage fantasies.

"What?" Her irises were grey, leached of colour in the night, but her stare was fascinated. "When you were his age...?" She ran the tip of her tongue over her bottom lip.

The rush of hormones stiffened his cock as though he were still seventeen. He bit back a groan. "Let's just say most guys at that age do nothing but think of women." He allowed himself a soft brush of his knuckle against her cheek and then guided her with a gentle hand on her arm as they retraced their steps. She strolled at his side, head tilted thoughtfully. "Do you really think he...I don't know...has a crush on me?" She sounded extraordinarily pleased at the idea.

"I'm sure of it."

A sliver of moon rippled silver on the waves in the bay. They stepped through an opening in the low rock wall separating the gravelly beach from the roadway. Stones gritted under Santos' sandals.

"I don't think anyone's ever had a crush on me. Even Ma—" She bit off the rest of her sentence.

He didn't want her feeling self-conscious, so he said encouragingly, "You were going to mention Martin."

She shot him a glance from under her lashes. "I'm sorry. I probably shouldn't talk about him."

"You don't have to hide him from me. You were together for how long?"

"Two years."

"He was obviously an important person in your life. It will take time to get over him." He was mouthing the right words, but they were empty, hollow. He wanted her to get over her ex quickly. He wanted her ready for him, ready for his kisses, his caresses. Now.

"This will probably sound awful," she said soberly as they sauntered along the edge of the water, "but I think I was only with Martin because he was convenient. He was simply there, and it was easier to go along with the relationship than break it off."

"If that's what you think, then you definitely did the right thing this morning."

"It's kind of scary, though. I'm not very good at meeting new people, especially men. I'm not exactly the type of person guys can't resist."

"You have nothing to worry about."

She chuckled. "Thanks for the confidence boost, but be honest. You didn't notice me for the first few days. If I hadn't k-kissed you"—he adored her embarrassed stumble—"you probably still wouldn't know who I was."

A few steps away, a wooden boat, overturned and stranded at the water's edge, waited quietly. He guided her to it and she sat on the smooth, rounded hull. He cupped her chin in his fingers. "Trust me, Abigail," he said. "It may have taken me a day or two, but right now?"—he bent forward, brushed his lips softly across hers, felt her shudder— "Victor's not the only one dazzled by you."

****

Santos nibbled slowly along her jaw until he reached the sweet spot just below and behind her ear. Her gasp was rough and raw against his cheek, and she sat stiffly, tension humming along her skin.

"Are we really going to do this?" Her voice trembled.

He leaned into her, a hand on either side of her hips, his mouth the only connection between them. "Well, it depends on your definition of 'this'," he said, his voice a low growl. "But we are definitely going to do something." He lipped her earlobe. "Touch me."

She didn't move. He nuzzled under her chin, breathed in her scent. The pulse in her neck thundered madly.

"Please," he whispered, astonished at his own need. He realized he was asking for more than a simple touch, craved more than the physical closeness, and a sudden start of panic had him drawing away—

Until she touched his chest. He watched her through lowered lids. Her expression was bewildered, confused, as if she wasn't controlling her own movements. Hesitantly she laid her palm flat over his heart. He held his breath, muscles rigid, waiting for her next move.

Her other hand settled next to the first. Then, with innocent daring, she swept both up his shoulders, down his biceps. She pushed up the sleeve on his right arm, uncovered the tattoo circling it, and traced delicate fingers over the inked design. He hissed in a breath, unbelievably aroused by her tentative caress.

Her eyes met his, her gaze unfocused, unsteady. He held tight to his willpower and refrained from crushing her to the cobbled beach, taking his release from her body, with her body, in her body.

"This is what your kiss started." He barely recognized his own voice. It gritted out rough and harsh.

"I know," she said.

Her voice, husky with passion, tightened his every sinew. His cock throbbed, eager and wanting. "Are you brave enough to finish it?"

She swallowed. He saw the muscles in her throat move. His imagination fired and he dug his fingers into the dried, flaky paint on the boat's hull.

"I don't know," she said.

The stark honesty floored him. What was he supposed to do with a woman like her? He couldn't read her, couldn't predict what she would do, what she would say.

"But I'm willing to give it a try," she said, her aching whisper proving his point.

A car drove by on the other side of the wall, the first one since they'd made their way to the beach. Its headlights slashed beams over Abigail's pale features, leaving him night blind for an instant, and recalling him to exactly where they were.

What the hell was he thinking? He was actually considering having sex on the beach, with a client. Not just considering it. Couldn't stop thinking about it, in fact.

"Come here." He reared off the boat and grabbed her wrist. She trotted after him, slipping occasionally in the loose gravel, but silent and willing, trusting him.

The hut was unlocked. Santos had known it would be. He tugged Abigail inside and shut the door. A long, narrow window, the only one in the building, ran along the back wall just under the rafters, letting in a hint of moonglow.

"Where are we?" She spun slowly on her toes, taking in the small space.

"The village council put up three or four of these shelters, thinking tourists might use the beach more if they had a place to change, to put their things, hide in if the weather turned bad."

"Do they?"

"No. There are nicer beaches elsewhere."

A bare wooden bench stretched down one wall, a raised counter with shelving below the other. No cushions, no towels, no blankets. But it had one thing vital to Santos.

Privacy.

Abigail leaned against the counter, hands behind her back. She wore a yellow dress in a flimsy material that swayed with every movement. Instead of straps or sleeves, it tied at the back of her neck, the ends of the bow hanging between her shoulder blades. Santos' fingers had itched to untie that bow all evening long, to see the cloth fall away from her body, reveal what he was sure was nothing but skin beneath.

"I want to make love to you."

"Now?" she squeaked, her eyes darting about the stark room. "Here?"

Yes, now, here, he wanted to answer. But she deserved better. "No. When we make love, I want you relaxed, comfortable, concentrating only on me."

Her eyes widened, dominating her face. Her mouth open and closed, but she didn't make a sound.

"Besides," he said with very real regret, "I only sleep with clients when they are no longer clients. I do have some principles." He stepped forward and ran his fingers through her hair, pulled loosely into its familiar ponytail. He twisted straight, silver-blond strands around his hand. "Tomorrow is the last day of the tour. Friday I take everyone either to the airport or to a hotel." His other hand caressed her waist, slid up her ribs, stroked her small breast. The heat of her seared his palm through the thin dress. "You told me you have another week on the island. Let me stay with you, Abigail. Take me to your room, let me love you, for the time we have left."

He wasn't sure if she was breathing. He knew he was having trouble taking in oxygen himself. He waited, yearning, anxious, for her answer.

****

Abigail was certain she was going to faint. What else would cause the black spots before her eyes, the faltering lungs, the inability to speak?

Santos' touch, that's what. His words. His hunger.

I want to make love to you, he'd said. *Let me love you. For the time we have left.*

He waited now, patient and kind, with a reassuring hint of anxiousness behind his confidence. She could no longer deny he wanted her. For some strange, inexplicable reason this man desired her. But she could not delude herself.

He wanted to have sex with her. That's all he meant when he said he wanted to love her.

"Abigail?" He cradled her face in both hands. "Say yes. Say you want me as I want you." His voice was as rough as the calluses on his palms, both raising delicious chills on her skin.

She was so tired of being safe, taking the line of least resistance. No matter what happened in the time she had remaining on the Azores, in just over a week she would get on a plane to fly home and never see Santos again.

It was time to jump off a cliff again.

She reached up, clasped his wrists with her hands, and pulled. He resisted at first, but she insisted, silently, and he gave in.

Stepping forward, she brought his hands behind her. He wrapped his arms around her with a gruff moan and drew her hard against his body. She reached under and up, gripping his shoulder blades, pressing tighter to him.

His lips moved, sure and determined, nipping and suckling her mouth. Electricity zapped through her nerves, tingled in her fingertips, liquefied her belly. He caught her to him, held her so fiercely her breasts flattened against the wall of his chest, her thighs snugged against his thighs. His erection was impossible to ignore, hot and heavy between them.

She was not a virgin. But one desperate night in college and two years of pleasant but passive sex with Martin had not prepared her for the volcanic, turbulent feelings swamping through her. Frantic for more touch, more taste, more taking, she scrabbled at the buttons on Santos' shirt.

"Easy, easy," he murmured, breathlessly soothing, in direct contrast to the feverishness of his hands as they streaked up and down her back.

"Get it off. I need it off." She was only on the third button, his shirt open to his breastbone.

He yanked it out of the waistband of his pants and tugged it over his head without waiting for her to finish the buttons, tossing it to the floor.

"Oh. Oh, yes." Now she could feel the heat of his skin, the bristly hair spattering his chest. She held her palms flat and swept them from collarbones to abs, circled them over his pecs, feathered them along his ribs. He sucked in air on a gasp, his stomach muscles tightening.

He reached behind her neck. "Fair's fair," he growled, and before she realized what he was doing the halter bodice of her dress fell to her waist.

She shrieked and made a grab for it, but he captured her hands, pressing them against the counter at her back.

"Oh, no, you don't."

She wriggled, battling embarrassment and frustrated desire, and only succeeded in brushing the taut tips of her nipples against his fiery skin. It felt so good she arched her back and did it again.

He swooped down, ensnaring her mouth once more. She stopped struggling and simply sagged into his arms, lust melting her bones, whirling through her veins. Minutes passed, hours maybe, his lips and teeth and tongue the sole focus of her world. When he dragged himself away, she whimpered, shocked to hear the panting need, the hungering sob emanate from her own body.

She was vaguely surprised to realize her hands were free, her fingers curled deep in his thick hair, tracing his skull in discovery. Hands grasped her hips and suddenly she was lifted up, her skirt billowing as he lowered her to the counter, cool and smooth on her ass, the bare backs of her thighs. She squealed softly and he laughed, low and deep.

"I should take you home." His lips burned a moist trail along her collarbone. "The others must be wondering where we are."

Her head dropped back and she clutched his shoulders. His lazy exploration continued to the upper slope of her breast. "Uh-uh." It was the best she could do, unable to form a rational thought as his questing mouth circled closer and closer to the throbbing peak.

"Should we go, Abigail?" He turned his attention to her other collarbone, nipping, nibbling, drawing ever closer to the wanting tip but still—still!—not touching.

"No," she moaned. "Oh, God, Santos, suck me."

His mouth locked on. The swirling sensation travelled directly from her breast to her womb and she almost shouted. While his mouth devoured one nipple, his fingers tweaked and played with the other and she fell back against the thin plywood wall. He followed her, standing between her thighs, and she wrapped her legs around his waist so she could grind her pulsing core against his cock, trapped behind his zipper.

****

"*Meu Deus*," Santos groaned against Abigail's breast.

She squirmed, and he could feel her sultry dampness through the cloth of his trousers. He dropped a hand to each of her thighs and held her. "*Calma*." He struggled to find his English as she wiggled under his restraining hands. "Be still. Be still, *meu amor*."

His pulse drummed furiously and he panted for air. Good Lord but he wanted to take her, right here, on the counter, on the floor, wherever he could. But it wouldn't be right. "We must stop. This isn't the time, or the place."

"It is. It is." Her hands moved restlessly over his body,

leaving a lava-like trail of need.

"No, *minha querida*." He caught her hands, clamped them at her sides, and waited. The hectic pace of his blood cooled agonizingly slowly. Abigail's breathing steadied, and her tense muscles gradually relaxed. He loosened his grip. He couldn't see much in the dim light sneaking in the narrow window, but he thought he might have bruised her alabaster skin.

"I hurt you." He skimmed a fingertip delicately along her inner thigh. "I'm sorry."

"I won't break." An oddly triumphant note in her voice drew his eyes to her face. She slouched languorously against the wall of the hut, her dress about her waist, her torso and breasts bared to his gaze. "I don't want you to treat me gently. You make me feel fierce, wild, uncontrolled." She licked her lips, swollen from his kisses. "I like it."

He gathered the strips of material that made up the top of her dress with fingers that still trembled. She dropped her head into the crook of his neck and shoulder as he clumsily knotted the fabric at her nape. When she was once more properly clothed, he lifted her to the ground.

"Are you sure you want to wait?" She hooked her ankle behind his and rubbed herself against him.

"I'm sure." At least, his brain was. His cock, however, was screaming for more.

He snatched his shirt off the floor and yanked it on, attempting to armour himself with the thin cotton. She insisted on buttoning it for him, so he gritted his teeth and suffered through it. The moment she was done, he took her hand and escaped from the mock privacy of the public shelter.

Maybe by the time they'd walked back to Quinta Carregado he'd have worked off his arousal.

He stole a glance at her, moonbeam hair glowing in the fluid light, expression sensuously soft, dress floating about her hips.

Maybe not.

HORSEBACK RIDING

Abigail stared Estrela in the eye, doing her best to appear calm, confident and in charge.

Estrela stared back, dark brown eye glistening, absurdly long lashes drooping coquettishly. She lowered her head and swung sideways at Abigail, butting her in the chest, staggering her, and whinnied in delight.

Abigail rubbed the heel of her hand up and down her breastbone but refused to move away. She had never been this close to a horse before. She was fascinated by the smooth, glossy, mahogany-coloured neck just begging to be stroked, the skin so sensitive a fly's tentative, tiny feet made it twitch.

Of course, the muscular haunches and dinner plate hooves were something to be wary of. But with Estrela tied securely to the fence, Abigail felt reasonably safe. She was pretty sure the head butt had been a friendly gesture. A little rough, but friendly.

Abigail had been introduced to Estrela by Lina.

"This lady will be yours today," she said cheerfully. "She's sweet and gentle, and should be perfect for your first ever horseback ride."

Abigail didn't want to doubt her—after all, Lina was the expert—but Estrela looked anything but sweet and gentle. Her big, beautiful eyes gleamed with fun, mischief and a wild intelligence Abigail wasn't sure she was prepared for.

Today was her final day at Quinta Carregado. Tomorrow everyone would be going their separate ways. She should have been feeling sad, wistful, a bit disheartened that half her holiday was over already. Instead she found herself torn between anticipation and anxiety.

Only one more night until she would be with Santos.

He and Lina worked their way through the corral, slipping bridles on the horses and bringing them to the guests. She tried not to be too obvious, but couldn't help watching him, wanting to store up as many memories as possible. This vacation had changed her life, and she knew she couldn't go back to the same staid sequence of days she'd left behind. But Santos had changed her soul, and she would need to remember how he made her feel in order to keep moving forward.

When everyone was ready to mount, Abigail stared in consternation at the hornless English saddle perched on top of Estrela's absurdly rounded body, at the stirrup dangling at her elbow. How was she supposed to get up there?

"Bend your left leg."

She looked over her shoulder and met Santos' amused eye, his expression eerily similar to Estrela's. She frowned.

He chuckled. "I'll help you mount. Just bend your left leg and grab the front and back of the saddle."

She did so, and with a sudden thump found herself on top of Estrela, who sidled restlessly.

"Hush," Santos reprimanded the horse as Abigail clutched for the reins. The animal settled.

The ground was a lot farther away than Abigail had

anticipated. Santos grinned up at her. "Comfortable?"

She nodded nervously. He slipped his hand from her calf to the back of her knee, a warm caress that brought back fevered memories of last night.

"Don't worry. Estrela knows what to do. Just hold on and enjoy the ride."

She nodded again. He tightened his grip on her leg momentarily, then moved one horse over to help Sabine with the same friendly professionalism he showed all the guests.

Except when he had one of them half-naked in a hut on the beach.

Abigail felt damp heat swirl low in her belly and squirmed on the saddle. Estrela, no longer tied to the rail, interpreted her movement as a command to start walking. She circled leisurely around and began plodding to the gate leading to the wide open pasture.

Abigail tugged on the reins, madly trying to remember Santos' instructions: "To stop, pull firmly back and down. Don't yank."

To her utter surprise, Estrela obeyed her amateur command. Abigail leaned forward, careful not to lose her balance in the tiny saddle, and patted the sleek neck. "Good girl. We're going to get along just fine, aren't we?"

Which was when she noticed the gate was still closed. Estrela hadn't stopped because of any guidance from Abigail. She simply couldn't go any further. The mare snorted indelicately through her velvety nostrils and tossed her head, eyeballing Abigail over her shoulder.

Who closed her own eyes and prayed.

****

When Santos first broached the idea of turning the farm

into a bed and breakfast, Lina's immediate response had been, "We have to keep the horses."

And he was so glad they had.

Every tour included at least one daytrip on horseback. It was the only excursion on which Lina accompanied the guests. When the family had divided duties for the fledgling bed and breakfast, she'd wanted to do more activities, to be out and about more often. But he'd needed someone in the office, and he and Serafina had overruled Lina. Her disgust at this decision still erupted once in a while in muttered comments and sharp glares. His concession had been the horseback tours. He was fairly certain if he hadn't given in on that point, Lina would have rejected the whole enterprise.

She rode at his side now, their guests straggled out in front and behind. Cordelia and Cedric, experienced riders, ranged far ahead, but they were in a large pasture, and there was little chance of trouble, even for the novice riders.

"Your sweetheart needs to get control," Lina said. "Estrela's taking over."

He quelled the urge to look back and check on Abigail. Estrela knew her job, knew all she had to do was follow the other horses. The result would be the same, even if Abigail did nothing but sit in the saddle. He slitted a glance at Lina. "Sweetheart?"

She grinned at him. "You can't take your eyes off her."

"I'm not looking at her now," he pointed out.

"You know what I mean." Lina clicked her tongue at her mount who had forgotten his manners and was trying to grab a mouthful of grass. He flicked his ears at his beloved mistress and snorted a resigned sigh. "It's not like you've never hooked up with one of our guests before—"

"Why does everyone say that?" he complained, insulted.

"—but she's not your usual type."

155

Ribeiro, Santos' horse, twitched his grey ears and dodged his head up and down as if in agreement. "Even you, old friend?" Santos laughed and tugged on the bristly black mane.

He gave in to impulse and swivelled in his saddle. Victor and Eric were only a few yards away, but Abigail trailed along dozens of metres behind them. Estrela's jaws moved lazily and long blades of grass dangled from her lips. Abigail's mouth was moving, too, and even though Santos couldn't hear her words it was fairly obvious she was pleading with the horse to pick up the pace. Her face was flushed with effort and possibly temper, and her hair wreathed about her face, plucked from her ponytail by the brisk breeze. He turned back to Lina, a wry grin twisting his lips.

"She's not," he agreed. "But I guess I'm tired of the usual type. When does the next group arrive?"

"Not until next Thursday. The *festa* is Sunday."

"Of course." The whole village turned out for the annual religious festival, when the church's beloved statues were paraded with pomp and ceremony through the streets. Ilha Verde Aventuras avoided taking guests around that time, partly so they could enjoy the centuries-old tradition, but also to allow them time to do maintenance on the converted barn and the house, prep activities, check the gear, work in the garden—the million and one things that needed to be done to keep the business running.

Santos calculated. "Do you mind if I take some time off? I can ask Jorge to come over and help." The teenage boy, another cousin, lived a couple of farms over and often picked up extra money that way.

Lina tilted her head and studied him thoughtfully. "What are you planning?"

"Abigail has another week on the island, before she goes home. I want to spend it with her. Or as much as I can."

They approached the far side of the pasture. Victor and Eric kicked their horses into reluctant canters and sped past Lina and Santos, joining the others as they waited at the gate as instructed. Abigail was still far behind, Estrela definitely in control now.

"You're starting to worry me." Lina regarded him, frown lines cutting between her eyes.

"I am?" He shifted uneasily under his sister's considering look. "Why?"

"I was teasing before. But I'm beginning to wonder whether you like her too much. Maybe more than you should."

He snorted. "I don't know what you mean." But the unease curling in his gut belied his nonchalant answer.

"She's not one of us." Lina gestured widely with one arm, encompassing the pasture, the quinta, the whole island. "She doesn't belong here. This is only a vacation, a break from reality. She's going to go home and forget all about you."

"I know. That's no different than before."

"I don't want you to get hurt."

He wanted to laugh, but couldn't toss off her concern that easily. He didn't want Abigail to forget him. Because he was beginning to worry that he would never forget her.

****

Abigail gritted her teeth and banged her heels against Estrela's barrel-shaped belly. It made no impression on the happily sauntering horse.

"Come on," she begged. "You're making me look stupid

here. We're the last ones." The rest of the group had already reached the far fence. She could see them patiently—she hoped—waiting for her. Despite her urging, Estrela took her own sweet time, but at long last she came to a juddering halt next to Lina and Santos.

The younger woman avoided Abigail's eyes but smiled at the horse. "She's a sweet old thing, isn't she?"

Abigail puffed out a breath, wafting her wispy bangs out of her eyes. "She certainly acts old. I can't get her to move above a walk."

"You need to show her who is in charge," Santos said. He clucked at his mount, a beautiful dapple grey, and the obliging animal took a few polite steps forward. "You're holding the reins too loose. Make sure you keep her head up. Once she figures out she can't do whatever she wants, she'll behave better." He slouched easily in the saddle, completely at home.

"I don't want to hurt her."

The corner of Santos' mouth twitched. "She's tougher than you think. Don't saw on the bit, but keep up firm pressure.

"Fine." Frustration still simmered. "I'll try to do better."

Lina opened the gate and led the group through. Santos sidled his horse closer to Estrela and his knee, bare below the canvas shorts he wore, bumped against Abigail's. Fire flared from that simple point of contact straight to her belly and she swallowed, dropping her eyes to the pommel.

His hands came into her view, and he laid them over hers, adjusting her grip on the smooth leather. "It's all about confidence," he rumbled, softly, sexily, directly in her ear. "You've got to let her know who the boss is, who is in control."

Her breath backed up in her throat. She watched his

hands on hers, his darker olive skin contrasting against her pale gold tone, afraid to look up and betray her longing, her lusting.

He leaned away, settling back in his saddle. She stiffened her spine and gathered her wits. "Confidence. Right. I've been working on that."

"I've noticed," he said, and she knew he wasn't talking about horseback riding. He didn't elaborate, but simply added, "Now, prove it to Estrela."

Abigail took a determined breath and grasped the reins firmly. Estrela tossed her head and she pulled back briskly. "Enough of that," she said matter-of-factly. "Now, get along." She clapped her heels to the mare's sides.

And as sweet as pie, Estrela stepped daintily through the gate, completely ignoring the lush clumps of grass lining the trail.

"That's my girl," Santos murmured behind her.

Abigail was pretty sure he was talking to her, not the horse.

****

During the rest of the ride, Abigail's confidence climbed to new heights. With a few more suggestions from Santos, she soon had Estrela behaving like a proper lady. But once they returned to Quinta Carregado she faced a new challenge—dismounting. Hours in the saddle had stiffened her muscles, locking them uncomfortably, and the hard-packed dirt looked a long, long way down.

The others managed to get off their rides with various levels of grace. Serafina, who had been working in the large vegetable garden near the corral when they arrived, nodded and smiled at her guests, drawing closer to share a few halting words over the fence with Richard and Tricia Thornton, on Abigail's right.

Very, very carefully she swung her right leg over Estrela's wide rump and dropped to the ground. She stumbled while getting her left foot out of the stirrup and clutched the cinch to keep from falling.

Despite an equal number of hours in the saddle, Lina strode out of the stable with long, smooth steps, carrying a bucket full of brushes, combs and what Abigail assumed was other horse grooming paraphernalia. "You will be sore tomorrow," she said, her teasing tone just a little too sharp.

Abigail replied warily, "Yes, I imagine I will." She wasn't quite sure how to read Lina. She was polite enough, but her attitude was more reserved, slightly standoffish. Abigail wondered if she was as happy working at Quinta Carregado as Serafina and Santos seemed to be.

"A shower might help your muscles." Lina dropped the bucket to the ground and began to undo the buckles on the saddle Estrela was wearing, causing Abigail to move between Estrela and the horse on her left, toward the fence edging the vegetable garden.

Her tiny bathroom had beautifully hot water, yet Abigail couldn't help commenting, a touch wistfully, "What I wouldn't give for a long, hot soak in a tub."

The sibilant sound of rapid Portuguese came from behind her. She turned to see Serafina standing on the other side of the fence, holding a large woven basket filled with carrots, their feathery tops drooping over the side.

Lina answered back in the same language. Serafina spoke again, her tone commanding. Lina sighed. "My mother asks if you would like to use our bathtub, in the farmhouse."

Abigail smiled at Serafina, but directed her words to Lina. "How did she know?"

"She understands more English than she speaks." Lina hefted the saddle of Estrela's back and the horse gave a huge, windy whinny. "So?"

It was more than obvious Lina didn't agree with her mother's offer. But the thought of stretching her aching muscles in soft, soothing, steamy water overcame any reluctance Abigail had in accepting it. "Yes, I do."

Lina shrugged, the metal on the saddle jingling. "Go into the kitchen. The door on the left leads to the hall. It's at the far end."

****

Santos showered off the scent of horses and grit of dust and grabbed a towel from the rack. It smelled of lemons and sunshine, and he smiled. When they'd renovated the barn he'd included an efficient laundry, which his mother used for the guest room linens. For the family washing, she preferred a set of stackable machines hidden in a small room off the kitchen, but she still favoured hanging sheets and towels on a line strung in their private garden to using the dryer.

Shrugging on his robe, he returned to his bedroom. A pile of clothes lay heaped on a chair in the corner, and he dug through it to find a relatively clean pair of shorts and soft, worn t-shirt. He might not be able to stop his mother from cooking for him, but he had managed to convince her to stay out of his room.

He glanced around the space and winced. A good thing, too. She'd have a stroke if she saw it now.

Not that it was a rubbish heap, he thought defensively. Sure, the bed was unmade, clothes were scattered about, books leaned in a precarious stack next to the bed and a few dirty dishes were piled on the nightstand. But you could still see the floor.

Mostly.

Late afternoon sun streamed in, glowing golden on the white walls, sloping ceilings and dark wood floor. It mocked the messiness of the room with its clean light.

Santos sighed and half-heartedly straightened the sheets. A band of brightness slashed across the bed, and he pictured Abigail spread out, her platinum hair lacing the pillow, her fair, fair skin glowing like a pearl. He sucked in a breath and clamped down on the erotic vision.

He'd done his best to act normally after Lina had stuck verbal pins in him during the first part of the ride. Abigail was different, he knew that. What he hadn't considered was that the situation wasn't. She was still a visitor to his island, she was going home, and he would have no reason to see her, ever again.

Why did the thought make him slightly queasy?

She fascinated him like no other woman ever had. And he wanted her in a way he'd never felt before. But that didn't mean the final conclusion would be any different. What did he think was going to happen—she would cancel her flight home and stay?

Hope grabbed his gut and wrenched. Abigail—stay? Was that what he wanted?

It couldn't be.

He shook his head, much like Ribeiro shook his when a fly settled on his long, sensitive ears. He needed to hold on to sanity for a little longer. As Lina had said, Abigail wasn't one of them. She wasn't part of his heritage, his culture. Surely after a week of sex—long, hot, sweaty, delicious sex—the vague depression he experienced when he thought of her leaving would evaporate.

He trotted down the stairs, relieved he'd finally made a

sensible decision. He reached the bottom tread, glanced casually to his left—

—and just about dropped to his knees.

Abigail stood outside the bathroom door, her hair wrapped in a towel turban, leaving her long neck bare except for two tantalizing tendrils, her slim, slender body clad in a heavy terrycloth robe with Ilha Verde Aventuras stitched on the chest. Her eyes shone like gemstones, her cheeks flushed like rose gold.

"Oh," she gasped. "You startled me."

Santos stared, mesmerized, as a lone drop of water trickled with excruciating slowness down her throat, over her collarbone, and under the lapel of her robe, exactly where the soft swell of her breast began.

"Lina said it was okay if I used the bath." She clutched the robe together at her neck. "Actually it was your mother that offered. Through Lina. Because I don't speak Portuguese, of course."

He nodded, not trusting his voice.

"I'll just go back to my room now."

He nodded again.

"Aren't you going to say anything?"

He shook his head. It was difficult to form coherent thoughts when there was no blood in his brain.

A mischievous smile trembled on her lips. She moved toward him and he was floored by the intoxicating perfume of moist, damp woman flesh. "I'll see you later," she said, and vanished into the kitchen.

Tomorrow couldn't come soon enough.

LEAVING QUINTA CARREGADO

Abigail did one last check of Quarto Violeta, making sure she was leaving nothing behind. She'd read somewhere that people subconsciously forgot items when they wanted to return to a certain place, but she didn't believe it. She would gladly come back to Quinta Carregado, and yet here she was sweeping it clean as if she was absconding with the linens.

It felt much longer than one week since she'd first seen the quaint little room. She'd packed more into those seven days than in all the years before. The resentment and anger she harboured when she thought of that wasted time eased into pity. Her mother had allowed fear to rule her and those she loved, denying herself of even a small taste of what Abigail now knew was possible. But she wouldn't let ambiguous nightmares ruin the rest of her life. She was going to reach out and grab it with all her strength—and she was starting today, with Santos.

Her heart pounded every time she let her mind drift to the coming hours. For a moment yesterday, when they'd met outside the bathroom door, she'd thought he would drag her to the floor and make love to her then and there. During those soul-searing seconds of stillness, the heat in his eyes had singed the dampness from her skin, stirred an answering warmth in her blood.

She both hoped and feared he would make good on all his eyes promised.

A brisk knock at the door jolted her out of her reverie. Lina poked her head in. "Ready? Do you need help?"

"I think I've got it. I just have to lug that beast to the van." She regarded her enormous suitcase with a crooked smile. "The next trip I go on, I'll know to pack lighter. A lot lighter."

"Are you looking forward to going home?"

Abigail shot her a glance, and Lina stared innocently back. Perhaps too innocently. "Uh-huh," she agreed vaguely, fiddling with the strap on her shoulder bag. "I have another week on the island, though."

"Yes, Santos told me you weren't leaving yet. Here, I will get that." Lina dragged the suitcase to the door. She studied Abigail, head tilted to one side. "You know, he does this sometimes."

"Does what?"

"Has an affair with a client. Well, ex-client."

A gaping hole, sharp edged and bottomless, opened in Abigail's stomach. Of course she was one in a long line of casual relationships; she wasn't naive enough to think otherwise. But that didn't stop Lina's words from sending a shaft of regret through her.

"He likes women," Lina said, "and they like him. It gives them one more memory to take home. He's an attractive man, with a lot of charm. Even I know this, though he is my brother."

The edge of the pit inside Abigail crumbled and she struggled to keep her balance. "Yes, he is," she said. She hadn't travelled far enough away from life with her mother to be comfortable with conflict yet, but forced herself to pull on a cloak of bravado.

"He likes to date women he knows will be leaving." Lina considered briefly. "He has not dated an island woman since he returned from Boston. Too worried they will want marriage, I think." Her grin was offset by the coolness in her deep brown eyes.

"What on earth made you mention marriage?" Abigail asked coolly, despite her trembling knees. "I'm not interested in Santos beyond my time here." This earned her a disbelieving look from Lina.

"Don't believe you're different, because you're not." Lina heaved the suitcase out the door and leaned back in. "You will get on a plane and fly home, and Santos will be here, on the island, meeting his next lady." She nodded once, eyes serious. "Think about it."

****

Santos hauled the last of Neve and Sabine's luggage out of the van and placed it on the sidewalk. The roar of jet engines drowned out the twittering of birds as a SATA Airline flight took off over their heads.

"That will be us in a couple of hours." Sabine sighed. "I wish we could stay longer."

"We'll have to come back." Neve raised an eyebrow at Santos. "Do repeat customers get a special rate?"

He laughed. "For you, of course."

"What about Abigail?" Neve asked coyly. "Would she get a special rate, too?"

He wondered what she had noticed. As far as he knew, no one but Lina and his mother were aware of his plans for the next few days, and he was certain Abigail had not confided in anyone. But Neve appeared to have her suspicions.

"Quit teasing the man." Sabine shook her head. "It's time to go."

"It's lucky I like her, or I would have put up a tougher fight," Neve said, slanting a look into the van where Abigail waited.

She sat in the second row, right behind the driver's seat, with Richard and Tricia Thornton behind her. Cedric and Cordelia, Eric and Victor, had already taken their luggage and headed to the Departure line ups. Santos felt the slight tug of melancholy he sometimes did when an especially congenial group split up, followed by a burst of relief that he wouldn't have to say goodbye to Abigail just yet.

Neve kissed his cheek and grinned. "Good luck. I don't suppose you'll need it."

He hugged her and the sedate Sabine. "Safe travels. Maybe we'll see you again."

He settled behind the steering wheel, acutely aware of the empty seat next to him. He'd half expected Abigail to claim it when they'd left Quinta Carregado, but she'd slipped in behind him as usual. He hoped she was simply being discreet, and that her actions didn't reflect a change of heart.

Because he wasn't letting her get away. Not now.

****

Abigail hadn't realized how bittersweet today's goodbyes would be. She'd only known these people a week, and yet she would never forget them. Sweet, protective Victor and his indulgent dad; reluctant Cedric and enthusiastic Cordelia; the athletic, competent Thorntons; quiet Sabine, gorgeous Neve.

The Dutch sisters lingered on the sidewalk, chatting with

Santos, yet she resisted the urge to look over her shoulder. Waiting impatiently, she pondered Lina's parting words.

At first she thought she should be offended. After all, who wants to be considered as simply the next available woman? Worse yet, a woman desperate enough to take what she can get for as long—or short—as the man was willing to allow her.

And then she thought she'd take it as a compliment. Santos didn't invite just any woman to spend time with him. He wanted *her*, desired *her*, Abigail Garsson. She should be proud.

But during the drive to the airport, she'd thought of a third response, one that chilled her to her fingertips.

What if Lina had been warning her off? What if she'd told Abigail about Santos' previous conquests because she didn't want Abigail to get hurt? Which meant Lina thought Abigail could get hurt. Not physically, of course, but emotionally.

Did Lina think Abigail was in love with Santos?

She tried to shrug it off. She wasn't, so it didn't matter if Lina thought she was. She was going into this with her eyes open. It was simply a fling, a few nights and days with a handsome, sexy man. And then she was going to go home to get on with her life.

In love with Santos? She'd only known him a week. Absurd.

The man in question slammed the back doors of the van and levered himself into the driver's seat. After her encounter with Lina this morning, she'd cravenly chosen her accustomed seat directly behind him. After all, why draw attention to herself now?

They sped along the expressway circling Ponta Delgada. The buzzing traffic didn't seem to bother a horse and rider, milk cans hanging on either side of the animal's belly, plodding along the shoulder. Negotiating past the slow-moving partners, Santos exited to the right and deftly joined the traffic in a roundabout before pulling into a small driveway in front of a ten-story, half-moon shaped hotel. Abigail followed Richard and Tricia out the side as Santos opened the rear doors.

"It was so lovely, getting to know you." Tricia hugged her. "We're planning a trip out west next year. We'll have to get in touch."

"It's time we explored our own country." Richard accepted their compact, efficient backpacks from Santos and handed Tricia hers.

Now there was a partnership, Abigail thought. She'd enjoyed watching the couple interact during the last week. Trusting each other, supporting each other. That's what love should be—respecting the other's abilities, allowing the other person a chance to grow, adapting to changes.

"I feel bad, knowing you're going to be on your own." Tricia searched Abigail's face. "Maybe we should arrange to meet up."

She and Santos had no reason to sneak around. But would he want her to broadcast the fact they would be together? "I'm not sure...I mean that's very..."

Santos broke into her stuttering. "You don't need to worry." He stood just behind her right shoulder, and her skin prickled at his proximity. "I have a few days off. She'll be with me."

That answered that question. And was she crazy, or did she hear a particularly possessive tone in his voice? Heat radiated from Abigail's cheeks and she was certain she looked guilty and embarrassed.

Richard shifted the pack on his shoulder. "I guess I can't

say I'm surprised." He slipped a hand around his wife's waist and Tricia smiled up at him. "Just remember, Abigail, if you need anything in the next few days, you can find us through the hotel here."

Wildly uncomfortable with the conversation, Abigail fastened her attention on the glittering buckle on the strap over Richard's shoulder. "Thank you."

He dipped a nod at Santos, took his wife's hand and headed into the hotel.

Abigail watched them go, awkward and shy now she and Santos were alone. A warm touch on her shoulder swung her around. She found herself staring at the dark, smooth skin in the vee of his throat. A pulse throbbed in the hollow, and she fought a sudden urge to kiss him, kiss that delectable spot, as they stood on the sidewalk.

God, she was a mess, swinging from lust to humiliation between every charged heartbeat.

He tipped up her chin with the pads of his thumbs. His face was serious, but his eyes smiled. "Breathe, Abigail."

She sucked in a lungful of soft island air.

"Do you need your medication?"

She shook her head and exhaled.

"Should we go to your hotel now?"

She paused, open and closed her mouth, then nodded jerkily.

His mouth quirked at the corner. "After we've put our luggage in the room, why don't we take a walk around the city?"

She found her voice. "A walk? You want to take a walk?"

"Relax, Abigail." His palms stroked her shoulders, soothing circles he might use to calm a horse. "I'm not planning on throwing you on a bed the minute we're near one. We'll explore Ponta Delgada a bit, have supper, see how things go."

The heaviness in her chest lifted. "It's not that I don't want to sleep with you—"

"I know." The lids of his eyes dropped. "This is new for you. And for me, too. There's no need to rush."

Given Lina's parting words, Abigail could only be grateful to Santos for pretending to share her own anxiety. At least he wasn't making her feel a fool for not being more sophisticated and worldly.

He opened the passenger door. "We'll start with small steps. It's not far to the hotel. Will you sit next to me"—he grinned, taking the sting from his next words—"or would you prefer to hide behind my seat as you've been doing?"

****

Santos leaned contentedly back in his chair, studying Abigail as she sat, chin in hand, staring out the restaurant window. She looked relaxed and peaceful, the candlelight spangling her pale blond hair with deeper gold, glistening in her soft blue eyes.

Lust simmered in his belly like a low-grade fever, and he'd been careful to keep it well banked through the last few hours. His usual companions didn't need seducing, soothing. They knew the rules and were more than willing to play by them. Abigail, on the other hand, was requiring more attention, more coaxing—and he was more than willing to follow that path. He felt in his bones she would be worth every moment of the wait.

"Do you see that ship?" she said quietly, "Way out there?" She nodded past the glass, past the curve of the pier twelve stories below, far out to the horizon where faint lights flashed on and off, on and off, the bulk of the ship itself invisible in the night. "I wonder where it's going."

"You're always looking for what's around the next corner." During their exploration of the city that afternoon, he'd been charmed by her delight in everything, from the black and white cobblestone streets to the narrow roads to the three arches of the Portas da Cidade. He'd left her briefly, slipping into a pharmacy to buy a box of condoms, and when he returned he'd found her staring upward at the clock tower on the Church of Saint Sebastian, oblivious to the pedestrians forced to dodge around her.

"The world is amazing." She had smiled at him dreamily as he'd taken her hand, interrupting her reverie. "So much to see, so much to explore."

Thinking of her wistfulness then, he asked her now, "Why have you never travelled before?"

A sigh drifted from her lips. "My mother could hardly bear it when I or my brother left the house, even if it was just to go to school or work. If I had travelled she would have been in agony, and I couldn't do that to her." She pulled her gaze from the darkness outside the window and faced him. "It made me so angry, sometimes, that I couldn't do all the things I wanted to do, travel all the places I wanted to go." Tears filled her eyes but didn't fall. "Now I can, but she had to die so I could get my wish. How awful is that?"

Her guilt was tangible and he reached across the table, tucking a stray strand of hair behind her ear, letting his fingers linger. "It wasn't your fault she died. And it's not your fault you wanted more from life."

"My brain knows it. But sometimes my heart simply seizes, because I'm here and she's not." She gripped his hand. "Today has been wonderful. This trip...it's been more than I could ever imagine. I wanted to prove to myself that I'm not afraid, that I can do anything, and I have." Her mouth twisted in a watery smile. "Paragliding just about beat me, except you wouldn't let it."

"I just helped you past your fear. It was your courage that did the rest." Her hand was delicate yet strong, and he could feel the pulse beating steady in her wrist. "That's what got to me the most. Your courage."

"Really?" Her face glowed.

"You battled up the hill at Sete Cidades, refusing to let it get the best of you. You dragged yourself over the edge at Lagoa do Fogo even though I'd never seen anyone so petrified. It's very attractive, very...arousing, your courage."

His eyes locked on hers and a silence settled over them—fraught with tension, heavy with anticipation.

"Let's go," Abigail said. "Let's go to our room."

HOTEL – FIRST NIGHT

Santos slotted the key card into the lock, heard the click, and held the door open with a sense of anticipation. Abigail edged past, moving quickly through the narrow hallway just inside until she reached the foot of the bed. There she turned, her hands gripping each other at her waist, and waited.

He approached her slowly, carefully. She looked as she had before paragliding, pale eyes huge, skin alabaster under her light tan. He wanted her to look as she had *after* the flight—wild and flushed and powerful. He wanted her to look like that, to *be* that. For herself, and for him.

Her throat moved as she swallowed and her tongue flicked the corner of her mouth. He stopped a foot away, well inside her personal space, but not touching.

"I'm trying to remember..." He let the sentence trail off deliberately, hoping she wouldn't be able to resist the suspense. He needed her to be active, engaged, not passively waiting.

Silence pulsed between them. "What?" she finally asked.

"Is this the second or third time we've been alone?" He paused, as if considering. "I distinctly remember the hut on the beach. I know we were alone then..."

A small vee formed between her brows. "Why? Why does it matter?"

He shrugged. "It doesn't, not really. I was just wondering."

Her frown deepened. "We were alone in the garden."

"Ah, yes. Although there was the distinct possibility we could have been interrupted."

Roses bloomed faintly on her cheeks. "That would have been..."

"...inconvenient?" he suggested.

"Embarrassing."

"You would have been embarrassed to be seen with me?" He felt a pang that she might not want others to know they were together. His thoughts jumped back to when they'd left Richard and Tricia Thornton. Abigail had had the chance to mention their plans then, but hadn't.

She was replying to his question, seemingly unaware of his distraction. "To be seen kissing you would be one thing. But we were...you were..." She lifted her palms helplessly when the words failed her.

She'd lost some of her taut nervousness, and no longer resembled a butterfly about to flit frantically away. He trailed the tip of one finger down the fragile skin of her neck. "What is it about our attraction that worries you, Abigail?"

She closed her eyes briefly. "I don't understand it. I don't understand...why me?"

"I told you partly why at dinner. Your bravery, your adventurousness. But is it necessary to understand it? Can't you simply enjoy the moment?"

His finger left her skin and traced a line between her breasts, over her pale green nylon tank top, down her belly, to the button on her tan hiking shorts.

"You're making it very hard to think," she gasped. Her

hands gripped his biceps as he flicked the fastening open.

"Perfect," he all but growled, sliding the zipper down tooth by tooth. Getting Abigail here, with him, had taken more skill and effort than any other relationship he'd been in. "No more thinking tonight. For either of us. Only feeling."

The shorts dropped to the floor.

Abigail made a small mewling sound, but before she could react he grasped her hips, pulled her against his body, and kissed her.

****

It was so easy to follow Santos' command. The moment his mouth covered hers, the thoughts racing about in her mind vanished, evaporated by the heat of his embrace.

She wrapped her arms about his neck and dug her fingers in the silky hair at his nape as he took advantage of her willing lips. His tongue demanded a response, teasing hers until she stroked back, tasting wine and bread and Santos.

He lifted his head just far enough so his lips grazed hers as he spoke. "What about your asthma? Should you take your medication before we make love?"

His questions were so unexpected she could only stare blankly. "Asthma?"

"Sex can be very—energetic." His eyes twinkled wickedly. "I don't want you to have an attack at an inconvenient moment."

She blushed at the fiery, erotic visions his words conjured up. "I've hardly needed to use my inhaler since I've come to the island. I think it must be the clean air."

"Don't be afraid to tell me. If you need it, let me know. No matter what I'm doing to you at the time."

His words sent her imagination rioting and her bones turned to wax. Then his mouth dropped to hers and she lost herself once more.

The coarse material of his jeans rasped her tender inner thighs as he thrust one leg between them. His hands cupped her ass and he snugged her against him, creating a delightful, tormenting pressure. She wriggled up and down, riding his thigh, tension blooming, moistness gathering. He groaned in her mouth and pulled her impossibly closer to him. Her breasts flattened against his chest and she suddenly, desperately needed to feel his skin.

"You're wearing too many clothes," she muttered against his lips, tugging at the shoulders of his shirt.

He grabbed her wrists, stilled her movements, and rested his forehead against hers. Their panting, heaving breaths mingled. "Maybe we should slow down."

"If we slow down, I'll start thinking again."

He chuckled. "We wouldn't want that, would we?" He stepped away and she wanted to whimper, her body suddenly chilled without the heat of him, the burn of him, near. But warmth flushed over her when his hands went to the buckle of his belt.

"Well, then," he said as the leather shushed through the loops and he dropped it to the floor, "maybe we should even things up a bit." He shucked his jeans and stood before her, the stretchy material of his boxers doing little to hide his arousal.

Her mouth went dry and black spots danced before her eyes.

She'd never wanted a man like this before. Hadn't known desire could be so fierce, so demanding. As if her very existence depended on the touch of his hands, his mouth.

"Undo your hair."

She pulled out the elastic and shook her head to swing the strands off her face.

"Take off your shirt."

She scrambled to obey, one part of her brain wondering where the hell this wanton, lustful woman had come from. The rush of the fabric against her over-sensitized skin was almost painful.

"Now your bra." Santos' eyes were hooded, lids drooping low, his gaze so intent she felt it like a brand.

She reached behind and deftly unhooked the straps, wishing she had brought lacier, sexier underwear, instead of plain cotton. Of course, the last thing she'd considered when packing was that she would be stripping for a gorgeous, hot man whose very voice was making her wetter than she'd ever been before. When she'd left Prince George...

"You're thinking." Santos pinched her chin. "Stop that."

She let the bra fall.

Air hissed through his teeth and his eyes darkened to near black. Surely now he would touch her?

"Put your t-shirt back on."

"But..."

"I want to suck your nipples through it."

His request stoppered her complaint like a cork in a bottle. She shrugged the tank top back on, her nipples hard points under the thin nylon. The sensation of being braless under her shirt was more disconcerting that simply being naked.

"Now get on the bed. Up against the pillows."

Abigail crawled backward from the foot of the bed, never taking her eyes off Santos. For a woman who was tired of other people dictating to her, she thought a tad wildly, she was obeying Santos' instructions without complaint.

She'd do anything, as long as he would touch her. Soon.

It wouldn't have to be much of a touch. She was ready to blaze into flames.

****

Meu Deus, Santos thought, she's gorgeous. Abigail sprawled on the bed, skin pale against the dark brown cover, fine fair hair fanned out over her shoulders, the pillow. A narrow band of white cotton covered her mound, the thin material of her shirt emphasizing, not hiding, her unbound breasts.

He wanted her naked as much as she wanted him to be, yet he was determined to take his time, to make this night worth the days of waiting. And if a few layers of clothes helped him control his raging need to find release in her warm wetness, he was keeping them on as long as possible.

The mattress compressed under his weight as he stretched between her legs, his ribs pressed against her sultry heat, his elbows holding him off her slim body. His hands lifted her breasts, squeezed them gently. Through the barrier of her t-shirt he could see her nipples, twin points of desire.

And he made good on his promise.

Abigail writhed beneath him as he sucked first one nipple, then the other. Her shirt darkened with the moisture from his mouth, clung to the rounded tips. She bucked her hips with such strength she lifted him off the bed and he felt a spurt of heat against his chest as his own t-shirt dampened. He lifted his mouth to gaze at her in wonder.

She lay back, panting, one arm thrown over her eyes, the other clutching the bed covers with whitened knuckles. He'd known she was responsive, sensual, eager. He hadn't known how incredible it would be to have her completely lose herself in him. How powerful, possessive, protective it would make him feel.

And they'd barely gotten started.

Without lifting her arm from across her face she spoke. "When I open my eyes you'd better have your shirt off or I won't be responsible for the consequences."

He laughed softly and rolled off her enough to pull his shirt over his head. "You can open your eyes now."

Her arm flopped onto the bed and her lids rose slowly, heavily. "You're looking very pleased with yourself."

He lay beside her, nose to nose. She threaded her fingers through the hair on his chest and he shivered. "It is my great pleasure to please you."

She traced the tattoo encircling his arm, followed the vein on the inside of his elbow to his wrist. His hand draped over his hip, and she continued her delicate exploration over the planes of his belly. His cock twitched in anticipation, but she returned to his chest, leaving him aching.

"I would like to please *you*," she said, long pale lashes hiding her eyes. "Tell me what to do."

Her innocent question froze the oxygen in his lungs. She'd responded with such willingness, such unabashed zest to his caresses he hadn't considered the possibility—
"Abigail. Are you a virgin?"

"No!" Her eyelids flew up. "No. It's just that...I don't want you to be disappointed. I don't have much experience with...with this."

"What do you think *this* is?"

"A holiday fling." She smiled uncertainly. "I've never had a holiday before, let alone a fling."

He clamped down an unexpected desire to deny that was all that was between them, to proclaim she was more, much more, than a vacation affair. He'd never felt so passionate about any other woman, and that thought alone was deeply disturbing. Realistically, though, she was right. He could see no way to a long-term relationship between them, even if he'd wanted one.

Which he didn't. Did he?

****

Abigail bit her lip as Santos' face grew shuttered. She'd done it now. Done what, she wasn't exactly sure, as she'd answered his question the way he would have wanted. Her time with Santos had always been too good to be true and she didn't want to jeopardize any of it by expecting more than he was willing to give.

"I'm sorry," she said.

"What for?" He focused on her intently, shrugging off whatever thoughts had gripped him.

She lifted one shoulder. "I wrecked the mood."

"I don't think we'll have much trouble getting it back." He cupped the back of her head and drew her closer. "Where were we?"

He nibbled her lower lip and she squirmed closer, tangling her legs with his. His erection once again pressed hot and heavy against her belly, and she was so relieved he still wanted her she could have sobbed.

"Do you really want to know how to please me?" he said between long, silky strokes of his tongue into her mouth.

She could only moan her answer.

He took her hand and placed it against his shaft, shrouded by the thin barrier of cotton. "Touch me. I need you to touch me."

She squeezed him gently and he shuddered, breathing sharply through his nose. Power surged through her and she stroked more confidently. With her free hand she pushed his shoulder, and he rolled to his back. Slipping her fingers into the waistband of his boxers, she eased them down. His cock sprang free and moisture pooled within her. She slid the material over his strong thighs, his muscular calves, and tossed it to the floor.

She grasped him again and his groan of pleasure turned into a gasp when her other hand came round and caressed his balls. He muttered unintelligibly in Portuguese as she explored him thoroughly, fascinated by his hard, hot silkiness.

She circled the pad of her thumb over the head of his shaft, spreading the dampness she discovered there.

Santos jackknifed forward. Before she could shriek, he tossed her on her back. "Enough." He reared over her. "Or this will be finished before either of us wants it to be."

He looked wild and wicked and heated red patches burned on his cheekbones. Abigail stretched languidly, revelling in the incontrovertible proof of his desire for *her*. "Could I do that?" She felt like purring. "I could make you come, just by touching you?"

"Keep looking at me like that and you'll see how easily you can make me come."

Laughter bubbled out. "What are you going to do about it?" God, she felt potent, sexy, fearless. If she could only capture this feeling and remember it forever, nothing would hold her back ever again.

He crushed her to the bed, the weight of his body a sensuous blanket, the taste of his mouth a heady wine. Dizzy, head spinning, Abigail could only hold on and ride the waves with him, soar the air with him, follow where he led.

Somehow her remaining clothes disappeared and they lay skin to skin, heat to heat. Santos' hands were everywhere, her breasts, her belly, her arms, her ass. She was as greedy as he, raking her nails over his back, squeezing his biceps. Whenever she reached for his cock, he blocked her and distracted her with his mouth on her nipples, her neck.

He growled incomprehensible words in her ear, but it didn't matter she couldn't understand. The tone alone told her of his passion, his hunger.

She writhed against him and he laughed breathlessly. "I cannot wait any longer." He ripped open a condom and rolled it on, then knelt between her thighs and gripped her hips in his hands. His shaft nudged her opening. "*Mãe de Deus.* You are so wet, so ready."

She could only moan, her head thrashing from side to side, her hips lifting to him, begging him for release.

In one smooth stroke he entered her.

For a moment they held still, savouring the intimacy, the newness, the wonder. As one they began to move, finding a rhythm, their rhythm.

Until the euphoria enveloped them, the bliss overcame them, and together they shattered.

AWAKENINGS

Even before he opened his eyes, Santos knew Abigail was not next to him in bed. He lay on his stomach, arms outstretched, and she should have been right there, but she wasn't. He could smell her on the sheets and his cock stiffened uncomfortably beneath him.

A faint blue sheen reflected on the wall. He rolled to his side, shifting beneath the light sheet, and saw her. The twist of abandonment he'd felt coiled in his belly eased.

She sat curled up in the round-backed, upholstered chair by the window, knees bent, her tablet resting on them. She wore his shirt, which looked a lot sexier on her than it did him. It puddled at her hips, baring a long stretch of thigh, the curvy roundness of her ass. The glow from the screen cast an eerie glow onto her face. Behind her the white sheers, drifting in the draft from the air conditioning, created a ghostly backdrop.

She typed silently on the screen, undisturbed by his movements.

"What are you doing?" he asked quietly, his voice hoarse with desire and sleep.

She lifted her head, and immediately shut off the display.

"Did I wake you? I tried to be quiet."

"You didn't wake me." His next words sprang out without thought. "I missed you."

She smiled. "I haven't gone anywhere."

"You're not in bed with me." He held out a hand. She placed her tablet on the table and uncoiled from the chair, taking his hand as she stepped toward the bed. He tugged her to him and looked up from his supine position, seeing her as only a silhouette against the window. Yet her touch, her scent, her very shape in the darkness was so familiar he felt he'd know her anywhere. It was a sobering, slightly terrifying feeling.

Unwilling to examine his own thoughts further, he said in a mock threatening tone, "You're wearing my shirt."

She smoothed it with her free hand, the material tightening over her breasts. "I woke up and couldn't get back to sleep, so I decided to check my email. It was handy, so I put it on. I hope that's okay."

"Borrowing my shirt without asking, hmmm?" Releasing her hand, he stroked up her calf to the back of her knee and felt her sway. "I guess you'll have to pay the penalty." He continued higher, fingers dancing over her hip bone, brushing the curls at the apex of her thighs. He bit back a groan. She was damp—still, already, it didn't matter.

"I guess I'll have to."

Her voice was breathy, trembling with uncertainty, yet he knew the courage that had ensnared him was there, just below the surface. She was innocent and willing, hesitant and ferocious. He'd hoped making love would settle his unnerving appetite for her. Instead he found himself hungrier than ever.

He gripped her hips and lifted her until she straddled him. She braced her hands on his chest, the erotic heat of her pressed to his belly. Her eyes gleamed in the muted light glowing in through the window.

"What is the penalty?" She licked her lips, her fingers gripping his muscles.

"Let me see." He pulled his t-shirt off her, her unbound hair falling in shining strands over her shoulders, her bared breasts. "How should you be punished?" He emphasized the last word, almost growling it, and watched, fascinated, as her nipples tightened into points.

Deus, would she ever stop surprising him? His timid little mouse was turning into a sensual tiger and he wondered if he'd be able to discover all he wanted to know about her in the few days they had left.

He shoved away the unwelcome thought as he lifted his hips and toppled her onto the mattress, following quickly to pin her beneath.

"Santos!" she gasped.

"Don't be afraid," he said against her eager lips. "I promise you'll enjoy it."

****

An annoying tingling in her fingers nudged Abigail to consciousness. She lay on her side, one arm trapped beneath her. Santos held her snug against his chest, his leg thrown over hers, as if determined to keep her from leaving the bed without his knowledge.

The sheets rustled as she shifted to her back and freed her arm. Santos mumbled, a frown slashing between his brows, and his hold tightened. She flexed her fingers to bring back the feeling and smoothed the furrows between his eyes with her thumb. His grip relaxed and he settled deeper into sleep.

She had no idea what time it was, but the quality of light outside their fifth floor window told of morning. Despite her sleepless night—she smiled as she recalled the many activities that had kept her from sleeping—she felt rested and peaceful.

Until she remembered Martin's emails.

In the less than seventy-two hours since she'd ended their relationship, he had messaged her no less than nine times. The first few were coaxing, and she'd had to grit her teeth to avoiding replying. Guilt told her she owed him that courtesy, but she knew if the break was to be clean she had to be resolute.

The last few were angry. They made her uneasy, and when she'd read the most recent one after she'd woken in the middle of the night she'd decided to answer in the hopes of calming the situation. Martin knew she was scheduled to leave Quinta Carregado and move to the hotel the day before. She'd be a lot easier to find by phone now, and the last thing she wanted was to taint her few days with Santos by having to take badgering phone calls from Martin.

She'd barely finished her quick note when Santos had awoken and lured her back to bed.

Not that she'd taken much luring.

She scrutinized his face, squirrelling away details she could take out and treasure later. The way his eyelashes, short, dark and thick, rested on his cheeks. The strong bridge of his nose. The heavy eyebrows.

His mouth.

Lips simply made for kissing. Supple and mobile, thin but not too thin, turning up slightly in the corners even in sleep.

Just looking at him made her wet. God, to think she might have missed this, might have let fear and passivity and plain old stupidity keep her from experiencing this. Experiencing him.

She couldn't ever remember lying with Martin after making love and experiencing this same sense of rightness. It made the idea of marrying him even more ludicrous. She was so thankful she'd found the courage to sever their ties.

Based on his last few emails to her, she thought he might be re-evaluating their relationship as well. But perhaps that was wishful thinking, a way of deflecting some of her guilt.

She wriggled her arms around Santos' neck, and with a soft sigh he buried his face in the crook of her shoulder. He was warm and solid and incredibly sexy—and he'd chosen her. Her confidence grew with every second they spent together. Content just to hold him, she drifted into a light doze.

Sometime later, she felt him wake up. His muscles lost their laxness, his breathing changed, yet he didn't move from their close embrace. He kissed her neck and she stretched against him. He nibbled his way up her jaw to her mouth.

"*Bom dia*, Abigail." His eyes, deep mahogany brown, studied her lazily.

"*Bom dia,* Santos." Her breath caught as the tip of his tongue flicked along her bottom lip. "Sleep well?"

"No." He nuzzled her ear. "Someone kept me awake half the night."

Her head spun in delight as he nipped her lobe, and she closed her eyes. "That's too bad."

"Oh, I'm not complaining." He switched to her other ear, his silky hair brushing her cheek, his chest rubbing her breasts.

She lost herself in sensation and only realized he'd asked a question when he repeated it, amusement creasing the corners of his eyes.

"What do you want to do today?"

She struggled to collect her scattered wits. "Well, I thought..." She blushed fiercely.

He grinned wickedly. "We'll do that, too," he said, "but you didn't come all this way to spend an entire day in a hotel room."

I wouldn't mind, she thought, as long as it was with you.

"I know what we'll do." With a loud, smacking kiss he rolled off her and climbed out of bed. "Let's go have tea."

CHA GORREANA

The scent of freshly cut tea was rich and heady, the air moist and humid. It was like being steeped in an enormous tea pot, Abigail thought, breathing deeply.

She and Santos stood in a long, airy room at the Cha Gorreana tea factory. The wooden planked floor, scarred and worn, creaked under her feet, but the sound was lost in the clattering and banging from the two machines before them. At one, fresh cut leaves travelled in a narrow trough, the correctly sized tips dropping into a wooden box below. The other, a large copper cylinder perhaps five feet in diameter, shook madly from side to side for no reason she could discern.

Santos leaned close to her ear so he could speak without yelling. "These machines are original to the factory, and have been in use since the 1880's. Cha Gorreana is the oldest remaining tea company in Europe, and this factory is basically a working museum."

She watched, fascinated, imagining these exact machines going through this exact procedure for more than a century and a quarter. The Azores was young by European standards—the islands only officially discovered in 1432, she recalled from her studies—but they made Canada look like a teenager on the world's timeline.

They strolled throughout the various rooms, Abigail entranced by the antique machines, the age-old procedures. In one room, two women sat at low tables, picking through mounds of dried leaves, discarding unwanted pieces at a blistering pace. Without missing a beat, one of the women pulled a smart phone from her pocket and checked the screen. The incongruity of the modern technology juxtaposed with an action that had been going on for more than twelve decades made Abigail smile.

She followed Santos into a dark, wide hallway. Glass cases lit from inside displayed memorabilia of the factory's past, and tables covered in wonderfully white linen offered the chance to test its famous blends. As she hovered, trying to decide which one to sample, a woman entered from the far end.

"Santos Carregado!" A flurry of Portuguese followed as she strode forward, hands outstretched. She kissed him enthusiastically on both cheeks and smiled, intimacy in every gesture.

He replied, dark eyes alight, patting her fingers as they lay on his arm.

Jealousy surged so fiercely through Abigail she had to clench her fists to avoid grabbing the other woman by the hair and yanking her away. A wave of despair followed in its wake, the clashing emotions leaving her nauseated.

The newcomer was the perfect complement to Santos. Only a few inches shorter, she matched his tawny, wild gorgeousness. Her long, straight hair flowed silkily down her back, a brown so rich it rivalled the unique hue of freshly dried tea leaves. She wore a white blouse and emerald green skirt, the business-like style of the designer labels doing nothing to hide the lush body beneath, voluptuous breasts and hips swelling the fabric in a way no red-blooded man could ignore.

In a way no pale, blond Canadian girl could ever compete with.

Abigail watched in mute misery as Santos and the other woman carried on a rapid, impenetrable conversation. The Portuguese beauty tossed her head back laughing at something Santos said, and the feeling deepened.

The confidence with which she'd started the morning drained out of her. She remained, invisible and awkward, by the tea table, staring blindly at a stack of soiled cups and saucers. With any luck, Santos would end this unexpected reunion without the embarrassment of introducing her. It was bad enough knowing about his ex-girlfriends in theory— meeting one of them would be beyond bearing.

Just then he called Abigail's name, and a doom-filled feeling of inevitability swelled inside her. Reluctantly she lifted her eyes.

With a small nod he gestured her closer. "Let me introduce you to a friend of mine."

Abigail gritted her teeth and forced herself to meet the other woman's knowing eyes. The smile on her face felt hardened in plaster.

"Abigail, this is Maria de Grace Devasa. She's in charge of Cha Gorreana's European sales division, out of Amsterdam. Maria, this is Abigail."

Oh, God. Could he have emphasized their differences any more clearly? Abigail, meet this amazing, sexy, smart world traveller. Maria, meet Abigail, a plain, boring nothing.

"Hi," Abigail said brightly, painfully. "It's wonderful to meet you. You must have a fascinating job. I love your factory." She clamped her lips together, pulling the corners up into another strained smile.

"Thank you. I hope you enjoy your visit. We're very proud of what we do here." Maria's English was as good as Santos' but harsher, more brisk, unlike the slight Boston drawl he had picked up during his years in the States. She turned back to him, red-tipped nails gleaming against the olive skin of his forearm. "It is so good to see you," she continued in English. "How long as it been?"

"A few months, I suppose," he replied. Abigail had to give him points for politeness; there was no hint of regret in his voice.

Maria swayed subtly toward him, and Abigail noted sourly how her breasts brushed his arm. "If I'd known you were coming, I would have arranged a private tour," Maria said throatily.

Abigail didn't think the invitation included her.

Santos deftly detached himself from her grip on his arm and shifted around to stand next to Abigail. "We only decided this morning. I didn't think you were expected back on the island until August."

Maria shrugged, elegant collarbones showing at the neckline of her discreetly buttoned blouse. "Jorge called me back for a meeting." She continued on in Portuguese too rapid and complex for Abigail to understand, then kissed Santos on the cheek, said a polite goodbye in English to Abigail, and sashayed out of the room.

"So, have you decided?"

Abigail dragged her thoughts away from Maria's obvious—*much* too obvious, she thought cattily—charms. "What?"

He gestured at the array of teas arranged on the table against the wall behind her. "What kind would you like to try?"

"Actually, I'm afraid I've got a bit of a headache. I think I'd like to leave now." She couldn't believe he fell for the clichéd excuse, but instantly he was solicitous and caring. Taking her hand, he led her through the cafe and gift shop, out to the parking lot and tucked her into the tiny BMW sedan in which they'd driven from Ponta Delgada. Lina had swapped vehicles sometime after they'd arrived at the hotel yesterday, taking the van back to Quinta Carregado.

He slipped into the driver's seat, but hesitated after putting the key in the ignition. "Do you need any aspirin? Tylenol?"

She shook her head and held up the bottle of water she'd stashed in the door earlier that morning. "I'm probably just dehydrated. I should be fine after I drink this."

He reached for the key again, hesitated once more. "Will you be okay here for a bit? I need to go back in, just for a minute." His eyes searched her face and he tucked a stray strand of hair behind her ear.

"Sure. I'll close my eyes. Maybe the headache will fade."

He strode into the factory and she leaned her head against the seat back, hoping against hope he wasn't making a date with Maria while she sat here alone, staring out over the waist-high, flat-topped, neatly clipped rows of tea hedges.

PRAIA DA SANTA BARBARA

Abigail's eyes were closed when Santos returned to the car, but she opened them when the vehicle shifted as he climbed in. The sparkle he'd seen there all morning was gone and she regarded him almost warily.

"I'm sorry, I was longer than I thought. How are you feeling?"

"I'm fine," she answered politely.

He frowned as he backed the car out of the stall and headed out on the main highway. "If you're not up to exploring anymore we can return to the hotel. Maybe a nap will help."

"I said I'm fine."

He raised an eyebrow at her sharp tone but said nothing. He had no idea what had upset her, but decided to let it ride. Even the women he knew best, his mother and sister, could still surprise him with their odd quirks and peeves, and he'd long ago learned there were some things he was simply never going to understand.

Take Maria for instance. Last summer he'd broken his long-held habit of never dating Portuguese women for her. He'd met her while escorting a group of his tourists to a tea festival, and had been immediately attracted by her cosmopolitan air. A few careful questions had revealed the fact her family was unknown and unconnected with his, so there would be little chance his mother would hear of her and begin dreaming of daughter-in-laws. Even better, she was already based in Amsterdam, and he'd seen the long-distance relationship as an advantage, lending piquancy to the times they could be together. Maria, however, soon began to complain about their separation, and had begun to hint he should join her in the Netherlands, with heavy overtones of commitment and marriage. She hadn't taken his refusal to move quietly, showing a shrewish temperament that had made the decision to end their affair easier for him. And yet today, she'd acted as if their acrid, bitter fight had never happened, and even as if she'd welcome his attentions once again.

He shook his head at the vagaries of women.

The road wound along the north coast of São Miguel, sheer, green hills on the left, craggy, ragged coastline on the right. After the tea factory, he had planned to bring Abigail to the main city on this side of the island, and they were fast approaching the roundabout where he would have to make a choice.

"Should we still go to Ribeira Grande?" he asked.

"I suppose." She hadn't looked his way for kilometres and still didn't as she answered.

He shook his head, faint flickers of frustration licking at the edge of his patience.

He had intended to take her to the beautifully landscaped riverside park that ran through the city, but when he saw the sign for Praia da Santa Barbara he swung around and followed the narrow road leading to the parking lot. They would have more privacy on the long, wide beach than the busy park.

"Let's walk," he said. "I think we could both use some fresh air."

She resisted half-heartedly when he took her hand, but when he refused to release her she sighed and gave in. They walked past the little snack shop and the tiny outdoor stage, dodged dripping children as they ran squealing into the change rooms, and stepped off the boardwalk onto the hard packed sand.

Santos toed off his sandals, and after a slight pause Abigail did the same. At first black lava rock, worn smooth by the waves that crashed and broke over it, created a barrier between them and the sea. They sauntered further along and soon wavelets advanced and receded before them, leaving the sand cool and moist under his feet.

Out on the water surfers bobbed, waiting for their next ride, while closer to shore dozens of people of all ages paddled and played in the water. He wound his way among the make-shift camps of wrinkled blankets and plastic coolers and umbrellas jammed in the sand until they left the crowd behind and found themselves alone at the far end.

He led her closer to the tall bank that formed a protective wall on the southern edge. "I didn't think to bring a blanket," he apologized. "But the sand is dry."

For the first time since the tea factory, she gave him a smile. It was small and weary, but a smile, nonetheless. She lowered herself to the ground and burrowed her feet into the shifting sand. He stretched out next to her, resting on one elbow.

"Are you ready to tell me what's wrong?" Seagulls screamed and squalled overhead, and in the distance breakers splashed against the large, square headland marking the western-most tip of the bay.

She reached between them and grabbed a handful of sand, pouring it slowly to create a cone-shaped pile. He waited, determined not to ask again.

"How long have you known Maria?"

"What?"

"You heard me."

The unexpected question had him scrambling. "About a year. We met when I was guiding a group last summer."

"Did you date her?"

"For a few months. It's been over for longer than we were together."

Abigail poured another handful of sand onto her pile. "She's beautiful."

Her wistful voice twisted in his gut. "Yes. And so are you."

She smashed her hand down, destroying her careful construction. "Don't patronize me."

"I'm not." He sat up and grabbed her hands. "Look at me."

She raised her eyes slowly.

"You are beautiful, Abigail. In so many ways."

"I'm a nobody. I don't jet across the Atlantic to have business meetings, or wear designer clothing. I've never been to the opera, or climbed the Eiffel Tower, or seen a Broadway play. I'm an accountant, for crying out loud. Could I be even more boring?" She tugged out of his grip and scuttled away from him. "I wouldn't blame you if you changed you mind."

Now he was truly befuddled. "Changed my mind?"

"You went back into the factory to talk to her again, didn't you? Have you arranged to see her, once you're rid of me?"

Santos couldn't remember ever being this angry. He

surged to his feet, yanking her up with him. "Is that what you think of me? That I am so fickle I will leave one woman to go lusting, *para ir cobiçar,* after another at the blink of an eye?" He gripped her upper arms and shook her, fine blond hair falling into her face as the messy bun on top of her head loosened. "I don't know when I've been so insulted."

"I thought...I was just trying...I wanted to be understanding, to be sophisticated." Tears puddled in the corner of her pale blue eyes.

Damn it, now he felt like a jerk. "Well, understand this." He gentled his clasp on her arms. Her skin was chilly from a cool breeze hinting of rain to come. "When I am with a woman, I am with *her*, not thinking of who the next one will be." His mind short-circuited at *the next one*. The thought of being with any woman other than Abigail seemed incredibly unappealing, even as he seethed with frustration over her insecurities.

"I'm sorry."

"You should be."

"It's just that—"

He closed his eyes. Women. They simply couldn't let an argument go.

"—I know this is only a short-term relationship. I leave in six days. I wouldn't blame you if—"

He opened his eyes and glared at her. Abigail swallowed and wisely changed tack.

"Well, if you didn't go in to talk to Maria, why did you go back?"

"Did it every cross that absurd brain of yours that I needed to use the washroom?"

She blushed lightly, then narrowed her eyes. "That's not why you went back, is it."

He'd wanted to do this in a romantic way, but she was

obviously not going to let him prevaricate any longer. "I went back in," he said, reaching into the pocket of his shorts and pulling out a small box, "to get you this."

****

Abigail stared in horror at the small white box laying on Santos' palm. He'd bought her a gift, and she'd accused him of—well, not exactly cheating on her, but close enough.

The tears burning her eyes throughout their confrontation welled onto her cheeks. "I'm so sorry." She choked on the words, her lips numb with shame.

He released an exasperated breath and scrubbed his hand through his hair. "*Não chore.* Don't cry." He offered her the box. "It's not much, but I wanted you to have a memento. Something to remember your stay on the island."

As if she would ever forget her time on São Miguel. Ever forget her time with Santos. "I don't deserve it." She clasped her hands behind her back. "You did something sweet and kind, and I ruined it by being jealous."

"You were jealous? Of Maria?" He seemed shocked at the idea. And also a tad smug.

"Heidi Klum would be jealous of Maria," she said grimly, "let alone a mere mortal."

"There is nothing between Maria and I any longer, and there never will be again." He met her gaze squarely.

She believed him, yet couldn't quite let it go. "Why not? You two look perfect together. Lina told me—" The sudden hardening of his face stopped her.

"Lina told you what?"

She swallowed, hoping the truth wouldn't give Santos an excuse to murder his sister. "She suggested you date ex-guests because you know they are leaving soon. That if you dated an island woman, like Maria, you might end up married, whether you wanted to or not."

He grumbled under his breath in rapid-fire Portuguese, heavy brows drawn tightly together. "Lina should keep her nose out of my business."

"It's none of mine, either," Abigail added hurriedly. "Forget I mentioned it." His expression remained thunderous and she backed away, only to find herself up against the sandy bank.

Santos clenched his fists. He stared down, as if surprised to discover he still held the small box. After a moment his shoulders relaxed. He sighed.

"It doesn't matter what Lina told you. It doesn't matter what you thought of Maria." He stepped forward and she caught his scent above that of the warm sand and salty ocean. She remembered rubbing her face on his chest last night, breathing him in, absorbing his essence, and her knees loosened. "I'm getting tired of repeating myself, Abigail, so listen and listen well." He brushed his knuckles across her cheek, bumping them along her jaw. "I want *you*. You, in my bed, at my side. These days I think of no one but you, your courage, your energy, your lips, your skin." She shuddered and he smiled devilishly. "And other parts of your body to be discussed later. We may not have forever, but we have now. So stop thinking about the future, and enjoy what we have, right here, at this moment."

She nodded, mesmerized by the intensity of his voice, the heat in his touch.

He lifted the box into her line of sight. "Open it."

Still reluctant, she lifted the lid slowly. Nestled inside, an exquisitely tiny teacup and saucer in delicate porcelain dangled on a thin silver chain. She bit her lip, waiting until she could trust her voice to speak.

"It's wonderful. But I can't keep it." She closed the lid and made to hand it back.

Santos closed his hand over hers, wrapping her fingers around the box. "Why not?"

"Every time I look at it I'll remember how stupid I was. How I overreacted when you left me in the car. I was catty and pouty and you didn't deserve it."

He chuckled. "Why don't we give you new memories then? Better memories."

She watched, puzzled, as he opened the box and lifted out the chain.

"Turn around."

She did so. Santos moved in behind her. His arms reached over her head, bringing the necklace into view. He draped the chain around her neck, the pendant cool against her breastbone, his fingers warm as he fiddled with the clasp. Goosebumps rippled down her arms when he leaned in closer and his breath ruffled the loose strands of hair on her nape.

She stared blindly at the crumbling sand wall as he trailed his fingertips down the slope of her shoulders, along the inside of her wrists, and grasped her hands. He wrapped their linked hands around her waist and snugged her against him, molding her to his body. She gasped when the stiff ridge of his erection pressed against her lower back.

"How can you think I would look at another woman," he growled, nuzzling behind her ear, "when simply holding you makes me hard?"

Her head fell back against his shoulder. He took advantage of her surrender and sucked on the sensitive skin of her neck. She moaned and wriggled, and he clasped her even more tightly. "You like that, do you? So do I. You taste amazing."

He continued to nibble, from the line of her jaw to under

her ear to the top of her spine, from one side to the other, until Abigail was limp with raw urgency. "I want...I need..." she whispered.

"I know, *querida*, I know." His voice was harsh but controlled. He spun her around and took her mouth.

She gripped his skull with both hands and rode with him, no longer simply submitting to his caresses but a full participant, demanding, taking. Her tongue tangled with his, jousting and tasting. She hooked her ankle behind his knee, the smooth skin of her calf rasping against the crisp hairs on his.

His hand slid up her thigh, under her flippy summer skirt and cupped her between her legs. The heel of his hand pressed against her most sensitive spot and she jerked her mouth away from his. "Stop that," she muttered frantically. "We're on a public beach."

He circled his hand and she meant to struggle away—she really did—but her thighs opened and her eyes closed.

"I will give you what you need, *meu amor.*" He fingered the edge of her panties, pulled them aside. "I want to give you everything." He played with her soft folds lightly, teasing.

"There are people...we'll be seen..." This was crazy, insane—and, oh God, she might die if he stopped.

"They won't see anything but two people standing on a beach." He slid two fingers deep inside her and she opened her mouth to shout, but he covered it with his own and swallowed her cry. "But people will definitely notice if you scream." His lips brushed hers as he spoke. "You must be very, very quiet."

The need for discretion only amped up her arousal. He curled his fingers and stroked her inner walls and her muscles clenched. She bit her lip to keep her whimpers and pleas buried inside. Her hips moved with him and the pressure started to build. It tingled in her thighs, spread to her lower back, gathered in her womb.

"I'm going...I'm going to..." she sobbed.

His voice was dark desire in her ear. "Let it happen, *meu amor*, let yourself go."

And she did.

****

Watching Abigail climax almost pushed Santos over his own edge. She shuddered and trembled in his arms, leaning limply against him. His chest suffused with a frightening tenderness, he kissed her temple.

Her panting breaths eased, but she remained nestled under his chin, her face hidden. A seagull shrieked directly overhead and she jerked, then settled back. "Ohhh-kay," she signed. "New memories, that's for sure. Definitely better memories."

He smiled into her hair. She shifted and he sucked in air as she bumped his groin. She stilled instantly.

"What about you? Do you want me to..." Her voice faded away.

"People would definitely notice that." He couldn't keep the humour from his voice and she looked at him shyly.

"It's not that I don't want to...uhm...help you," she said. "I think I might rather enjoy it."

The image of Abigail, on her knees in the sand before him, gazing up at him with those incredibly blue eyes, her pale pink lips wrapped around him, hardened his already painful cock even more.

"I know a different beach," he said. "A private one."

"Let's go," she said.

HOTEL – SECOND NIGHT

Abigail wobbled as the hotel elevator jolted to a stop. Santos steadied her with a hand on her elbow. They grinned at each other, Abigail wondering if the expression on her face was as goofy as his. Their visit to the second beach had been a rousing success, despite the fact she now had sand in places she didn't want to think about.

Light-headed from sated lust, she felt half-drunk as they made their way down the hallway. She was also starving, but food would have to wait until she showered. Santos gestured her into the room. She kicked off her sandals and a small dusting of sand speckled the carpet.

A light flashed on the phone lying on the nightstand. "I wonder who that is?" Santos moved between the beds. "Lina would have caught me on my cell if she needed me." He reached for the receiver.

Abigail knew without a shadow of a doubt it was Martin. She rushed past Santos and snatched the phone from his hand. "What makes you think it's for you?" She tried to sound playful, but Santos raised a disbelieving eyebrow. "It's probably Tobias. My brother. You remember, I told you I had a brother."

"*Sim*, I remember." He smiled and tapped the tip of her nose. "The easiest way to find out which of us is right is to listen to the message."

"I am." She pressed the correct sequence, held the phone tightly to her ear and waited.

"Hello, Abigail, it's Martin." She white-knuckled the receiver and angled slightly away from Santos. "If you can possibly fit it into your busy schedule, I would appreciate a phone call." Martin rarely used sarcasm, but she had no trouble discerning it this time. "I will expect a call before close of business, my time, today. At the office, of course." A click snapped in her ear.

She plastered on a smile before turning to face Santos. "Yup," she said, desperately cheerful. "Tobias, just as I thought. He says everything is fine, but he would like me to phone him back."

"Why don't I leave you alone for a while? You'll have a better chance to talk if I'm not hovering." He checked his phone for the time. "I'll go sit in the lounge. Call me on my cell when you're done."

"You wanted a shower."

"So do you. Maybe we'll take one together when I get back."

She was too anxious to react to the nuances in his invitation. "Thank you. I'll try not to be too long."

"*Não e nada.*" He kissed her, quick and casual. "Take your time. I'm sure you have lots to talk about."

The door snicked shut behind him and she collapsed onto the edge of the bed.

Lying to Santos made her sick to her stomach. But telling him the truth wouldn't do any good, and might possibly harm their fragile relationship, especially after her silly display of jealousy over Maria earlier.

She began to dial Martin's number, her hand heavy, reluctant. As she finished off the area code, her fingers disobeyed her weak will and she found herself connecting with Tobias' cell phone.

It rang once, twice, three times, before a gruff voice answered.

"Tobias?" She checked the alarm clock next to the phone. Minus seven hours from six-seventeen… "It's almost eleven thirty. Are you still sleeping?"

"Not anymore. Wait a minute." Muffled sounds came over the line, as if the phone had been dropped on something soft. When next she heard his voice, he sounded slightly more awake. "Is everything okay, Abigail? Why are you calling?"

She tangled her fingers in the phone's spiralling cord. "I was supposed to call Martin, but dialled your number. By accident."

"Uh huh." The doubt was clear, even in his sleep-roughened voice. "When were you going to tell me you broke up with him?"

"Oh." Every time she'd emailed Tobias, she'd planned on giving him the news. And every time she'd avoided it. "When I got home?"

"He's livid, you know. Keeps calling me to see if I've talked to you."

"I'm sorry he's bothering you. I should have warned you, but I didn't think he'd tell anyone. I get the impression from his messages to me that he hasn't accepted the fact yet."

"If it's any consolation, I think his pride is hurt more than his heart."

"I hate to ask you to do this, but can you phone him, tell him I got his message, but that I won't be calling him? When I get back he can yell at me all he wants."

"Okay. But you owe me." A long, hollow yawn echoed through the receiver. "Since you woke me up, the least you can do is give me the details. Why break up with Martin now, like this? Time to spill it."

The words were out of her mouth before she had a chance to block them. "I think I'm falling in love."

Silence.

She lay back on the bed, her legs dangling over the side, and stared at the ceiling. "Tobias?"

"I thought you were in love with Martin."

Her laugh felt remarkably close to a sob. "I thought I was, too. But when he asked me to marry him—"

"He asked you to marry him? When?"

"A couple of days ago. It was less of a proposal, and more of a command."

"Bastard."

"Tobias!" She jolted upright, shocked at the venom in Tobias' voice.

"How insensitive could he be? How could he spring something so serious on you like that?"

"He wants to take care of me."

Tobias snorted explosively. "You? You don't need to be taken care of. You're the strongest person I know, putting up with Mom's issues all these years, shielding me from the worst of them. He's looking for someone to take care of *him*."

It was wonderful, knowing Tobias understood her so well. And disturbing, realizing she didn't know him nearly as well. "I had no idea you disliked Martin."

"I don't, not really. If you loved him, I'm sure I could have found a way to get along. But if you're in love with someone else.... I don't suppose he's a Canadian tourist who just happened to be in the right place at the right time?"

She hadn't realized how badly she wanted to tell

someone about Santos. "Actually, he's the owner of the tour company. He's...amazing. Handsome and smart and charming."

"Does he make you happy?"

She considered the question. Excited, anxious, aroused, exasperated...happy? "Yes," she said slowly. "Yes, he does. I can be myself with him. And he makes me better. Stronger, more in control, more adventurous."

"Is he falling in love with you?"

The sunshine inside her dimmed. "It's not like that, for him. He enjoys my company, I know that. And it's not only that we have good...I mean, that we're..."

"Stop right there. I get the picture."

She laughed shakily. "Thank God."

"Are you still coming home next week?"

"Of course I am." The stab of sorrow was so sharp she sucked in a breath, released it gradually to contain the pain. "This started as nothing more than a short-term affair, and it still is, for Santos."

"Santos, huh? What kind of name is that?" He continued without waiting for an answer. "You deserve to be happy, Abigail. If you want more than a holiday fling, go for it."

Her throat closed, tears tightening behind her eyes. "It would never work out. Even if he did want something more, he belongs here, on the island, and I belong home, with you."

"You're not the only one that's done some changing over the last week, you know. I kind of like living on my own."

He almost fooled her, but she caught the hint of loneliness in his voice. She knew better than to mention it. "Of course you like it. I'm not there to nag."

"Exactly. And I can walk around naked anytime I want."

"Ewwww. That's a visual I didn't need." She tried to match his cheerfulness, but couldn't quite get there. "I didn't mean to bomb this on you."

"No worries. I guess that explains why you don't want to call Martin, hey?"

She collapsed back down onto the bed. "I can't talk to him, not now. When I come back I'll explain everything. I owe him that at the very least."

"I suppose."

"I dated him for more than two years, Tobias. Breaking up with him over the phone was awful of me, but I couldn't let him go on thinking we had a future."

"What about this Santos? Are you going to tell him how you feel?"

"What good would it do?" The tears she tried so hard to hold back trickled from the corner of her eyes and scalded down her temples into her ears. "I love him, but it means nothing if he doesn't love me back."

****

Early evening sun gilded the hotel lobby, slanting in through the huge wall of glass overlooking the marina. Santos slouched comfortably in a chrome and white leather chair tucked behind a giant feathery fern and sipped his Sagres.

The beer quenched his thirst, but did nothing to sate his hunger for Abigail. They'd been together for approximately twenty-four hours, and he had had her in bed—the same bed, twice—and on a beach—two different beaches, once each—and if anything, he craved her more than ever.

It was unsettling, to say the least. He swallowed his drink moodily.

The light tapping of high heels approached and a woman strode into view. His eyes wandered over her, starting at her siren red shoes, travelling up slim calves to well-toned thighs barely hidden beneath a tight multi-coloured skirt. A loose, floaty top drifted around high, rounded breasts. Her rich, dark hair was piled artfully on top of her head, baring a long, slender neck, and when she smiled at him, her glossy, ruby lips parted to reveal straight white teeth.

"Do you mind?" She pointed at one of the empty chairs across from him.

"Of course not."

The waiter approached and she ordered red wine, then leaned forward to rummage in the large leather bag she'd placed on the floor. The neck of her blouse gaped open and he caught a hint of white lace, a glimpse of satiny flesh. She pulled out a tablet and tapped the screen.

He waited for the insistent tug of desire such an overtly sexy woman should inspire. Waited for the surge of sensuality she should motivate. Waited, almost desperately. And waited.

Other than a connoisseur's appreciation for a lovely piece of art, he felt nothing.

Yet all he had to do was picture Abigail as he'd last seen her—phone in hand, slightly awkward smile on her face, dried sand crusting the ends of her hair—and he stiffened immediately.

He felt a bit of a cad, thinking about sex when he was pretty sure something had her worried. She'd acted odd about the phone call, and he hoped everything was okay with her brother. He wondered if there was something going on back home she hadn't told him about. The thought gave him pause.

Of course there was something going on back in her unusually named hometown. She had a life there, completely separate from this tiny oasis of a holiday. Some of that life had crossed the ocean with her—Martin, for one—but who knew what else she was dealing with?

He frowned and tipped the last of the beer into his mouth. It shouldn't matter, what her life was like in that cold Northern country. But it did. He realized, with a deep, gut-wrenching shock, he wanted to know everything about her. Know each tiny minutia of her wants, her needs.

His phone rang before he had time to analyze what that discovery meant.

"I'm done," Abigail said. "Ready for a shower?"

Images of a wet, naked Abigail erased any coherent thoughts from his brain. "I'll be right up."

****

Abigail lay draped over Santos' chest.

"I don't think I'll ever move again." His exhausted voice rumbled beneath her ear.

She wanted to smile, but every muscle in her body was so relaxed she couldn't even twitch up the corner of her mouth. "Me, either." Her heart still thundered and nerves fired tiny bolts of electricity through her body. Then her stomach growled. "Except to eat," she said.

His chuckle shook her gently and she raised herself, resting her weight on her hands on either side of his shoulders. She welcomed the cool, air-conditioned air on her sweaty breasts.

"Hungry?" He traced a finger around her nipple.

She scooted away and slapped his shoulder. "Stop that. I'm starving, and now I have to have another shower." She scowled down at him, and he gazed smugly back.

"You weren't complaining a few minutes ago. In fact, I distinctly remember you saying..."

She pressed a hand over his mouth, trying to keep a stern

face but losing out to laughter. "Don't you dare repeat what I said in the throes of sex. That's not fair."

His tongue tickled her palm and she quickly released him. He grinned. "All right, I'll play nice. Go, have your shower. I won't join you this time."

The memory of the two of them under the spray, slippery with soap, hands sliding in and out, up and down, burned a flush on her throat. The love she'd so recently realized slammed into her. It wasn't only the physicality they shared. It was the fun, the discovery, the shared adventures.

"Abigail? Are you all right?" Santos sat up and reached for her.

She smiled. "Of course. I was just..."

"I'm sorry, I'm an ass." He shifted so he could wrap his arm around her shoulders. "I never even asked, how is your brother? Is everything okay?"

"Yes, everything's fine."

"And the rest of your family?"

"There is no one else."

"No uncles or aunts? No grandparents?"

She shook her head. "My parents were both only children, and their parents were gone even before my mom and dad married."

"You had no family around you? No one to help you with your mother, your brother?"

"No. It was just the three of us." She wrinkled her nose. "I suppose it seems odd to you, someone who has so many relatives you can't keep track. Why do you ask?"

He twined his fingers through hers and avoided her gaze. "We're sleeping together. Is it so odd I'd want to know more about you?"

She stared at his profile. "Even though we're going to be together for less than a week?"

He raised his head at that, eyes hot and intent. "I care about you, Abigail. It doesn't matter how long or how short our time will be. I still care about you."

His words were more than she had allowed herself to dream. If he didn't love her, at least he liked her, cherished her. She cupped his cheek in her hand. "I care about you, too." He rubbed his jaw against her palm and she shivered deliciously at the day's growth of bristles.

"Is there anything particular you want to do tomorrow?"

Other than spend it with you? she thought. "No."

"My village is having its parish festival. We decorate the streets with flower petals, and the statues from our church are paraded through." Red stained his hard cheekbones. "It's quaint, but charming."

"I suppose your mother expects you." Disappointment balled in her gut. One less day together, when already they were numbered on one hand.

"I told her I wouldn't be there this year. But if you thought it might be interesting," he said, lids downcast as he played with her fingers, "we could go, help my mother and Lina decorate, take part in the procession, have dinner with my family."

"I would love to do that." The heavy weight of dejection vanished and she felt buoyant, light and bright. "It sounds fascinating." And it would give her one day to be a part of his life, not as a tourist or a guest, but as family. Temporary family, but still.

"All right. That's settled, then." He rubbed her thigh gently, his hand dark against her paleness. "Go have that shower. It's time to eat."

THE *FESTA*

"Here, carry this." Lina shoved a large bag at Abigail. Bigger than a king-sized pillow, it was unwieldy but light and decorated with a red band of cows, chickens, horses and pigs. She peered in and saw it was full of soft, blue hydrangea blossoms. Lina grabbed a similar bag and hefted a wooden frame about two feet by four feet onto her shoulder. "Mom and Santos will bring the rest, but we might as well get started." She crunched across the gravel of Quinta Carregado's forecourt.

Abigail and Santos had arrived at the *quinta* around three in the afternoon. Unlike her first warm, friendly arrival at the farm, this time tension hung in the air. Senhora Carregado greeted her formally, without the pleasant ease she'd shown when Abigail was a paying guest, and had ushered her into the family's painfully neat living room. Two small sofas, stiffly upholstered in a brown and red floral print, faced each other across a lovingly polished dark wood coffee table, on which was set out a beautifully presented offering of tea and cold drinks and biscuits. Abigail sat next to Santos, their combined weight barely denting the hard-stuffed seat, and sipped her tea. After a few stilted sentences in English,

Senhora Carregado had slipped into Portuguese. Abigail thought her tone sounded sharp and demanding, but Santos replied calmly, his expression unaffected, and slowly the older woman's posture eased.

Santos turned to Abigail. "My mother apologizes that she cannot speak better English."

Abigail shook her head, smiling. "Tell her I'm sorry. I should be able to speak her language."

"Why not tell her yourself? Say this: *Minha desculpa. Eu deveria ser capaz de falar a sua lingua.*"

"I'll make a mess of it."

"Give it a try." He repeated it. "I promise I won't laugh."

She stumbled through the unfamiliar sounds. True to his word, Santos didn't laugh, although the corners of his mouth tucked in. His mother allowed her demeanor to soften further and giggled behind her hand, her eyes dancing.

Lina entered the room, wearing grubby jeans and a threadbare t-shirt with green stains streaked across it. "I thought you were coming to help." She smacked Santos on the shoulder. "And instead you are here, in the best room, like company."

"We were just on our way." He stood and lifted the drinks tray. "You're a wreck."

She looked down and shrugged. "I was painting the guest room doors. You might be on holiday, but I am not. And making the flower carpet, it is messy, too. I will change after."

"Let me help clear." Abigail reached for the biscuit plate.

Senhora Carregado beat her to it. "*Não, não.* Go with Lina. We come, we come."

So now Abigail trailed after Lina, gripping the lip of the bag filled with flowers. She stepped into the narrow street and watched as Lina lowered the wooden frame onto the cobblestones. Chattering and shouting echoed around her as other groups of people prepared the sections in front of their own homes. Most of the houses opened directly onto the roadway, not having the luxury of a front yard.

"You have the hydrangeas. They go here." Lina pointed to the two diamond shapes in the centre of the wooden guide. "Spread them out, in *punhados*." She demonstrated, taking a big double handful and dumping the petals in the frame. "*Muito*. Use *muito*."

Abigail dug her hands into the bag and spread the soft, silky fragments on the ground. "How do they stay on the road? Don't they blow away?"

"If it is very windy, yes. But when my *preguiçoso* brother brings the hose, he will spray them with water. That holds them."

"I am not lazy. And if you're not nice to me, I'm not going to help," Santos said as he and Senhora Carregado joined them. He handed Lina another bag, dropped a snaky green hose, grabbed one end and dragged it toward the neighbour's house. Pulling open a small wooden hatch low to the ground next to the front door sill, he uncovered a faucet, attached the hose and returned.

Senhora Carregado, who brought yet another bag, knelt next to Abigail and began filling parts of the frame with deep reddish-brown cedar chips. Lina used delicate, brilliantly green fronds of cedar for the remaining spaces. Once the guide was complete, Santos soaked everything with a healthy dose of water.

"Grab your side, Abigail, and lift straight up," Santos directed. They boosted up the frame, moved forward a few steps, and lowered it back to the ground.

"And again," Lina said with a small grin. "Many, many times." She nodded at Santos and rattled off something in

Portuguese.

He turned to Abigail. "Lina tells me she's offered my help to the neighbours, just around the corner." He must have seen the slight panic she felt at the thought of being left alone with Senhora Carregado. "We'll be right back," he reassured her. "It'll will be fine." Abigail wasn't so certain, but knew she had little choice." He kissed her quickly on the cheek then strode up the street with Lina, greeting everyone as he went.

Abigail squatted across from Senhora Carregado and gathered her courage to try her very rudimentary language skills. "The flowers," she said haltingly in Portuguese as she held a handful of the blue blossoms. "Name?"

"Ah. *Nuvelaos.*" Her busy hands scattered the cedar chips briskly as she nodded at Abigail. "In English?"

"Hydrangea." She added in Portuguese, "Pretty."

Silence fell between them. They finished the second frame, Abigail sprayed it down, and they moved on. She searched for another conversational opening, but the only question she could think of was beyond her capabilities, so she spoke slowly in English, hoping for the best. "Who picks them?"

Senhora Carregado sat back on her heels and cocked her head to one side. "*Que?*"

Abigail had resorted to mime, acting out gathering flowers, when Santos appeared. "Playing charades?" he asked, one eyebrow raised.

"I was trying to ask your mother who picks the flowers."

"There's a committee that organizes the festival. They take care of those details."

It didn't take much longer for the three of them to finish their stretch of street. Senhora Carregado spoke rapidly— Portuguese always sounded fast to Abigail—handed her a broom, gathered up the empty bags, pointed a finger from Santos to the wooden frame and headed into the courtyard.

"My mother wants—"

Abigail held up a hand. "I don't need to be fluent to figure that out," she laughed. "We're on clean-up detail, aren't we?"

"Mom is going to tidy up for the procession, and as soon as we're done we can do the same."

Abigail looked down at her denim capris, the knees damp and gritty from kneeling on the stones, and the flecks of petals dusting her light pink t-shirt. "I'm glad you warned me to bring a change of clothes."

"I'm looking forward to seeing you in that dress again." She'd brought her yellow sundress with the halter top, the one she'd worn to dinner with the tour group. The one Santos had taken halfway off in the hut on the beach. His eyes slid deliberately down her body and back up to her face. "Especially now I know exactly what's underneath it."

****

Santos winced at the boom of the big bass drum thundering rhythmically only two metres away. Abigail, standing in front of him, clapped her hands in delight.

She glanced over her shoulder, pale eyes sparkling. "Three marching bands? I love it!"

He hadn't meant to invite her to the *festa*. And certainly hadn't meant to tell her he *cared* for her. He did, of course—he wasn't a monster, unable to like the women he spent time with—but he would never have admitted it to her if he'd been in his right mind. Because the only excuse his scrambling brain had come up with was that he'd gone crazy.

Lina had certainly thought so when he'd called to say he

was bringing Abigail to the *festa*. "You're getting in too deep," she had warned him last night. "Someone is going to get hurt." His mother had been more direct. "We know nothing about her, about her family, who they are, what they believe. Why do you bring such a woman home? Do you feel sorry for her?"

No one would feel sorry for her if they saw her now, he thought. She glowed with excitement, looking like a buttercup in her bright yellow dress. It swirled about her knees in the light ocean breeze, molded itself to her slim torso. The bow at the back of her neck was tantalizingly close and he curled his hands into fists, resisting the urge to untie it.

They had walked from Quinta Carregado, joining a stream of villagers and tourists gathering in the small square before the main village church. The festivities began only three-quarters of an hour later than expected—practically on time by Azorean standards—and so far three bands had marched to the formal front door of the church, each playing a deafening selection of music with vigour and enthusiasm.

As the echoes of the final *bom-di-bom-bom* faded away, the doors of the church opened. Six men wearing red capes stepped out, carrying between them a platform decked with flowers and cedar branches. They carefully heaved the stage to their shoulders, the statue perched on it swaying above their heads.

A respectful hush settled over the crowd. Abigail leaned back so she could whisper her question. "Who is that?"

"Our Lady of Fatima. Do you know her?" He spoke quietly in her ear. Abigail shook her head, her fascinated gaze never leaving the figure as it was conveyed along the floral carpet and came to a stop a few metres away. "Mary, our Lord's mother, appeared to three Portuguese children near the Mainland village of Fatima in the early part of the twentieth century. She visited them from May to October, and by her final appearance thousands of believers were with the children, although no one saw her but them. Many Portuguese are deeply devoted to her."

Another group of men clad in red exited the church, carrying an image of a bearded man in a brown robe carrying a child on his shoulder. "St. Anthony," he told her without waiting to be asked. "Carrying the Child Jesus."

If possible, the quiet grew even deeper when a third statue was carried out. "*Nossa Senhora da Luz.* Our Lady of the Light. This is our Lady, the Lady of our very own church."

Three priests dressed in white robes joined the procession. They marched in great dignity beneath a large, heavy canopy supported on long poles and carried by teenage altar servers. Santos remembered *festas* from his childhood, when he and his friends accompanied the local pastor for the long, slow parade. He'd participated under duress, bowing to his mother's will, although he realized with faint surprise those were some of his most vivid memories of his youth.

As the statues, the marching bands, the priests and attendants began their pilgrimage, some of the watchers joined in at the back, while others drifted away.

Santos touched Abigail's bare shoulder, warmed by the late afternoon sun. "Do you want to walk with them?"

She wiped her cheek, and he frowned. Tilting her chin, he saw teardrops dance on her lower lids, and his heart clenched. "Abigail?"

"It was just so...so lovely." Her smile was soft and pensive. "I kept thinking of the decades of tradition, the generations of families that have taken part in this, who still do. I've never experienced anything like it."

"Your family must have customs of its own, perhaps not so elaborate." He took her elbow and they strolled in the opposite direction of the procession.

"No, not really. For so many years it was only the three of us. And now it's just the two of us." She leaned her head briefly against his shoulder as they walked. "You're so lucky, to have family, friends, a community like this, so close, so tightly knit. I envy you."

The loneliness in her voice stirred up his protective instincts. He couldn't do anything about her life back in Canada, but he could help her belong, at least for tonight. "You may change your mind about that after dinner. My mother is expecting about twenty people, and you're going to get a stiff dose of that togetherness you're wishing for."

"Should I offer to help? That sounds like a lot of work." Her low heels clipped on the cobbled street as they neared Quinta Carregado. She stretched out a longer step to cross over the flower carpet without disturbing it.

"You can ask, if you want to. But it's not necessary." He opened the gate and she passed through. He caught her scent, sunshine and soap.

"I'd like to."

"In a minute." He twined his fingers in hers and tugged her around the corner of the house out of sight of the street, away from any windows. "First, I need to do this."

Her lips were welcoming and he took his time, savouring her taste, her warmth. She came into his arms, willing and eager, and he splayed his hands against the supple skin of her back, bared by the low waist of her dress. The tips of the ribbons trailing from the bow at her nape tickled his wrist, daring him to give the one gentle yank that would free her.

"It's going to be hours before we get back to the hotel room," he muttered against her mouth. "I want to be alone with you now."

"We can't leave yet." She gasped as he brushed the pad of his thumb over her nipple, protected only by thin fabric. She didn't wear a bra with this dress, and the thought had tortured him all afternoon.

"I know. But I couldn't go any longer without touching you. Without you touching me." Her hands grasped his hips, clinging to him as he bent her over his arm, pressing her snugly against his groin. "Kiss me. Kiss me again, and then we'll go in."

Sometime during the last forty-eight hours, Abigail had lost her shyness. When their mouths met she controlled the kiss, she stoked the fire. Her slim strength burned in his embrace, and she left him panting.

"Okay, enough. We have to stop." He rested his forehead against hers. "God, I don't want to stop."

She laughed weakly, her breath drifting on his cheek. "I don't want to either."

"I can't get enough of you." He braced his arms against the rough wall behind her to prevent himself from snatching her up again. "I want all of you, all the time."

"You have me." She leaned away, far enough so she could meet his eyes.

His breath caught, froze in his chest. She looked at him with such trust, such passion, such...love?...he forgot to exhale.

"Whatever you want of me, you have only to ask." She raised a trembling finger, caressed his lower lip. "I don't have the strength to say no to you."

The temptation to ask her to stay on the island, not to go home, swept through him with such momentum he clamped his lips together to stop the words from blurting out. She hadn't meant anything of that magnitude. She was talking of sexual adventures, not life-changing choices.

He forced himself to reply lightheartedly. "Now that's a dare if I've ever heard one." He nudged her toward the door. "We'd better get inside quickly, before I take you up on it, right here and now."

AFTER THE FESTA

"I don't think I'll ever have to eat again." Abigail groaned as she climbed out of the car in the hotel parking garage. "I've never seen so much food. And it was all so good."

"My mother was disappointed you only had two helpings of everything. She was worried you wouldn't be strong enough to survive until breakfast." Santos pushed the button for the elevator and leaned his shoulder against the wall as they waited. "So, was your first Portuguese family meal all you thought it would be?"

"Oh, yes. Loud and crowded and wonderful." The elevator dinged and the doors slid open. They stepped inside. "And I know it's probably only my imagination, but I swear I could understand a lot of the conversation. I can't speak well enough to be understood, but I'm starting to have an idea of what people are saying to me." She looked at him anxiously. "I hope no one was upset with me, because I couldn't speak to them. I did try."

"My family liked you just fine. Even my cranky Aunt Dorotea told me you were sweet." He reached out and sleeked her ponytail through his fist. "I know my cousin, Cesare, was impressed by you," he added dryly.

Abigail giggled. "He didn't mean anything by his kiss.

He was just saying goodbye."

It was almost worth having to stand by and watch Cesare ogling Abigail to see her so gleefully confident. Yet Santos still planned on having a private chat with Cesare the next time he saw him on the etiquette of flirting with another man's woman.

The car slid smoothly upward. Abigail hid a yawn. "Oh, I'm sorry. I'm so full it's made me sleepy."

He tugged on her hair. "I have plans for you tonight. Plans that don't involve sleeping for a very long time."

She studied him from beneath lowered lids, no longer looking the least bit tired. "You do, do you?"

"You said I could ask you anything, remember?"

The tip of her tongue wet her bottom lip. "I suppose I did," she said, her husky voice sultry.

The doors slid open on their floor and he grabbed her hand. "You. Room. Now."

She laughed as he dragged her down the hall. "You'll have to wait a little longer." He unlocked the door and she slipped past him. "It was awfully hot in your mom's dining room. I'm all sweaty."

"You're going to get sweatier." He made a grab for her, but she dodged and put the door of the bathroom between them.

"I won't be long, I promise."

He heard the lock snick shut, the rattle of the shower curtain, and the sound of running water. He wasn't an animal. He could wait patiently. But if she was in there longer than five minutes...

He toed off his shoes and loosened his tie, pulling it over his head and dropping it on the bed. As he started undoing the buttons on his shirt the phone rang. He tucked the receiver under his chin as he fidgeted with unfastening his cuffs. "Hello?"

Only the hollow sound of static greeted him. "Hello?" he repeated.

"Is this Abigail Garsson's room?" a man asked.

"Yes." He finally conquered the cuffs and shrugged off his shirt. "Did you wish to speak with her?"

"Who is this? Why are you in her room?" the voice demanded.

"Are you Abigail's brother? She's in the shower but should be out in a minute if you want to wait." Please say no, he begged silently. I've waited all day to have her alone. He reached for the fly of his slacks.

"I am not Abigail's brother." The man's furious tone crackled through the line. "I am her fiancé. And I ask you once again—who are you and what are you doing in Abigail's room?"

****

Abigail sighed in bliss as she stood under the steaming water. She raised her face to the spray and let the heat burn away her loginess.

The evening spent with Santos' family had been amazing, but nerve-wracking at the same time. A number of his relatives spoke English well enough to inform her that Santos *never* brought his girlfriends home.

"Not since he return from America." The banty little man who shared that tidbit might have been an uncle, but she wasn't positive. Three long tables had been placed end to end, and still there had been barely enough elbow room to raise a fork. She'd lost track of the introductions about three people in.

Lina sat across from her, next to a tiny old woman

dressed completely in black, thick framed glasses magnifying her eyes enormously. She pointed at Abigail and chattered at Lina, who had grudgingly translated. "My aunt says you are not what she expected for Santos, but she hopes you will be very happy," she'd said, making it clear she didn't share the sentiment.

Abigail *wished* she could believe what Lina seemed to be worrying about—that bringing Abigail to the *festa* meant she held a special place in Santos' life, meant she *was* different than the others. Yet she was afraid to believe, afraid to allow her heart to even contemplate the possibility they were right.

Yet she couldn't stop herself.

If Santos did care for her enough to let her meet his extended family, what difference would it make? Was it possible he would ask her to stay? And if he did, what could she say? Tobias was waiting for her at home. And she still had to deal with Martin. So no matter what, she would be leaving in a few days.

But she could come back.

If Santos wanted her to, she *would* come back.

****

Buzzing filled Santos' ears. "Martin? This is Martin?"

"Yes. Who the hell are *you*?"

He lowered himself to the bed. "My name is Santos Carregado. I am the owner of the tour company Abigail booked." He gripped the receiver and straightened his neck cautiously, conscious of muscles that had suddenly tensed and tightened. "What do you mean, you're Abigail's fiancé? She told me she'd broken off with you."

"Aaaah, I understand." Martin's condescending tone had

Santos gritting his teeth. "I assume you are the reason she did? Abigail is not normally so impulsive. I should have known some outside influence was affecting her."

"I had nothing to do with Abigail's decision."

"And yet you are in her hotel room. Just having tea, are you?"

Santos clenched his fist. "What is between Abigail and I is not your concern." He knew he should simply deny any relationship between them, but wouldn't give the other man the added ammunition.

"Abigail has been acting oddly since her mother died. It was a horrible shock to her, and since then she has been doing things she would normally never consider. I'm sure breaking up with me was an act of impulse, one she will come to regret."

"I think you underestimate her." Santos could appreciate the man was under stress. Saying goodbye to Abigail after knowing her for only two weeks was going to be difficult, so he could imagine how losing her after two years would affect a man. "Abigail has told me about her life prior to coming to the Azores. She has amazing courage, and she's only getting stronger."

"This is her first trip away from home, the first time she has truly been on her own. She is unsophisticated, unworldly. The perfect prey for a man like you."

"Prey? What the hell do you mean? The last thing I want to do is harm Abigail." Santos defended himself automatically, but his gut acknowledged the blow. He'd known she was naive from the first moment he'd seen her. Yet he'd conveniently ignored her artlessness when his attraction to her couldn't be denied.

Martin's voice took on a man-to-man tone that did nothing to change Santos' first impression. "I don't blame you for wanting to be with Abigail. She may not be beautiful, but she has a certain charm."

Santos pulled the receiver away and stared at it. Was this guy for real? Tinny words continued to flow out of the speaker. He held it to his ear again.

"...really, what can you offer her? A few days and nights together? And then what? She'll be coming home, to me."

Damn it, how did the bastard know what buttons to push? The thought of Abigail returning home, returning to Martin, made him queasy. Yet it was going to happen, and there was nothing he could do to stop it. "This is not about what I can offer. It's about what Abigail wants."

"She doesn't know what she wants. Why else would she reject a two-year relationship for a short-term affair?"

Why else indeed? It was more than possible Abigail had gotten caught up in the excitement of new experiences, and once she returned home would slip back into her old ways, old dependencies.

He became aware the water had stopped running in the bathroom. "Look, you need to discuss this with Abigail. I'll tell her you called." Martin's voice continued to squawk out of the receiver until Santos broke the connection.

The silence that followed echoed uncomfortably. As much as he hated to admit it, Martin had forced him to face some unpleasant realities.

What had started as a fling had become so much more than he had expected. Santos realized with niggling horror that, when Abigail left, he wouldn't be able to walk away with his usual composure. If he wanted to return to his old life, live with his accustomed casualness and freedom, he was going to have to do something soon, before he fell even deeper.

Fell deeper into *what* he didn't want to contemplate.

FLIGHT

As Abigail rubbed the towel over her breasts, her belly, her thighs, she tingled, anticipating Santos' touch. For now, she would simply live in the moment, take what he was willing to give, and not let thoughts of tomorrow overwhelm her.

She wrapped the towel sarong-style about her torso and walked out of the bathroom.

Santos stood between the beds. She sauntered toward him, her eyes roaming over his naked chest, delighting in the well-defined muscles, the dusting of dark hair. She noted the button of his slacks was undone, erotically, tantalizingly, and her mouth went dry.

Her gaze rose to his face, and she stumbled, catching herself against the foot of the bed.

He stared at her with an expression she couldn't decipher. Gone was the carefree adventurer, the tender lover. In his place stood a polite, distant stranger. Dread balled in her stomach.

"Santos? What's wrong?"

"There was a phone call. While you were in the shower."

Fear raised the hairs on the back of her neck. "From

who?"

"Martin." His voice was flat and calm, but undercurrents she didn't understand swirled beneath its surface.

The air whooshed out of her lungs as if she'd been punched. "What did he want?" From the looks of it, it hadn't been to leave a "best wishes" message.

"I gathered he is refusing to accept your decision to break up with him."

Her knees gave out and she dropped to the bed. "He keeps emailing me, now he's calling. Why won't he leave me alone?"

"He seems to think you only split from him because you are infatuated with me. And that when you return home, you'll change your mind once again and be prepared to marry him."

She shuddered. "That's not going to happen." She held her palm out in supplication. "I've come too far in the week I've been here to ever go back to the life Martin wants me to live. It would crush me to be that cautious, that staid, ever again."

Santos ignored her hand and she dropped it to her knee. Her vision shrank until it seemed as if she was looking down the wrong end of a telescope. The blood rushing in her ears made her dizzy.

"He did make a valid point." He strode to the sliding glass doors, gripped the drapes and slid them to the side. He stood, arms crossed, legs apart—battle ready—and stared out at the night. "A couple, actually."

"What? What did he say?"

"You're experiencing so many things for the first time. It's bound to shake your belief in your ordinary life. But once you go home, once you're back where you belong, it's likely you will realize the choices you made here weren't the right ones."

"I'm never going back to Martin," she said fiercely. "Never. No matter what."

"But you are going back home." He turned to face her. "You will be leaving the island. Leaving me."

She stared at him helplessly. "Tobias is there. My job is there." Although she couldn't envision working in the same office as Martin any longer.

Santos stood stock still for an endless moment. Then he stepped forward one pace, then another, then strode past her and grabbed his duffle bag from the closet. "This was a mistake."

Panic had her pulse racing so fast her hands shook. "What do you mean a mistake? Santos, what are you doing?"

He yanked open a drawer and tossed his clothes into the bag, his movements clipped and deliberate. "I thought we could spend a few days together, have fun, enjoy each other in bed."

"We can. We are." She raised herself cautiously.

He jerked a t-shirt over his head, buttoned up his slacks. "But then what, Abigail? Would we go our separate ways, happy never to think of each other again?" He shoved his feet into his sandals, threw his loafers and runners into the bag.

In a moment of blinding clarity Abigail realized she'd done a horrible, terrible thing. Had done something she would never, ever be able to make right. Would never be able to recover from.

She'd fallen in love with Santos.

"I could never forget you." The damp towel clung uncomfortably to her skin. Cold water trickled from the tips of her hair. She felt vulnerable, defenseless, and clutched the cotton closer, wishing it were armor. Wishing it could protect her from the agony rising to a crescendo inside her.

"And that's the problem. You're not cut out for this sort of game. You don't know the rules, the most important of which is don't look back." Santos stared at her, and in his eyes she saw remembered passion, the memories of shared kisses and laughter.

And goodbye.

"I know we have no future," she forced herself to say. "I can accept that. All I want are these last days with you."

The furrows in his face deepened. "That's exactly what I mean. This already means too much." He slung the bag over his shoulder, jerked his jacket off the clothes hanger, which rattled briefly before falling to the floor. Neither of them paid it the least attention.

She staggered, battered by his words. "Don't do this." Her voice wavered, heavy with unshed tears. "Don't take away what little time we have left."

Santos backed to the door. She followed him, fighting for control.

"It's no good, Abigail. This is for the best."

This is for the best.

Those words dammed the misery flooding through her. It was as if she stepped out of herself, and could see the scene spooling out like a play. Once again someone else was making her decision for her, forcing her to accept what she didn't want because it was "for her own good."

"I can't believe you said that." The words dropped from her mouth like shards of glass.

"It's true. This was going to end, anyway. Why stretch it out longer than it has to?"

"You coward. If you wanted out, you just had to say so." She spun on her heel and stalked away.

"Abigail—"

She whirled in the narrow gap between the foot of the

bed and the dresser. "Stop. Don't say anything more. If you want to go, go. But don't you dare make it about me, about what's best for me." Her fists clenched the towel so tight her hands shook. "What I want—no, what I *wanted*—was to spend my last days on the island with you. *That's* what would be best for me. But if that's not what you want, fine."

Santos pressed his lips together but stayed silent. He turned and reached for the handle.

"There's just one more thing."

He froze, facing the door.

She had her pride, so wouldn't tell him the whole truth. But she would make sure he knew just what he was rejecting. "I could have loved you." She refused to let her voice tremble. "I could have loved you like no one else ever has, or ever will."

He remained rigid, unmoving. The faintest flicker of hope licked at her icy stomach. Then he opened the door and disappeared, leaving her staring into the empty hallway.

****

Santos could never remember the details of his drive home that night. His shock blinded him to the road. He parked at Quinta Carregado, fingers cramped from gripping the steering wheel, the pain a welcome distraction from the confusion tormenting him.

He leaned against the head rest and closed his eyes, breathing deeply through his nose. His last sight of Abigail weighed on his chest like granite, constricting his lungs. Platinum hair darkened to silver from her shower. Skin glowing golden ivory against the stark white of the hotel towel, the tiny teacup pendant he'd given her glinting in the hollow of her neck. Eyes huge with defiance as she'd blasted him. She'd been so magnificent he'd had to tear his eyes away. He would have been lost if he'd looked at her a moment longer.

But the knife in his gut had been her final words. The future she'd teased him with had been so tantalizing he'd had to escape quickly, before he could plead for her to take him back.

He groaned and rolled out of the seat, controlling the urge to slam the car door. All he needed now was his mother or Lina to realize he was home. He wasn't ready to explain what had happened. Didn't know if he could explain it.

His shoulders throbbed and a tension headache pounded behind his eyes. Every muscle in his body was taut. He wandered into the family's private garden and slumped onto a lounger. The velvet night overhead was thick with stars, the sleepy silence heavy as a blanket.

He had wanted to scoff at Martin's refusal to accept Abigail's decision to break off their relationship. Where was the man's pride? Why wouldn't he give in gracefully, instead of making a scene from seven thousand kilometres away?

It was those seven thousand kilometres that had finally decided Santos. His life was here on the island, Abigail's on the other side of a continent. He couldn't ask her to stay, and how could he go? As much as he hated to admit it, Martin was right about one thing. When Abigail returned home, she would see things differently. Decisions made in the halcyon days of a holiday would be regarded with loathing and regret once her life was back to normal.

So he'd made the decision to leave. He'd hoped to mitigate the damage by severing their ties immediately.

He welcomed the stabbing sensation knifing through his chest. He deserved it. He would never forget how the colour in her face drained so fast he thought she would faint. He'd rejected his first instinct to protect, to comfort, and instead had been steadfast, keeping himself unmoved.

It was the hardest thing he'd ever done in his life.

He rubbed a hand over his face as adrenaline trickled away, leaving him empty and hollow. Moving stiff as an old man, he struggled out of the chair, slipped into the house and up the stairs to his room.

Where he lay, wide eyed and sleepless, into the darkest hours of the night.

AFTER ABIGAIL

A shriek jolted him awake the next morning. "Santos! What are you doing here?"

He dragged his eyes open and propped himself onto his elbows. His mother stood in the doorway, a dust rag clasped to her chest, a broom in her other hand. He would have laughed at the expression on her face, if he could have summoned the energy.

He'd finally fallen asleep as eerie dawn light had crept through his window. "What time is it?" he croaked.

"Almost eleven o'clock." She approached the bed. "I was going to tidy your room while you were away. I didn't realize you had come back."

He flopped back onto the bed and hid his face in the crook of his elbow. "It's not your job to clean up after me." Thank God he hadn't bothered to undress last night and simply crashed onto his bed fully clothed.

"I'm your mother. It's a habit. Where is Abigail?"

The sound of her name twisted his gut. "At the hotel."

"Ah."

He uncovered his face and peered up at her. "What does that mean?"

"Get out of bed, come to the kitchen. I'll make you something to eat." She disappeared from his field of vision, leaving him staring at the slanted ceiling.

He slouched into the kitchen ten minutes later and dropped into his chair. Serafina studied him for a long moment, then filled two mugs with coffee, automatically added two sugars to his, and sat down on the other side of the table. "What did you do?"

The corner of his mouth tugged up slightly, but not in amusement. "Do you have so little faith in me? I didn't do anything. Anything wrong, that is."

"When you said you were bringing her to the *festa,* I was not pleased. She is a stranger, to our island and to our ways. But I saw the way you looked at her, the way she looked at you. I also saw a woman willing to appreciate another culture. And I saw man willing to share it with her."

He closed his eyes briefly. His mother's disapproval had been another of the frail, straw-like reasons he had clung to during his sleepless night. He wished she hadn't spoken.

"What happened to bring you back here alone?" she asked.

He stared into the slightly oily surface of the coffee. "It was never meant to be more than an affair." Serafina snorted and he glanced up at her. "Sorry, you asked."

"Maybe so. But I've seen you at the end of your affairs before." He shot her a look and she shrugged. "You may not have introduced any of those women to me, but I knew about them. And never do you look like this." Serafina rose from the table, moved to the work counter and began slicing bread.

"Abigail was...different." The admission was sour as lemon juice, and his mouth dried with the speaking. He sipped his coffee. "But that doesn't change the circumstances. She was going home in a few days. It was better to end it now than later."

Serafina placed a plate of bread in front of him, along with butter, soft cheese, and rhubarb jam, and then sat down again. "Why does this bother you so much? A day here, a day there—why does this make you angry?"

"I'm not angry." He pushed his coffee mug aside so abruptly the liquid sloshed over the rim. "I might be...disappointed. We might have had more time together, but she wanted more. More than I can give. "

She calmly spread cheese on a slice of bread and bit into it. "What did she ask for?"

Santos was silent. Abigail had asked for nothing but the few days she had left on the island. She'd told him she knew it could go no further.

And yet he'd run.

Serafina chewed, swallowed. "If you cannot answer that, then what could you not give her?"

Habit had him reaching for a piece of bread, but he only picked at the crust, ripping it off the soft, inner dough. "I couldn't give her what she deserves." He tossed down the bread and leaned back in his chair, scowling at the patch of bright blue sky outside the window.

"You say she is different. Maybe it is you who are different. Maybe you are different because of her."

His troubled night hadn't dulled the pain in his chest, but it must have fogged his brain, because it took him a few moments to realize what his mother was trying to say.

"You think I'm in love with her, don't you?" He wanted to jeer, wave a dismissive hand, but for some reason he couldn't.

Serafina sipped her coffee. "I've always known a woman would take you away from me. I had hoped she might be someone I knew, the daughter of a friend. Someone I could understand, who would understand me. Not just our language, but our life." She smiled sadly. "But I want you to be happy, so if Abigail is your choice, so be it. Except, right now, you are not happy. You are angry."

"I told you. I'm not angry."

"You might not be stomping about the room, shouting and yelling, but you are angry. I see it in your eyes." She rose from her seat and rounded the table to stand before him. She smoothed his hair back from his forehead and he felt twelve years old again. "Maybe you wouldn't be so angry if you didn't care for her so much."

"Of course I care for her." He didn't sleep with women he didn't care about.

"Where is she now?"

He shrugged. "Sightseeing somewhere, I imagine."

"Will she return to the hotel?"

"Probably. She has to sleep somewhere. Her flight doesn't leave for a few days yet."

"Go to her. Talk to her. But most importantly, listen."

The thought of seeing Abigail again sent a jolt of joy through him. Immediately followed by a stubborn refusal to acknowledge that joy. "We have nothing to discuss. I've done what's right, for both of us."

Serafina tweaked his earlobe between her fingernails. "You will do what your mother tells you. You will go back to your Abigail and you will listen to what she says. She's a grown woman, capable of making her own choices. Don't treat her like a child."

The irony was impossible to ignore. "I'm a grown man, and you're treating me like a child."

"Yes, but you are my child. Abigail is your lover, and deserves to be treated with respect. Now that you've both had time to think, you need to talk." She patted his cheek, moved to the counter to pull a neatly ironed apron out of drawer and tied it around her waist.

He rose slowly to his feet and looked down at her. "You're bossy."

"I know." She reached up and patted his cheek again, perhaps a tad harder than necessary. "I'm also right."

"And you won't give me any peace until I go back, will you?"

She smiled serenely.

He went to get his keys.

****

Santos stood outside the hotel room door and tapped the key card against his palm. More than once on the drive back he'd considered taking the next exit and returning home. He'd kept on going, however, and here he was.

He took a deep breath, slid the key in the slot and pushed the door.

It didn't open.

He pulled the key out, slid it back in, but the light remained stubbornly red.

Had Abigail had reception change the codes on the room so he couldn't return?

He knocked, but there was no answer. If she heard him at the door and was avoiding him, there wasn't much he could do. But the more logical conclusion was she was out for the day. He decided to have his key re-coded at Reception and wait for her. If he went home too soon his mother would only send him back, and he hunched his shoulders at the thought of her disapproval. Here he was, almost thirty years old and still bowing to her will.

While he'd never been a guest of the hotel before, his

work had brought him in contact with the staff many times before. A woman with a cap of dark blond hair working the reception desk greeted him as he approached. "Santos! *Como está?*" Her accent was much better than Abigail's, but he seemed to remember she'd only come to the islands a couple of years ago from England.

He lied. "I'm well, Teresa, *obrigado*." He handed his card over the counter. "My key card doesn't seem to be working. Can you check it for me?"

"Did you forget something?" She smiled at him as she tapped the card against her palm. "I can't let you back in, but I can have housekeeping look for you."

Confused, he shook his head. "No. I'm looking for Abigail—the woman I've been staying with?—but I can't get in the room."

Teresa stared at him uncertainly. "But Ms. Garsson checked out this morning."

He blinked to clear away the fuzzy grey spots floating before his eyes. "What do you mean?" he said from between stiff and numb lips. "What do you mean she's checked out? She wasn't scheduled to leave until the end of the week."

A concerned frown crossed Teresa's pale face with its scattering of freckles. "Are you okay, Santos?"

He resisted the urge to shout, to pound his fist on the counter. "Where is Abigail, Teresa? I need to know."

"I'm not supposed to talk about the guests." Her eyes searched his before sliding a glance at her colleague at the far end of the counter. She leaned toward Santos and spoke quietly. "Claudio changed her airline ticket this morning. Something came up, and she had to cut her holiday short. He helped her book a new flight to Toronto."

Santos gripped the edge of the counter. "When? When is her flight?"

Teresa regarded him with something that looked like pity. "She said she had to get home today. Her flight left ten minutes ago."

****

Abigail hadn't lived in the new apartment for long before heading to the Azores. Certainly not long enough for it to feel like home. So she hadn't expected the huge rush of relief she felt when she walked in the door, but it was definitely welcome.

Maybe it was simply being back in Canada. She'd felt enveloped in familiarity as soon as she'd walked off the SATA flight at Pearson International, and even the night she'd stayed in Toronto, waiting for her connecting flights to Vancouver and on to Prince George, had filled her with a comforting sense of belonging.

Too bad it did nothing to fill the jagged hole in her soul.

"I'll take this to your room." Tobias jostled past her, dragging her giant suitcase. "The next time you go anywhere, pack lighter, won't you? This just about gave me a hernia getting it out of the car."

She collapsed onto the couch and stretched her legs out, luxuriating in the wealth of space after hours in cramped economy seats. Her body clock was completely out of whack and her lids drooped even though it was only—she had to check the clock on the wall behind her—one in the afternoon.

Tobias sat on the coffee table and leaned toward her, resting his elbows on his knees. "So, are you going to tell me what happened?"

Tears welled and she squeezed her eyes shut. She was overtired, overwrought and had survived this far only by ruthlessly refusing to think of Santos. Since she'd made the decision to cut short her holiday and return home, she'd blocked all thoughts of him, terrified she'd be reduced to a sobbing, hysterical mess.

"Come on, Abigail. You can tell me. Was it that man you met? Did he hurt you?" His voice was raw, edgy.

She opened her eyes and met his steady gaze. She sensed a new maturity, a strength of character, in him. She'd been gone slightly over a week, and yet he seemed so changed. Or maybe it was her own changes that allowed her to see him differently.

She swallowed back tears and tried to speak calmly. "It was my fault."

"No." Tobias gripped her knee. "Whatever he did, it was not your fault. Should I...do you need..." A bright flush climbed his neck.

"Oh my God." She straightened, abruptly realizing what Tobias was thinking. "He didn't *hurt* me, not like that. We had a fight, sort of. And then he left me."

"He didn't...touch you." The red receded.

She patted his hand. "Not in any way I didn't want."

"But it must have been bad, for you to come home early."

She slumped against the back of the couch. "I couldn't stay. He didn't want to be with me anymore. He tried to make it sound as if it was for my own good, but it was only an excuse." She rubbed her temple, hoping to ease the turmoil in her brain. "I couldn't bear the thought of being on the same small island with him any longer."

"What do you mean, 'for your own good'?" Tobias swung off the coffee table and sat next to her on the sofa. "What was he trying to protect you from?"

"Himself." She leaned against his shoulder, wondering when their roles had reversed, but thankful for his comfort, support. "He said I wasn't ready for a holiday fling, that I didn't understand the rules. Which meant it was no use spending time together, because when I went home I'd realize I'd made a mistake breaking up with Martin and regret that I'd ever been with him, with Santos." A spark of anger lit. "I told him I was never going back to Martin, no matter what happened between us. But he was sure he knew what was best."

"It does sound like he was just looking out for you," Tobias said tentatively.

The spark strengthened. "Maybe he was. I'm sure he thought so. But that doesn't give him the right to make decisions for me." The anger felt good, cleansing. "I've spent too much of my life being told what to do. It's part of the reason I broke up with Martin. I thought Santos understood that. I thought he understood *me*."

"You only met him a few days ago. Is it possible you didn't know him quite as well as you thought?"

"It's hard to explain." Too exhausted to nurture her faint fury, she let it fade. "During a couple of our tour activities I was so afraid I thought I was going to pass out. He wouldn't let me give in. He gave me the courage to believe in myself, just by expecting me to do what I'd set out to do. We had a connection, I'm sure of it. Especially when we...I mean...not only..."

"I get it. You had sex."

"Oh, God. Yes." She chuckled wearily and attempted to change the subject. "So, what have you been up to while I was gone?"

"Never mind me." He nudged her gently. "You were saying..."

She sighed. "It doesn't matter. We weren't in the same place, I guess." Her heart gave a sharp stutter and she pressed a fist between her breasts. "You know the worst of it?"

"What?" His arm came around her shoulders and hugged her.

"He was right."

"What do you mean?"

She clasped her hands, her fingers twisting so tightly the skin went white and bloodless. "I didn't understand the rules. I broke the most important one."

"What's that?"

"I fell in love with him."

And then the tears came.

****

Abigail made Tobias promise not to tell Martin she had returned early.

"He's going to go crazy, not knowing where you are." He returned from the bathroom with a wad of toilet paper and handed it to her. "Sorry, no tissues."

"That's why I need you to call him, tell him I'm safe, and that I will see him on Thursday as planned." She blew her nose vigorously. Her weeping fit had left her limp and shaky and the thought of her upcoming altercation with Martin didn't help. "I need time. I need a couple days on my own." Maybe by then the gaping wound in her chest would start to heal.

She listened to Tobias' half of the conversation with trepidation. She could tell Martin was trying to browbeat him into revealing where she was, but he held firm. When he finally hung up, he shot her a dirty look. "You owe me."

"I know."

"And you look like crap. You should go to bed. You look like you haven't slept in days."

"I'll try." She hauled herself to her feet, her body weighed down with exhaustion and despair. She ruffled Tobias' blond locks. "Thanks. For everything."

He ducked out of her reach. "No problem. Go. Sleep."

She shut the door of her room carefully, as if too loud a noise would break her. Tobias had left her suitcase beside the bed and she stared at it numbly, before climbing up from the foot of the bed and dropping face first onto the pillows.

The rush of traffic outside the window magnified the silence inside the room. The ache in her chest grew and grew until she feared her heart would explode. She curled onto her side and hugged her knees, trying to contain her agony, but it didn't help.

Her body shook as she held back sobs, trembling with the force needed to keep silent. Tobias had been concerned enough during her first crying jag. She didn't want to worry him more.

Her happiness the day of the *festa* seemed to belong to another age, another person. She allowed herself to remember glimpses of that day and her pain and sorrow intensified. She'd sensed something different, sensed possibilities beyond her wildest fantasies. It only made what happened that night more bitter, more crushing. In a matter of moments she'd discovered she loved Santos—and then lost him forever.

Her breath sliced through her lungs like a serrated knife. She'd tried to prepare herself for leaving him, tried to curtail unrealistic hopes and dreams, and she'd thought it would be enough if he looked on her with affection. Even if he couldn't love her, at least he would remember their time together with fondness. She would have been able to hold that tiny consolation close, take it out and bask in its warmth, long after she had faded from his thoughts.

She'd been a fool. She didn't want him to like her, to remember her as a pleasant interlude in his life. She wanted his love. Wanted him to need her more than his next breath.

Just like she wanted him.

Knowing that would never happen was killing her.

Scalding tears tracked her face and soaked the comforter, but she didn't make a sound.

FAREWELL

Abigail drew a long, deep breath and let it ease out. Gathering her courage, she gripped the handle and opened the door to Martin's office.

For two days she had huddled inside the apartment, trying to deal with the past and decide on the future. Yesterday she'd finally found the courage to call and reveal she had returned. He rightly demanded an explanation, and she agreed to meet him, knowing she'd put it off long enough, but sick to her stomach with dread at the confrontation to come.

He sat behind the desk, swivelled slightly toward his computer monitor. He must have heard the door open, but he didn't look up. Long fingers tapped with swift competence on the keyboard, pale wrists protruding from the immaculate cuffs of his pinstriped shirt. His subtly patterned tied was neatly knotted, his thick blonde hair tamed into a smooth, business-like style.

She stood patiently until he finished typing. When he finally turned to her, his stiff, unyielding expression didn't bode well, yet something in the set of his shoulders told her he felt more than anger. She knew in his own controlling way he cared for her, and she had confused and hurt him. It was time to clear the air, to make a new start. Separately.

"Hello, Martin."

"Abigail."

She closed the door behind her and sat on the edge of the chair in front of his desk. She cleared her throat. "Before anything else, I want to say I'm sorry."

"Tell me what you are apologizing for, and I'll decide whether to accept it."

Less than two weeks ago she would have flinched at the ice in his tone. Now she simply straightened her shoulders and spoke quietly. "I treated you badly, because I wasn't brave enough to acknowledge the truth. I should never have let our relationship get to the point where marriage seemed inevitable. I should have had the courage to break it off months ago."

He sat rigid in his chair, his tie perfectly knotted, his pocket handkerchief pressed neatly. His hands lay flat on the desk, and only the tapping of one finger betrayed his turmoil. "I knew I shouldn't have let you go alone. If you hadn't left me, this wouldn't be happening."

Sweat beaded under her arms but she continued firmly. "It's true that certain...events...while I was away did bring everything to a head." She swallowed around the dry knot in her throat. "But I honestly believe the end result would have been the same. I hope that, in a little while, you'll see I am right."

"Two years," he said. "We've been together for two years. You can't tell me you were unhappy that entire time."

She recognized his tone. It was the way he spoke when he was explaining procedure to a not particularly bright intern. It only stiffened her resolve. "Not unhappy. But what I felt for you...it wasn't enough to build a life on."

Silence stretched between them. Martin's finger continued to tap restlessly. "It's that man, isn't it?" he said dismissively. "The one who answered the phone."

She'd cravenly hoped he wouldn't confront her with Santos, but now that he had she wouldn't retreat. "Yes."

"You are putting aside a life of comfort and respect, all because of a man you met on holiday?" His disbelief was palpable. "Where is the future in that?"

Comfort. Respect. Now that she'd discovered passion, known what it was to love, she couldn't settle for such pallid emotions. "There is none." It was a relief to admit it so bluntly. "But it doesn't matter. I can't go back to the way I was. Too much has changed." In her thoughts. In her heart.

"There's where you're wrong," Martin stated. "Whatever you experienced on this misguided adventure is in the past. Next week you'll return to work, and in a few days everything will be back to normal."

"You don't understand—" she began, but he cut her off.

"Abigail." He held up his hand, palm out. "You know I'm right. This man you met"—Martin gestured around the room with an exaggerated motion—"he's not here. He was never really a part your life, was only a childish daydream. You need to be mature about this."

Heat rushed up Abigail throat, her cheeks, as frustration overwhelmed her. "Stop telling me what to do!" She almost yelled the words, and it felt so good she continued at the same volume. "I am a grown woman. I don't need a man— *any* man—to look after me, to make my decisions for me."

Martin's eyes widened. If she hadn't been so furious she might have been amused. But she hadn't jumped off a cliff, hadn't lost her heart to a near stranger, simply to slip back into her sedate, stolid, stultifying life.

She reached into her handbag and pulled out an

envelope. "Here's my resignation letter," she said in a calmer tone, "effective immediately. I think it's best I look for another job." She slid it across the desk to Martin.

His expression shifted from surprised to wary. Charged moments passed, and then he let out a long breath. "I see." The starch leached from his posture and he looked older, tired.

"I'm sorry."

He nodded slowly. "Perhaps I am wrong. If you are serious about taking this step, then maybe you truly have changed."

She said nothing, determined not to give in to the guilt swamping her. Martin had been good to her, in his own way. But good enough was no longer what she deserved.

"What will you do?" he asked.

Long hours in her room, alone, hadn't answered that question. She only knew she couldn't continue living her life the way she had for so many years. "I don't know. I'll need some time to figure things out."

Martin stood and rounded the desk. She rose to meet him. He placed his hands on her shoulders and met her gaze, sadness and regret in his own. "I will always care about you. But perhaps this is for the best."

"It is. I'm sure of it. We would not have made each other happy."

He brushed a kiss gently on her forehead. "Good luck, Abigail. Good luck and goodbye."

****

The roar and rumble of a departing jet rattled through Santos' chest. He welcomed the sensation. At least it filled the hollowness echoing inside him. The hollowness left by

Abigail's unexpected departure ten days ago.

He yanked open the rear doors of the van and unloaded luggage. Ilha Verde Adventuras' most recent group of tourists gathered on the sidewalk and laid claim to their suitcases. He smiled and laughed and accepted their thanks, but truth be told, he would have had a hard time remembering their names, despite having spent the last week ferrying them around. Now all he wanted was to send them on their way so he could stop pretending everything was okay.

Because it wasn't. His life was a mess, and he didn't know how to fix it.

"This was the best holiday ever." A hand on his arm halted his mechanical movements. Long, purple nails gleamed against his skin and he looked up, meeting blue eyes bright with invitation. Linda? Lorraine? He couldn't recall. "I only wish I had more time on your island. I would have loved to explore more of it." The tip of her tongue darted out, teased her upper lip. "With you."

He couldn't miss the innuendo in her voice. It left him cold. "I'm glad you enjoyed your time with us," he replied politely.

"Maybe I'll come back again."

"Ilha Verde Adventuras would be pleased to welcome you." He forced the corners of his mouth into a replica of a smile. "Have a good trip home."

He climbed into the driver's seat and headed toward Quinta Carregado.

São Miguel was a tiny island, and while Abigail had been on it they had travelled almost everywhere. Now, no matter where he went, he was reminded of her.

As he circled Ponta Delgada on the ring road, he saw the hotel where they had stayed rising in glass and steel above older, smaller buildings. He couldn't remember what exactly he had said, after Teresa had told him Abigail had left him, but he distinctly remembered his heart collapsing in on itself. Disbelief and denial had weighed him down for days, until one morning he woke to find the heaviness had dissipated. Unfortunately, the emptiness it left behind was even harder to bear. At night he lay sleepless, aching for the scent of her hair, the silk of her skin. During the day he operated on autopilot, and while it wasn't difficult to hide his disconnect from the tourists, he often caught Lina and his mother watching him with concern.

Neither one of them mentioned Abigail. Not to his face, anyway. At first he'd been relieved, but as the days wore on irritation set in. Had they simply dismissed her from their lives? Maybe they hadn't known her like he had, but she had eaten with them, been a part of the family, if only for one brief night. Had they forgotten about her completely?

He put the van in park in the courtyard outside the farmhouse. And blinked. Damn it, he'd done it again—lost himself in thoughts of Abigail when he should have been concentrating on something else. Like driving.

He stepped into the hall and hesitated. The next group of tourists would arrive tomorrow, and he knew he should really get to work on the maintenance that always needed be done. He just couldn't summon the energy.

Lina's dark head popped out from the kitchen doorway. "Good, you're home. Come have a cold drink." She disappeared.

He trudged after her. Maybe he was coming down with the flu. He couldn't seem to shake the lassitude, the dreariness that had assailed him the last few days.

His mother was also in the kitchen. Two pairs of eyes watched him as he dropped into his usual seat. "What?" he demanded, unable to remain silent under their intent scrutiny.

"We've given you time to deal with it on your own. Since you can't seem to do that, we're having an intervention." Lina loomed over him, arms crossed. Serafina stepped from the counter to stand at her shoulder.

"Deal with what?" As if he didn't know. "Where's that drink you offered me?"

Serafina took a tall pitcher of lemonade from the refrigerator, poured a glass and handed it to him. "We have been worried about you. Since Abigail left."

He sipped the tangy liquid, the tart taste easing the dryness in his mouth. "Don't be. I'm fine." Lina snorted and he worked up a glare. "Maybe I was upset at first, but I'm over it. It's not like we had a future together. You told me yourself, both of you. She was always going home. So what if it happened a couple days early. It was always going to end." He lifted the glass to his lips and glugged a few mouthfuls. It was either that or keep blathering.

"I was wrong." Lina uncrossed her arms and planted them on her hips. "Is that what you want to hear? I...was...wrong."

"As was I," Serafina said.

His brows lowered in confusion. "Wrong about what?"

Lina and their mother shared a look he couldn't read, and then Lina continued. "I told you she didn't belong here, on the island. That she would forget you as soon as she was gone, that you would do the same. I've changed my mind."

He stared at her. "Changed your mind," he repeated stupidly.

"I don't think you're going to forget her."

Torn between laughing and bellowing, he said, "You think that changes things? Abigail didn't leave because of you, because of what either of you thought or didn't think. She left because of..." He broke off, clamping his lips shut.

He placed the empty glass on the table and fisted his hand, damp with moisture.

"She left because of you?" Serafina's voice was soft and sympathetic. "Is that what you were going to say?"

Whatever fight he had in him whooshed out like air from a balloon. "Of course she left because of me." He rubbed the heel of his hand between his eyes. "I was jealous and confused. So I did exactly what everyone else in her life had done—forced her to accept my choice, without taking into account what she wanted. I screwed up so bad that when she did make her own choice, she chose to go home early instead of taking the chance of seeing me ever again." And she hadn't even left him a message.

Serafina moved to his side and patted his shoulder. It didn't make him feel better. Somehow he knew there was worse to come.

"It isn't good, the way she left," Serafina said. "She should have stayed, given you the chance to come to your senses and talk to her."

He bristled at her criticism of Abigail. "Why should she have stayed? I gave her no reason to believe I ever wanted to talk to her again."

"Because that's what people who love each other do. They fight, and then they work it through."

He stiffened under her comforting hand. "We don't love each other."

Lina snorted again. "Everyone could see it, the night of the *festa.* Watching the two of you was like watching pigeons cooing."

He winced. "Attracted to each other, yes." He cut a glance at his mother who met it serenely. "In love? That wasn't part of the plan."

Serafina shrugged. "Who plans to fall in love? It just

257

happens."

Santos opened his mouth to deny his mother's words once again, then closed it. Did he love Abigail? Is that what this horrible, dragging depression was? A broken heart?

"Wouldn't I have known it? If I loved her?" Desperation coloured his voice, as the realization began to grow. "How could I have been in love and not known it?"

"Ah, *querido.*" Serafina leaned over and wrapped her arms around his shoulders. "Sometimes it is hardest to see what is right there, in front of our face."

****

One of the rock walls hemming the back pasture at Quinta Carregado needed repair. Santos decided it was the perfect job for his current frame of mind.

He changed into his grubbiest jeans and a tattered, long sleeved shirt. Grabbing a pair of heavy canvas gloves, he strode to the wall and surveyed the section that needed mending.

Chunks of volcanic rock had toppled out of the fence, dislodged by the wear and tear of wind and rain and backscratching cows. Others tottered precariously, held in place only by the heavy morning-glory vine twining along the wall's length.

With a ferociousness born of frustration, Santos began tearing the wall apart, hefting the jagged stones out and tossing them to the spongy earth. He ripped the leafy green plant away, knowing it wouldn't take long to recover in the island's easy-growing climate, but showing far less care and consideration than he knew he should. Sweat formed in the hollow of his neck and between his shoulder blades, but he kept on going.

Abigail had accused him of being a coward, of using what was best for her as an excuse to leave. Had she been right? Had he really been protecting himself by leaving her? Protecting his heart, not hers?

He cautiously allowed himself to think those three frightening words.

I love Abigail.

Instead of gut-churning panic, a sense of rightness enveloped him.

He rested his elbows on the wide top of the wall, his breath coming in pants and sweat dripping from the end of his nose. He wiped it away with his wrist.

He'd been raised to believe he would marry some day— a nice Portuguese girl, one who understood his past, would carry traditions into his future. And because he hadn't been ready to settle down with that nice Portuguese girl, he'd whiled away his time with former guests of Ilha Verde Aventuras. Those women were doubly safe—not Portuguese, and only temporarily on the island.

No wonder the knowledge that he loved Abigail had him feeling like he'd been hit by a truck after falling over a cliff.

She had been right. He was a coward. If he hadn't been so afraid to examine his fascination with a woman so unlike any other he'd ever dated, the opposite of any woman he'd thought he'd end up marrying, he might have realized what was happening sooner.

He'd tried to justify running from the hotel room that night as the best decision for both of them. But even then he'd felt a different emotion scraping at his nerves. He hadn't recognized it as fear, but just the memory of it made his stomach clench.

He backed away from the wall and studied the holes gaping in it. Scowling at a particularly recalcitrant rock, he slammed at it with his fist, the ragged edge bruising the side of his hand through his glove.

Now she was seven thousand kilometres away, home with Martin. The two of them might be reconciling even as he battled this stubborn wall.

The strength drained out of his legs. He sank to the ground and leaned against the knobbly stones.

A green vista of field stretched ahead of him, dropping down and down in steeply terraced levels until it reached the lip of the cliff, where the land sheared off abruptly to the sea. Generations of Carregados were connected to this land, and every metre was familiar to him, was rooted in his bones and blood. While he'd been reluctant to return after his father's death, he'd rediscovered a new love for his island in the years since then, and the thought of leaving it again was disquieting.

Because how else was he to try and get Abigail back? He'd rejected her, cruelly and unnecessarily, and the best way to convince her of his regret was face to face. If she had reunited with Martin—the thought spasmed in his gut—he'd be able to see for himself that she was happy, that Martin was treating her as she deserved. At the very least, he'd get to see her one more time.

And at the very best, she might agree to give him a second chance.

PAST, PRESENT, FUTURE

"I think that's my last question for you." Tracy Calogheros, Chief Executive Officer at the Fraser-Fort George Regional Museum, closed the folder on the desk in front of her and smiled at Abigail. "Do you have anything you'd like to ask me?"

"No, I think we've covered everything." Her head spun slightly from the intensity of the last hour. "Thanks very much for choosing me to interview."

The tall, curly-haired woman rose from her seat and Abigail followed suit. Tracy reached across her desk to shake Abigail's hand. "You have excellent qualifications, and I enjoyed meeting you. We do have a few other interviews to do, however, so we won't be making our decision until late next week."

"I look forward to your call."

Abigail let herself out of the administration offices. As soon as she was out of sight around a corner, she collapsed against a wall and allowed herself a deep sigh of relief. It had been years since she'd interviewed for a job, and she'd been nauseously nervous since receiving the invitation two days ago.

She texted Tobias, who replied he would be there to pick her up in ten minutes or so. With a bit of time to kill, she wandered through the galleries, exploring what might be her new place of work.

She'd been home for two weeks, and told herself life was getting better. It had been two days since she'd spontaneously burst into tears over nothing, which she took as a good sign. While thoughts of Santos cropped up at unexpected times, she assured herself she was better able to deal with them when they did.

Except at night. In the dark, alone in her bed, she still wrapped her arms about her waist and huddled in on herself, holding tight to sanity, to courage, to whatever would get her through the long, quiet hours.

She felt good about the interview she'd just completed. The museum needed an office manager, someone to take care of book-keeping and ordering supplies and performing the other assorted duties necessary in any organization. She wouldn't be part of the curatorial staff, but there was something appealing about being, even if only remotely, involved in preserving the history of her home town and area. She hoped Tracy would call with good news.

She stepped from the cool, humidity-controlled comfort of the museum into warm sunshine. Tobias was yet to arrive, but she felt no urgency, no impatience. Losing her mother, losing Santos, had stripped life to its essentials. Adhering rigorously to a schedule was no longer a priority. Getting the most out of every moment was.

The museum was situated in Lheidli T'enneh Memorial Park, a large acreage adjacent to the Fraser River. She crossed the parking lot and strolled across the grass, stopping to watch a Canadian National train chug its way along the tracks snaking below the sandy cutbanks on the far side of the river.

Her sense of moving into a completely new time in her life was enhanced by the errand she and Tobias were about to do. Their childhood home had been listed for sale a month or so before Abigail had gone to the Azores, but they hadn't had any interest in it until this morning. Their real estate agent had called with a solid offer, and they had set up an appointment to meet her and go over the details after Abigail's interview.

She heard an engine behind her and turned toward the parking lot, flinching as her efficient and economical, boring and bland, grey four-door sedan bounced and shuddered to a halt in front of her. Tobias grinned at her from the driver's seat. If she got the job at the museum, Abigail promised herself, she would buy a new vehicle. Something quirky and sporty. In lime green. Maybe a totally-impractical-for-Northern-British-Columbia convertible.

"You drive like a maniac," she said as she climbed in.

He ignored her criticism. "How'd it go?"

"Good. Really good." She crossed her fingers. "Here's hoping."

"It's going to work out. I have an excellent feeling about it." He put the car in drive and merged onto the main road at a sedate pace. "Are you ready to do this?"

Abigail considered for a very short moment. "I think so."

"That's how I feel, too." He signalled right and made another turn. "I guess I'll be a bit sad. It is the last piece of our old life."

"I know. But it's time to move on. Build new lives."

"So much has changed in the last few weeks. Sometimes I don't recognize myself when I look in the mirror."

Abigail nodded in agreement, but didn't say anything. Couldn't. She turned her head and stared out the window, hiding her face as a tear traced silently down her cheek.

She knew exactly what he meant.

****

Tobias and Abigail were ushered into a small boardroom at the real estate office by their agent, Yolande Paluski.

"I think you'll be very happy with this offer," she said, gesturing them to be seated. Comfortably rounded and in her mid-forties, Yolande radiated a soothing sense of friendly competence.

In the days after her mother's death, timid-and-tentative Abigail had chosen Yolande after much research, a recommendation from a colleague, and Martin's approval. While she had no issues with the realtor, if she were to make her decision today, impulsive-and-intrepid Abigail might do it differently. Perhaps by sticking a pin in the Yellow Pages.

Yolande sorted through the piles of paper she carried with her. "The interested buyers are a lovely young family, just moving into town. The wife is a lab technician, expecting their second child, and the husband will be working at the new mine up north." She slid over the contract. "And they are willing to accept the listed price."

Tobias whistled. "Really? That doesn't happen often, does it?"

Abigail lifted an eyebrow at him.

"What? I watch Home and Garden Television."

Yolande laughed throatily. "It's not the norm, but in this market, not completely unusual, either. We priced the house to sell, after all."

"It just seems, I don't know, sudden." Abigail brushed the papers with a fingertip. "I know it isn't, not really, but now that the decision has to be made..."

"It's the right thing to do, Abigail." Tobias reached for a pen. "It might be an end, but it's also a beginning."

"I won't pressure you into anything," Yolande said with understanding and compassion, "but think of this. It's only a house."

"That seems an odd thing for a real estate agent to say," Abigail said.

"You take your memories with you, both good and bad." Neither Abigail nor Tobias had told Yolande about their mother's illness, although she knew about their parents' deaths. "Signing this contract won't erase those years. And it will give you a solid financial foundation for moving on."

"We can do this, Abigail." Tobias signed his name in his tiny, illegible writing and handed her the pen. "It's time."

She studied his face, so familiar, so loved. More than once in the last few weeks she'd felt their roles shifting, moving from big sister and little brother to adult and adult.

Drawing a deep breath, she signed away her past, affirmed her future.

ARRIVAL – PART TWO

Santos peered out the oval airplane window, fascinated by the white tipped peaks far below. Snow! It was the summer, and there was snow on the mountains.

The plane levelled off after the steep climbing bank out of Vancouver International Airport. In one hour he'd be in Prince George. And as soon as possible after that, he would be with Abigail again.

His gut churned. He had no idea how she would react to his sudden appearance. He hadn't wanted to give her the chance to tell him not to come, so he'd made no contact with her after his decision to fly to Canada. There was no turning back now.

At first he'd refused to consider abandoning Ilha Verde Aventuras during the high tourist season. But when his need to see Abigail grew more and more impossible to ignore, he hesitantly broached the idea to Lina. She jumped at the chance.

"I'm tired of being stuck in the house and office most of the time," she said. "A friend of mine is looking for work. Give me a day or two to show him the ropes and then go get Abigail back." She hugged him, then smacked his cheek lightly. "Besides, the pathetic look on your face is getting on my nerves."

The rugged rocks below levelled out to tan and brown stretches of wild pastures, interspersed with thick carpets of spiky green trees. He shifted in his seat, itchy to see Abigail again. The closer he got, the tighter his skin grew.

By the time the plane was on its final approach to Prince George he was so jittery he could barely sit still. After his shoulder brushed against his seat mate, a late middle-aged man with a fringe of stark white hair and a ruddy complexion, for the third time, he felt obliged to apologize.

The man smiled. "No worries. Anxious to get back?"

"Actually, it's my first time here."

"Ah." The man nodded. "You sound like you're a long way from home."

His accent always got stronger when he was nervous. "I am. I'm Portuguese, from the Azores."

"You'll find most Canadians very friendly to new immigrants. I'm sure you'll be feeling much more comfortable in a few months." The seatbelt light dinged on and the man checked to make sure his was secured.

Santos didn't bother to correct his assumption. He had no idea what would happen after he saw Abigail. He intended to invite her back to São Miguel, but it was very likely she would not be able to simply pick up and go. She had a brother, a job. Friends and responsibilities, of which he knew nothing. He'd discussed the possibility with Lina.

"I've booked a return flight in two weeks. If I haven't convinced Abigail to come with me by then, I'll have to play it by ear. If there's even the smallest chance I might be able to change her mind, I'll probably switch the ticket for later."

She had wagged her finger in front of his face. "If you can't convince her in two weeks, it's not meant to be. Don't waste your time. Tell her you love her...and then bring her home."

A subtle change in pressure signalled their descent, and he craned his neck to see as much as he could out the small window. Pale green fields dotted with dark roofed buildings checkerboarded the landscape, and the distinctive layout of a golf course came and went. The hydraulic shriek of the landing gear cut through the ambient hum of the jet engines. A few minutes later the ground rushed up, black with new asphalt, white lines flashing, and the pilot lowered the large aircraft inch by inch. The wheels screeched sharply as they rejoined the earth.

The terminal building reminded Santos of the same facility in Ponta Delgada—long and narrow, with honey-gold wooden beams instead of concrete, but comfortingly small and accessible. The rental car counters were right next to the baggage carousels, and in a very short period of time he was manoeuvring his way out of the airport parking lot.

The wide, smoothly paved roads leading into Prince George gave Santos an amazing sense of space and freedom. Greyish-green pine forests lined the shoulders, interspersed with long, narrow driveways leading to houses with plots of land that would be the envy of most homeowners in the Azores. The highway curved down and around a large embankment and the city spread out before him, ringed by round crested hills. He crossed a double-lane bridge over a silty brown river, an impressive expanse of water glittering far below.

It had been a simple exercise to use Google Maps to work out the route from the airport to the address Abigail had provided when she'd booked her stay with Ilha Verde Aventuras. Following his carefully noted directions, he wound his way through a residential area with broad green lawns, double car garages and neatly tended gardens. He made one final turn and slowed down, reading house numbers as he inched along.

****

"I can't believe this is it."

Abigail glanced at Tobias, sitting in the passenger seat. They were on their way to take one last walk through their old home. One last check to make sure they had packed up everything. One last chance to say goodbye. Yolande would be meeting them there to take the keys once they were done.

"I know. Once we signed that contract, things move so quickly. Barely a week for all the conditions to come off." She waited for a woman pushing a stroller to cross the road, then pulled away from the stop sign. "I guess it was meant to be."

"I'm sorry about the job at the museum."

Tracy Calogheros had called yesterday to give her the bad news. Abigail sighed and gripped the steering wheel tighter. "Thanks. I really thought I had a good shot at it."

"Don't worry," Tobias said with his new, surprisingly mature, confidence. "Something else will come along. Something better. Like the house, if it's meant to be, it will be."

"And I do have some breathing room, now that the house is sold." The money would be safely squirrelled away in various sound, solid investments. She didn't want to have to touch it, though. Tobias planned on returning to the University of Northern British Columbia in the fall, and who knew what unexpected expenses might come up? Besides, she needed a job, simply for her own sanity. She was starting to go stir crazy.

She turned onto the quiet, tree-lined street, achingly familiar and yet no longer home, and pulled into the driveway, manoeuvring around a small blue car. She caught a glimpse of the driver and for a heart-stopping moment thought *Santos* before sternly controlling her imagination. For a long time she'd seen him in every dark-haired, strongly built man, only to be crushed over and over again. It was disappointing to realize she still couldn't control her daydreams.

She and Tobias climbed out of the car and headed for the front door. She'd barely taken two steps when a hoarse shout fixed her in her tracks.

"Abigail." Softer this time, still raspy, but pleading, not commanding.

She twisted slowly toward the voice, refusing to believe what her hammering heart was telling her.

Her eyes stretched open in disbelief at the man standing at the end of the driveway.

Santos.

DECISIONS

Santos vaulted out of his seat at the sight of Abigail. He vaguely noted the young man with a matching shock of white-blond hair, but couldn't tear his eyes from her, afraid even to blink.

"Abigail!" Nerves roughened his voice and he cleared his throat. He'd come seven thousand kilometres for just this moment, and now all he could do was say her name. "Abigail."

She turned, excruciatingly slowly, her eyes so wide white circled the pale blue irises. He soaked in the sight of her. Her pale hair was piled on top of her head, leaving her neck bare. She wore a lavender-coloured blouse with short sleeves and figure-hugging jeans. Her long, elegant feet were buckled into heeled sandals with purple jewels sparkling on the straps. She looked strong and vital and he exulted. She hadn't retreated back to the pale, wan woman he'd first met. She'd used that well of courage he found so arousing and claimed victory over the challenges she'd faced.

The very confidence she exuded held him prisoner at the end of the driveway. This wasn't a woman waiting for her man to come rescue her. He shifted from one foot to the other, uncertain what to do next.

She took a step toward him. His breath jammed in his lungs.

She took another step. And another. Each one quicker than the last until she was racing down the concrete. He held out his arms, ready to catch her, ready to hold her close. She stopped just out of reach. Her breath snorted indelicately in and out of her nostrils and rosy flags of colour highlighted her cheekbones.

"You." Her eyes narrowed and she lifted her chin, rearing like a snake readying to strike.

He lowered his arms warily, and took an involuntary pace back. She followed, lengthening her stride enough to reach him. She poked him viciously in the sternum.

"What are you doing here? Nothing for weeks"—she poked him again—"weeks! And then you simply show up on my doorstep?"

Maybe he should have called first.

****

Abigail revelled in the fury burning bright through her veins. Her lips twisted into a fierce grin at the shock on Santos' face. If he'd come all this way expecting her to fall weeping with relief into his arms he had another think coming.

Even though the romance of it tightened her lungs.

He opened his mouth and she attacked again. "You parade out of our hotel room like a martyred hero, without even discussing whatever the hell your problem was, and now you're here?" Righteous anger fuelled her barrage, but underlying it was the uncomfortable knowledge that if she let herself remember those bitter, arctic hours after he'd left she might drop to her knees and beg him never to leave her again.

He captured her hand as she stabbed him with her finger a third time. "Abigail, wait. Just listen, would you?"

The warmth of his touch and the plea in his voice melted the surface of her resolve. So much for convincing herself she'd heal from his betrayal, assuring herself she'd survive without him. Need shrieked through her nerves, need she didn't dare let him see. She yanked out of his grasp.

"Fine. I'm listening. What?" She crossed her arms under her breasts and glared.

"Um, Abigail?" said a hesitant voice from behind her.

She'd forgotten all about Tobias. He sidled into her line of vision, shifting his weight from foot to foot as he stood between her and Santos.

"Do you want to do this here? Or should we go into the house?" Tobias said.

Once more aware of her surroundings, she noticed curtains twitching in the kitchen window across the way. "Mrs. Sanford always was a nosey old bag," she muttered, earning a startled glance from Santos. She spun on her toes and tossed an ungracious invitation over her shoulder. "You might as well come in." Without waiting to see if either of the men followed, she stamped up the front steps. Her hand shook so badly she fumbled with the key, and her mood darkened further.

The living room greeted her sadly, naked and desolate. A discoloured patch on the wall echoed the faded memory of the last family photograph taken before her father was killed, deep circular indentations in the carpet the ghostly remains of the fussy, elaborately curved furniture her mother loved.

Tobias and Santos spoke in deep, quiet murmurs behind her but she didn't bother to listen. The lull had dampened her anger and she clasped the last shreds of it around her, a flickering, fading shield against the hunger clawing at her heart. She drifted to the white brick fireplace and fingered a small, chipped edge, evidence of an errant Frisbee Tobias had smuggled into the house.

Santos. Here. He could only have come for her.

What was she to do? What would he ask of her? She closed her eyes briefly, held her breath a moment to calm her racing blood, and turned to face him.

He stood square in the centre of the room, thumbs hooked in the pockets of his jeans, his casual stance belied by the tension in his shoulders, the twitching muscle in his jaw. Tobias leaned against the far wall, his leery gaze flashing back and forth between her and Santos. He caught her eye and nodded, once.

She gathered her courage about her. "All right, I'm listening," she repeated. She couldn't help but add, "Which is more than you did that night," and had the satisfaction of seeing him wince.

"I've had weeks to think of what to say, and now"—he waved a hand in the air—"every word is gone, vanished." He rubbed the back of his neck, scrubbed the edge of his jaw, heavy with more than a day's beard. "I guess I should start with an apology."

She eyed him stonily, refusing to give any encouragement.

"I am sorry." He met her gaze, dark eyes soft and serious. "I'm sorry I didn't stay that night. And I'm sorry you left before we could talk."

Her mouth gaped. "You're blaming me?"

"No, no." He held up both hands, palms out. "I'm saying this all wrong. That night, after I left, I went home. The next morning"—he paused, rolled his shoulders— "after I'd had some time to think, I went back to the hotel. But you were gone."

A ragged piece of her heart began knitting back together. It had eaten at her, believing he could walk away from her so easily. Knowing he'd come back, made an attempt to see her again, eased that pain.

"At first I was furious. With you for leaving, with myself for driving you away. I thought I'd be able to forget you." He paced forward cautiously. "But I couldn't."

Her body felt weighted, the pull of gravity an unbreakable force. His eyes trapped her, held her captured. She couldn't move, could barely breathe.

Step by guarded step he approached until he stood scant inches away. The muffled click of a door closing jolted her, and she realized Tobias had gone outside, leaving her and Santos alone.

His hand lifted, oh so haltingly. "I couldn't forget you, Abigail, no matter how hard I tried." He brushed a strand of hair off her cheek, tucked it behind her ear. "Everywhere I went I was confronted by memories of you." A corner of his mouth quirked. "I have always known my island is very small, but never has it felt so crowded, so claustrophobic, and yet so empty."

She swallowed, tongue desert dry, all the moisture in her mouth having migrated to the palms of her hands. "I couldn't forget you, either."

An iota of tension left his body. "For now, that is enough." He clasped her hand. She tried to tug it away, but he cradled it in both of his. "I know I shocked you, arriving so unexpectedly. I was afraid to call, afraid you would tell me not to come."

"I might have," she said bluntly.

He tightened his grip. "We have more to talk about, I

know. But we have time. I have two weeks."

She stared at him. "Two weeks? It's the middle of summer—this must be your busiest season. Can you afford to be gone so long?"

"Lina is looking after everything." His thumb rubbed her knuckles absently. "I couldn't wait any longer."

She searched his face, seeing nothing but naked honesty. "I can't believe you came all this way."

"I had to see you."

"I need some time." If he wasn't holding her hand, she might have wondered if she was only dreaming. "I need to think." To decide whether she was willing to risk her heart again.

A loud rattling at the door gave them warning only seconds before Tobias came back in, with Yolande right behind. "Yolande's here," he announced unnecessarily.

The realtor's eyes swung from Santos to Abigail and back. "I'm sorry, I'm a bit early. Should we wait outside?"

"That's fine." Abigail slipped her hands from Santos' and stepped away. "Santos was just leaving."

He hadn't taken his eyes off her for a moment. Heat and longing and loneliness burned in their depths, and she took a firm grip on her willpower.

"I'm staying at the Holiday Inn." He dug a business card out of his wallet. "My cell number is on that. Call me, when you are ready to talk." He backed away a few paces. "Please, Abigail. Please call."

He strode past Tobias and Yolande and disappeared out the door.

****

Abigail nibbled at her thumbnail and eyed her phone.

It lay on the table before her, black and blank, silent and still.

Taunting her.

Santos' business card lay next to it, a small white rectangle with green print. Gingerly she prodded it until it aligned precisely with her phone.

"Why don't you get it over with?" Tobias stepped into the kitchen and rested a hip against the counter. "You know you're going to call him. How much longer will you put it off?" The late afternoon sun glowing through the window over the sink framed his head and shoulders, created a shimmering nimbus around him.

"You need to get your hair cut."

He tossed the too long bangs out of his eyes. "That's a pretty weak attempt at distraction." He dragged out the chair opposite her and folded into it. "Call him."

"I don't know if I'm brave enough."

She'd stumbled through the meeting with Yolande, earning a few concerned glances from the kindly agent. Thank God they hadn't had anything important to discuss, and it was only a simple matter of one last check of the house and a handing over of the keys. Still trembling from the shock of Santos' arrival, she'd been more than pleased to have Tobias drive home.

Her decision seemed easy, on the surface. He had come after her, so she must mean something to him. But she'd been wrong before.

"Abigail." Tobias shook his head in mock sorrow. "He travelled across an ocean and an entire continent to see you. You aren't cruel enough to refuse to see him again. Besides, you want to."

She did. She wanted to see him again so bad her fingers cramped from the effort needed to stop herself from grabbing the phone and dialling his number.

"What does it really mean? Why *did* he come all this way?" She picked a shred of fingernail off her tongue and flicked it away.

"That's disgusting."

"I'm sorry. I can't seem to stop myself." She shoved her hands down under her thighs and hunched forward. "What does he want? He says he couldn't forget me. Maybe he just didn't give it long enough."

"You need to ask *him* these questions."

"I told him I was falling in love with him."

The sentence hung in the air, bald and blunt. Tobias sat, frozen. "What?"

"I told him I was falling in love with him. I wanted him to know what he was giving up." Quivers of remembered humiliation raced over her skin. "He still left."

"You didn't say you *did* love him, right? You only said you *might* love him?"

"What difference does it make? I used the word love and he left me standing there."

"Maybe you scared him off. Guys are weird that way."

She laughed tremulously.

"What about now?" Tobias voice was gentle. "Do you love him now?"

She rocked back and forth on her chair, the restlessness of her body matching the whirling in her mind. "I think I must. I don't think it would hurt so much if I didn't. Am I crazy? I only knew him a few days." She scrubbed her hands through her hair, grabbing hanks of it and pulling. "I don't think I could stand it, if he left me again," she blurted. "What happens if I give in, we see each other for the next few days, and then he gets on a plane and goes home? Without me." She gasped in shallow breaths, her lungs locked tight. "I need...my inhaler," she wheezed.

Tobias strode from the room, returning in an instant. She grabbed the medication and sucked in a dose.

"I haven't seen you use that since you got home."

Because she'd been using it mostly at night, when the cold, lonely dark triggered uncontrollable thoughts of Santos, and the resulting emotions cut off her breath. She inhaled tentatively and air scraped through her narrowed windpipe. The next breath was easier, the next easier yet. Her muscles relaxed and she could speak without choking. "I almost stopped using it in the Azores. It must be the stress."

Tobias crouched next to her and looked up, worry lines creasing his forehead. "Look, I know I'm just your silly little brother, but for God's sake, Abigail, grow a pair and call the man." He snatched up her phone and pressed it into her hand. "He came all this way to see you. No guy spends that kind of money, commits that kind of time, without a good reason." He wrapped her chilled fingers around the phone. "Spend some time with him, decide what you feel. Everything else will fall into place."

"I don't know if I can."

"You jumped off a damn cliff, Abigail. After that"—he puffed on the tips of his fingers, spread his hand out as if releasing fairy dust into the wind—"after that, you're brave enough to fall in love."

BEGINNING AGAIN

Santos paced the sidewalk, dodging pedestrians and short, blue lampposts. After leaving Abigail, he'd driven on automatic pilot to his hotel and checked in. But he couldn't face the thought of staring at the walls in his empty room, so he'd taken to the streets.

He patted his jeans pocket, compulsively checking for his cell phone. Yes, it was there. Silent.

Struggling for patience, he reminded himself he had left her less than two hours ago. Maybe she was still tied up with the realtor. God, he hoped that was it.

He halted at an intersection. A teenage boy in baggy shorts, an enormous basketball jersey and a knit cap over lanky bangs rolled up next to him, flipping his skateboard neatly with his toe into his hand. When the light changed, the boy jogged briskly across the street, dropped the skateboard on the opposite sidewalk and rolled away. Santos followed more sedately.

A large, white clock supported by red, iron beams was framed high above the ground at the end of the street, and for want of a better destination he headed that direction. A familiar ring tone had him stopping short, to the irritation of a woman in a business suit following him. She muttered as she dodged past, answering her own phone as she shot him a dirty look and marched on. Santos checked his phone just to be sure, then shoved it back in his pocket, his sense of defeat growing.

Why hadn't she called? If she loved him, wouldn't she have put him out of his misery by now? Oh, God, what if he'd waited too long, and she'd come to her senses and felt nothing for him? Questions tunnelled through his brain like ants.

He heard ringing again. This time he ducked into a doorway to get out of the flow of walkers before checking. His hand shook when he saw the display on the screen. The phone buzzed and beeped again, unlocking his muscles. He hurriedly answered. "Hello, Abigail."

Silence.

His grip tightened on the thin rectangle. "Abigail? Are you there?"

Nothing, and the trembling in his hands spread to his gut. Then— "We should probably talk."

He was so relieved she was finally speaking to him he didn't care that her opening remarks were less than positive. "I'd really like that. When? Where?"

Another short pause. He waited impatiently.

"There's a Tim Horton's, a coffee shop, downtown near a big plaza. Do you think you could find it?"

"Does the plaza have a red clock tower?"

"Yes."

"I can find it. When?"

"Fifteen minutes?"

"I'll be there."

She disconnected. He stared at the white face of the clock in the near distance, letting his rattled nerves settle, before stepping back onto the sidewalk and striding forward.

Time, he thought. All he needed was time to show Abigail he was serious. About her, about their life together. He would prove his love for her.

If only she gave him enough time.

****

Santos and Abigail ordered their coffees to go and found an empty bench next to the fountain. They sat down, careful inches away from each other.

Abigail fussed with the lid on her cup. The dregs of unresolved emotions swirled between them, much like the damp breeze curling off the sprays of dancing water. She opened her mouth, couldn't decide how to begin, and closed it again.

"How have you been?" Santos' voice rumbled under the bright pattering of water droplets. "You look well."

"I'm doing okay." She sipped her drink, the scent comforting and familiar. "And you?"

"Okay. I'm doing okay, too." He rested his ankle on his knee, then put both feet flat on the ground and shifted straighter on the bench. He took the lid off his cup, blew across the liquid, put the lid back on, but didn't lift it to his mouth.

He's nervous, she thought. It was so out of character she almost smiled. A few of the manic butterflies in her belly settled down. "Your mother and Lina are well?"

"Yes, they're fine. They said to say hello."

"They did?"

"Of course."

She knew she hadn't imagined Lina and Senhora Carregado's disapproval, especially during the day she'd spent with Santos at the festival. But she had enough to worry about at the moment so shrugged off the thought.

"What did you tell them?" she couldn't help asking. "About us."

She could feel him studying her profile, but she kept her eyes on the sparkling water. On the far side of the fountain, a young mother held her toddler son low enough so he could dangle his feet in the water. His giggles pealed across the plaza.

"I told them the truth," Santos said quietly. "I told them I couldn't see a future for us, so I left you."

"I see." The back of her throat burned and tears scalded her eyes. She scrabbled in her purse and dug out a pair of oversized sunglasses. Once hidden behind the dark lenses she felt brave enough to meet his gaze.

"Do you want to know what my mother said to that?"

No. "Sure."

"She said I was an idiot."

Abigail hiccupped a half-laugh, half-sob. "I don't believe you."

"Well, not in so many words. But she pinched my ear. That still gets my attention."

Her laugh was stronger this time. "So you came all this way because your mother told you to?"

His face was solemn. "No. I came all this way because she was right. I was an idiot."

This time the tears pricking her eyelids were caused by hope.

"I don't want it to end. Whatever we have between us. Not this way." He leaned his elbows on his knees and dangled the still full paper cup from his fingers. Her centre tightened, burning memories of what those hands had done rising unbidden. She lifted her gaze, only to have it focus on the back of his neck. He'd cut his hair since she'd last seen him on São Miguel and his nape was bare but for short, dark bristles. She squeezed her lips together, quelling the urge to bend forward and press a kiss on the sun-browned skin.

He glanced over his shoulder, not quite meeting her eyes. "I'm not ready to give up on us." A muscle in his jaw flexed.

"Do you know how much strength it took for me to be with you? To believe you wanted me?" She forced herself to speak calmly, disguising the constriction at the back of her throat. "And then you tossed me away, without a backward glance."

He placed his cup on the ground and swung sideways on the seat, bending one leg up onto the seat. "I suddenly realized how much I hated the thought of you leaving me. So I left first. But the only way I could justify it to myself, convince myself to go, was to say it was what was best for you."

Her fingers tightened on the paper cup dangerously. "That's what's so infuriating. You knew about my mother, about Martin. You knew the last thing I wanted was someone else making important decisions about my life, without any regard to what I wanted."

"I know."

She steamrollered on. She hadn't dreamed she'd ever get the chance to confront him about what he'd done, and now that she had started she couldn't stop. "You could have been honest with me. You could have just told me you had changed your mind, didn't want to be with me anymore. Instead of trying to sugarcoat it by saying it was for my own good."

"*Mãe de Deus,* is that what you thought?" Santos tugged carefully at the cup clenched in her hands, placed it next to his on the ground, and clasped both her hands in his. "Did you really think I was making excuses simply to get away from you?"

"What else was I supposed to think?" She tried not to revel in the sensation of his warm fingers embracing hers. "I was leaving in a few days, anyway. It's not as if we were starting a long-term relationship. But obviously you couldn't bear to be with me even for that short a time. You were just too much of gentleman to tell me the truth."

Santos' deep brown eyes snapped with strong emotion. "I told you the truth, Abigail. At least what I thought was the truth at the time." His grip on her hands tightened, almost painfully, and she wiggled her fingers. He gentled his hold, but the fire in his eyes didn't lessen. "As much as I hate to admit it, Martin made me see how little I had to offer you. How could a few days of sex compare to a lifetime of commitment?"

"There was no lifetime of commitment," she shot back. "I told you. I was never going back to Martin. I wanted to be with you." I loved you, she wanted to cry out, but didn't. "And instead of believing the woman you were with, you believed a man you'd never met, a stranger with no right to a say in my life."

"I panicked, okay? I panicked." He released her hands, almost tossing them in her lap, jumped off the bench and began to pace. "All of a sudden I was wondering—What if Martin is right? What if she really does love him and is only rebelling with me?" He stopped in front of her and stared down, hands clenched at his hips. "And I was jealous. Jealous because no matter how great it was between us, you were going home. To him."

He stalked to the edge of the fountain, ranging back and forth and muttering to himself. She studied him in worried wonder. He looked thinner than she remembered. Had her leaving upset him so much?

He strode back to the bench and dropped beside her. She sat silently, lost as to what to say next.

Jets of water shot out of the concrete, glittering rainbows forming in the bright summer sun. Swallows swooped by, diving through the spray, whistling past them in a loose squadron.

Finally, she found her voice. "Where do we go from here?"

His shoulders lowered, as if her words had uncoiled a spring inside him. "I'm here for most of two weeks. I know you're probably working, but I was hoping we could spend time together. Take things day by day."

"As it happens, I'm out of job right now. I worked with Martin, you see. It would have been much too uncomfortable to continue, so I quit."

"I'm sorry for that, too. Will you have trouble finding another position?"

"I'm being picky about where I apply. There's no hurry, especially now we've sold the house. I thought I had one lined up, but I found out yesterday I didn't get it."

"I'm sure you'll find another soon."

She appreciated the confidence, but it only confused her more. What was his goal, coming to see her? It had to be more than simply to clear the air. Was it possible he intended to ask her to return with him? But then why would he offer her hope in finding a new job?

She pushed those questions aside, willing to take things at face value for now. He wanted to spend time with her. That was enough. "What that means is that, at least for the next few days, I'm free. So I say it's time to turn the tables."

Santos gave her a puzzled look. "Turn the tables?"

"This is my town." She smiled. "This time, I get to be your tour guide."

****

The next evening, Abigail studied the clothes strewn across her bed and bit her lip. Santos was taking her to a late dinner, his only hint it would be "somewhere nice." What did that mean? Dress jeans and spiky heels? A flirty summer skirt?

She plucked her go-to black dress off the bed and held it in front of her, swishing the material from side to side, then tossed it into a crumpled heap and slid open the closet door. Surely she had something fitting to wear—not too elegant or casual, too prudish or sexy. Yellow bloomed in the dimness of her wardrobe and she slid out the sundress she'd worn on São Miguel.

She and Santos had spent the day exploring Prince George, its streets and shops, its parks and rivers. At first Abigail had felt a sense of restraint, of shyness, but soon the reversal of roles became amusing. She enjoyed being the knowledgeable one, the one that knew where to go, what to see, what to do, and Santos had given every appearance of appreciating his part as tourist.

They never did quite attain the level of contentment they'd reached during the *festa*. And even as they worked to reach an easy companionship, Abigail was aware of tension building inside her. Every casual touch and warm glance tightened a need she couldn't ignore.

Santos was waiting for her to make the first move, she was certain. It was up to her to take the next step. All she had to do was gather that courage Santos said she had and act.

She hooked the dress hanger on the hinge of the bifold

door and rustled in the closet for a pair of strappy silver sandals. The only time she'd worn them, Martin had declared them unsuitable and she'd tossed them in the depths. Now she dusted them off with a faint hint of rebellion and set them neatly by the bed.

Tobias was right. It had to mean something, that Santos was willing to come so far to see her again. He'd done so with no guarantees, only hope. All she could do now was trust it was enough to build a future on.

Rifling through her meagre selection of jewellery, she pulled out a pair of plain silver hoop earrings. Dangling from one was the delicate teacup necklace Santos had given her.

Her fingertip touched the pendant gently, setting it swaying. She'd worn it constantly after Santos had fastened it for her at Santa Barbara, and only noticed it was still round her neck after her frantic flight home. Unwilling to continue wearing it, yet unable to throw it away, she'd buried it under the costume jewellery she kept in a small box.

She untangled it from the earring and laid it on the dresser, then shrugged out of her robe and stepped into the silky yellow dress. The last two times she'd worn it Santos hadn't been able to keep his hands off her. Maybe the magic would strike again.

****

Tobias opened the apartment door to Santos' knock.

"Come on in. She's still getting ready." He turned and walked into the small living room, expecting Santos to follow without ceremony.

The younger man was overtly protective, suspiciously watchful. Santos had no problem with that—after all, he was Abigail's only family.

"Have a seat." Tobias gestured to the couch. "I don't know how long she'll be. She's been in her room for an hour. You know women. Want a beer? "

Santos hid his amusement, genuinely pleased at the man-to-man comment. Poking fun at Abigail wasn't just a branch, it was an entire limb from the olive tree. "No, thanks. I'll wait for a glass of wine at dinner."

"Mind if I have one?"

"Go right ahead."

Tobias disappeared into the narrow galley kitchen. Santos sank onto the couch as he listened to the open and close of the fridge door, the rattle of cutlery, the clink and snap of the opener.

Tobias dropped into the arm chair next to Santos and sipped from the long-neck bottle. "What are your plans?"

"Just dinner."

"Somewhere fancy?"

"I thought Fraser River House. The concierge at the hotel suggested it."

"Nice." Tobias picked at the label on the bottle. "And then what?"

"And then I'll bring her home."

"I won't be here." Tobias looked up from the partially shredded label. "I'm heading to a friend's house. He's got a new video game. I'll probably stay the night. Come back tomorrow morning."

Santos tilted his head, considered the faint flush rising under Tobias' jaw. "Are you giving me permission to spend the night with your sister?"

The flush deepened. "Look, here's the thing." He swallowed but met Santos' gaze squarely. "Before Abigail went to the Azores"—his eyes flicked to the bookshelf next to the TV where a photo of their mother rested—"she had never really done anything just for herself. She was too busy looking after me, after Mom. Even...well, you know, Martin...she just kind of drifted into that, it wasn't like she was ever really excited about it." He rose and paced to the hallway, where there was still no sign of Abigail, then returned to his seat. "She was a mess when she came back, though, and I was prepared to hate you, for hurting her so bad." He hunched his shoulders, their wide breadth not yet filled out into adulthood. "But I've seen how she looks at you. How you look at her. If you ask her to go back to the island with you, I think she'd say yes."

Santos battened down an inward leap of joy. *I think she'd say yes.* He leaned forward. "What about you? Do you really think she'd leave you?" It was hard for him to imagine having but one living relation in the entire world. His immediate family was small, with only Lina and his mother, but he was surrounded by uncles and aunts and cousins and second cousins and family friends who might as well be related. How could he ask her to leave her only family behind?

"It's time she lived her own life. If she chooses you, and I think she will"—Tobias smiled, yet Santos could see the uncertainty behind it—"I'm old enough to take care of myself."

Santos hesitated, not quite sure how to respond to this unselfish statement without sounding condescending. The click of a door and the quick snap of heels on the wood floor forestalled his answer.

"Tobias, I can't get this darn clasp." Abigail strode into the room, her arms crooked behind her head, wearing the yellow dress Santos oh-so-fondly remembered. "Can you help me—" She stopped short. "Oh, Santos. I didn't know you were here already."

His breath caught and blood rushed to his groin. He'd

promised himself he would give her romance, would go slow, would give her the chance to trust him once again. Waiting would be a near impossible task, if just the sight of her was so painful. "That's all right," he said hoarsely. "I was early. Tobias has been keeping me company."

She lowered her arms and whatever charm it was that dangled on the chain shone dully. "I'm having trouble fastening my necklace."

"Let me help." He circled behind her, breathing in the crisp, citrusy scent of her hair. Their fingers brushed as he took the ends of the chain from her and he felt her shiver. He focused desperately on the tiny loop and hook, distantly amazed to see his hands trembling. "There you go."

She turned to face him, their bodies separated by a scant inch. "Thank you." She lifted her hand to the hollow of her throat where the pendant rested. His gaze dropped to the pale, fragile skin, and now he was closer he could see the charm more clearly. Shimmering faintly as it pulsed along with the beat of her heart was a familiar porcelain teacup.

He met her eyes. Promise and passion glimmered deep in their depths. His gut clenched and air whooshed out of his lungs. When he could trust his voice again, he said quietly, "I like your dress."

"I know."

Appreciating the confidence in her demure reply, he stepped forward, closing the tiny gap between them. He brushed his hands down her bare arms and saw her eyelids flicker.

Tobias cleared his throat and Santos moved away reluctantly.

The younger man approached. "Have a good time tonight." He patted Abigail on the shoulder. "I'm heading to Justin's. I'll see you tomorrow." He shook Santos' hand. "And

I imagine I'll see you tomorrow, too."

The door closed quietly behind him.

****

Abigail turned to Santos with a puzzled frown. "Is it just me, or was he acting kind of weird?" She wondered if she should go after him, find out what was going on.

"He's fine. You, on the other hand, are much more than fine."

The hunger in his tone ruffled over her skin, raising prickles of awareness. She plucked a silky, daffodil-coloured pashmina off the back of the couch and wrapped it around her shoulders. "Are you going to tell me where we're going yet? I had a hard time deciding what to wear since you are being so secretive."

Santos stared at her from under lowered brows. "You're perfect, no matter what you wear." Colour rode high on his cheekbones and his nostrils flared.

"Oh." Primal, elemental need swelled deep inside her and she relaxed, instinctively, subtly, offering herself.

"As for Tobias...I think he left because he was embarrassed." Santos held up a foil packet between two fingers. "He palmed me a condom when he shook my hand just now."

Her mouth dropped open. "He what?"

"He told me earlier he was staying the night with his friend. He implied he was doing so to give us some privacy." Santos tucked the condom in his pocket.

"But that's...he shouldn't..." She covered her eyes with her hands. "Why would he do that?"

"He told me it was time you lived your own life. And that he thought you might choose me to be a part of that life."

292

She dropped her hands and simply stared. "Am I that obvious?"

He reached out slowly. The tip of his finger brushed the sensitive skin along her collarbone to the base of her throat. She felt him toy with the teacup charm.

"Remember the memories we made, on the beach, the day I gave this to you?"

Her heart pounded so hard against her breastbone she thought it might crack. "Yes."

"I want to make more of those memories."

Her nipples tightened and liquid warmth pooled between her thighs. "Me, too," she whispered.

Santos stood with his back to the sliding glass doors leading to the minuscule deck. Light outlined his solid shoulders, gleamed on his sooty hair, highlighted the tension in his body.

The significance of what was about to happen grew weightier with each passing second. As life changing as making love the first time had been, this would be even more resounding.

His hands cupped her chin, warm and controlling, and she shuddered. "You have no idea how many times I've had to stop myself today."

Her eyes focused on his mouth. "Stop yourself from what?"

"This." He lowered his head and drifted his lips across hers.

Lost in sensation, she didn't notice her eyelids closing. She gripped his hips, as he tasted, teased, would have stood there forever if he hadn't drawn away.

"Will you take me to your bed?" He linked a chain of kisses from the corner of her mouth to the hollow of her ear. "So I can make love to you until we forget our own names?"

She struggled to think rationally. "What about dinner?"

"I'm only hungry for you."

Desire sizzled even brighter at his words. She nodded, dazed and aroused. Arms about each other, they made their way down the hall, into her room. The shadows were deeper here, leaching colour from the daisy print duvet, the soft yellow walls.

He stood behind her, wrapped his arms about her waist and kissed her neck. She sighed with pleasure and leaned back, one arm curving over her head to bury her fingers in his thick hair. Shivers chased up and down her arms as his mouth slowly, leisurely, explored her bare shoulders, her nape. The dangling ends of the ribbons holding up the halter top of her dress grazed her spine.

His hands curved up her belly to cup her breasts and she gasped. His fingers circled her nipples, hard points under the silky material, then trailed down her ribs, up her spine. With a couple of quick tugs, he released the bow. In a smooth, satiny glide the dress puddled on the floor at her feet.

"There," he said in satisfaction. "I've finally taken that dress off you, just the way I've fantasized."

She giggled breathlessly as his hands roamed freely over her heated skin. "You've seen me naked before."

"There's something about you *in* that dress that makes me want to see you *out* of it." He turned her around and with both hands on her ass, nestled her against his groin. "You're not quite naked yet."

She didn't think the tiny scrap of lace snugging her hips counted for much, but then his mouth was on hers and there was no time to do anything but feel.

****

God, she felt good in his arms, Santos thought hazily. And she tasted even better. His tongue dove into her mouth, exploring the seductive moistness. Soft and supple, she molded and melded to his body perfectly. The nearly-not-there material covering her ass did nothing to hide the heat of her skin, and still he wanted more, wanted her bared to him, body and soul.

While they'd been apart, he'd tried to convince himself he had exaggerated the feeling of connection, of closeness he experienced with Abigail. That feeling blasted through him now, shattering his composure, his control. He revelled in it, greedily, hungrily, certain more than ever she was the one for him, that he would love no one else the way he loved her.

Her fingers worked busily at the buttons on his shirt. "Why are you always still wearing clothes when I'm already naked?" she muttered.

"Good planning on my part?" He tugged at the thin ribbon at the side of her panties. "Are you emotionally attached to these?"

She frowned. "They're new, but..."

He snapped the fragile material with a quick tug.

"Hey!"

He lifted her and the panties slithered off her legs. With a grin, he tossed her on the bed. Before she could do much more than shriek he yanked off his shirt, shucked off his pants and joined her.

He gathered her in his arms and she twined her legs with his, burrowing close. He buried his nose in her hair and breathed deeply, inhaling her scent, imagining it swirling through his body, absorbing into his cells. "*Meu amor, meu unico amor.*"

"Truly?" She raised her head from his chest.

He'd wanted to say it in his own language first. "My

love, my only love," he repeated. "Truly."

Her bottom lip trembled. "I thought I'd never hear you say that."

The faint light from the window glimmered on a tear tracing down her cheek. He brushed it away with his thumb. "It took me a while to admit it, after you left. God, I was miserable, but I couldn't let myself think about you."

She stretched herself on top of him, folded her arms and propped her chin on her hands. "Why?"

He trailed his fingers up the subtle bumps of her spine, loving every inch of her. "Because I was sure I had lost you, that I would never get you back. If I loved you, I had ruined my life. So I decided I didn't love you. It was the only way to survive."

"I wanted to get over you. Tried to stop thinking about you." Her eyes gleamed, silver in the dim light. Thanks goodness no more tears overflowed. "I couldn't. I was learning to live without you, scrambling through every day by my fingernails. Then you showed up."

"I had to see if you'd give us another chance."

"I'm so glad you did." She shifted up, her breasts flattened erotically against his chest, and kissed him.

Love added an entirely new dimension to sensation. Gone was the almost frantic need to explore all, to experience all, quickly, instantly. Instead he was free to savour, to sip, to glory in every touch, every sound, every scent.

Abigail slithered onto him, silken skin gliding from chest to groin, thigh to calf. His erection, trapped against her belly, pulsed hot and hard and he groaned. As much as he longed to sink into her body, feel her warm wetness wrap around him, he wanted even more to give her pleasure, send her spinning into stunning satisfaction.

He slid down, underneath her body as she straddled him. Her breasts hung soft and full above him, and he cradled them in his hands, bringing the rigid tips together so he could suckle them.

Abigail arched her back, thrusting toward his mouth. Tension wracked her body, her arms, braced over his head, trembled. Soft, mewling gasps seemed torn from deep within her and he set himself to drive her even higher.

She rocked on her hands and knees as he tortured her breasts, then collapsed onto him, her ass on his thighs, the hot, wet damp between her legs against his balls. His hips bucked and he flipped her over so he lay between her legs, propped on his elbows over her.

Her chest heaved and she gazed at him through lids weighted with passion. One hand fluttered through his hair, the other curved against his jaw. "God, I love you."

"And I love you."

"I want you inside me."

He shuddered at the rawness of her command. "But there's so much more..."

"Later." She cut him off. "I want you inside me, now." She hooked her ankles behind his knees and lifted her hips.

His cock strained at her entrance, eager for the warmth, the wetness, the welcome. "Wait." He leaned over the side of the bed and scrambled for the condom in his jeans. *Thank you, Tobias.*

Determined not to rush, wanting to cherish every instant, he eased into her. She wriggled, adjusting the angle, and he breathed harshly through his nose, clenched his fists.

He stared down at her. A small frown creased between her eyes, smoothed out as he sheathed himself completely. Her lips curved, softly, sexily. "You feel so good," she purred.

He rocked his hips and she moved with him. Hands glided, caressed, explored, lips discovered, searched, stroked. Pleasure grew beyond the boundaries either had known before, and each found their reward in the other's roaring release.

TAKEOFF

Abigail put down the phone and smiled at Tobias. "One left," she said.

"What do I always say? If it's meant to be, it's meant to be."

She moved toward him as he stood by the sliding glass doors in the apartment. Although he had been taller than her for years, it could still surprise her when she had to tilt her head back to look into his face. "Are you okay with this?"

He nodded. "You need to do it."

"I know. I just worry—"

"Don't. Don't worry about me. I'll be fine."

"It's a habit. But I'll try not to let it get in your way." She hugged him, felt his arms come around and squeeze her back. Despite the strength in his hold, the breadth of his shoulders, there was still something unformed, undeveloped about him. He was so young, caught between boy and man. How could she leave him to make that transition alone?

She opened her mouth to second guess her decision, then closed it again. Tobias had helped her make it, knew what it meant for both of them. She had to respect his opinions, his choices, as he respected hers.

A knock sounded at the door. She tightened her hold briefly then let him go. "I love you, little brother."

"Love you, too."

She opened the door and her face broke out in a smile. Santos stood, a sheepish grin on his face, clutching a colourful bouquet of mixed flowers.

He held them out. "For you."

She caressed the bright orange petal of a Gerbera daisy. "Thank you." She stepped back and gestured him in.

Tobias strolled to the door, hands tucked into the back pockets of his jeans. "Hey, Santos."

"Hello."

"See you later." He winked at Abigail and swung into the hall, whistling.

Santos embraced her before the door closed. His arms encircled her waist and he kissed her soundly. "There," he said in satisfaction. "Now the day can begin."

The searing heat in his eyes made her dizzy. "I missed you last night."

"You should have stayed with me, at the hotel."

She had spent the night before last there, too self-conscious to sleep with Santos while Tobias was in the apartment. "I needed to spend some time with Tobias."

"I understand. I don't have to like it, but I understand." He tugged her to the couch and pulled her onto his lap.

"I should put these in water." She waggled the bouquet.

He took it from her and dropped it on the coffee table. "In a minute. For now, I want to hold you." He gave a masculine grumble of approval when she relaxed into his hold, tucking her head under his chin.

He was constantly surprising her with such statements. She supposed she shouldn't be—he approached life with such joy, such abandon, she should have realized he would do the same once he admitted to being in love.

She simply hadn't dared hope it would be with her.

His heart beat, steady and sure, under her cheek as she curled her legs up onto the couch and lounged against him. "These have been the most amazing few days," he said as he stroked her hair.

"For me, too." She rested her hand on his chest and fiddled with the collar of his shirt.

"It's probably way too early to mention this, but..." His voice trailed away.

"But what?"

"When I go back to the Azores, I don't want to go alone."

A thrill of relief shuddered through her. And still she waited.

"I want you to come with me," he said.

She shifted to straddle him on the soft cushions, knees beside his hips, hands resting on his shoulders.

"Santos—"

His palm on her lips stopped her. "Wait. Let me say something first." She nodded and his hand slid from her mouth, down her arm to clasp her waist. "These last few days with you...I don't know how to describe them. You fill a place in my life I didn't even know was empty. Before you, I was content just to let things be. I accepted friendship, companionship—"

"Sex." She couldn't help butting in.

"—and sex," he agreed amiably. "I accepted them as they came, but I didn't work for them. You made me work for it, work for *you*."

"I'm sorry."

He scowled. "Stop interrupting. And don't you dare be sorry. You deserve someone who respects you, who appreciates you." He tapped the tip of her nose. "Who loves every part of you. Like I do. Like I will."

****

Her eyes, hydrangea blue, regarded him steadily. She cupped his jaw with cool hands and her thumb rubbed his bottom lip. "You're right. I do deserve you," she said confidently. "And you deserve me."

He could barely remember the hesitant, shy woman he'd first met. In her place was an Abigail who aroused his pride with her fearlessness, his love with her spirit. He turned his head to kiss her palm. "I have a question." He blew out an unsteady breath. "Do you remember what I asked you, just before we went paragliding?"

Her brows drew together. "I was too freaking petrified to remember much until after we were in the air."

He grinned. "I suppose so. But you didn't let that stop you, did you? I asked you if you were ready to jump of a cliff with me."

"I must have said yes."

"Will you say yes if I ask you again?" His heart thumped wickedly, erratically. He could only hope it wouldn't stop.

She looked at him warily, then scanned the room. "I don't see a cliff, Santos."

"We're standing on the edge of one. You and I. If you step back, I leave as planned. We try and keep this, what this is between us, going long distance." Sweat sprang up on his palms. He grasped her hips, snug in well-fitting jeans. "I love you enough to try to make it work that way, but it will be tough. I know it."

"And if I step forward?" she asked softly.

"You come with me." He spoke in a rush, determined to

block her objections before she could utter them. "Tobias and I talked. He's an adult, ready to be on his own. You haven't found a new job yet—I know, I know, you haven't been looking since I got here, but maybe that's because you're meant to come with me. Come back to São Miguel."

"Couldn't you stay?" A corner of her mouth trembled.

"I can't, not right now," he said regretfully. "I have commitments, obligations, to the business, to Lina, my mother. But if you can't go, if you can't leave Tobias, I'll make arrangements to come back. I don't know how long that will take, what exactly I will do, but—"

Her lips cut him off.

He sank into her, her sweetness, her spice. Desire sprang up at the touch of her tongue, the caress of her mouth. The edge of panic dulled, softened.

She raised her head, smiled brilliantly. "I bought a ticket this morning."

He stared at her, dazed. "You bought...what?"

"It was meant to be. There were seats left on all your flights, from Prince George to Vancouver to Toronto to Ponta Delgada. Every step of the way."

Hope ballooned in his chest. "You're coming to São Miguel?"

Her eyes glinted mischievously. "I haven't booked anywhere to stay. I'm hoping you'll have a suggestion for me."

He felt as if she'd smacked him with a club.

"You're coming back with me? You had it all planned, even before I asked?"

"It was my decision to leave. I thought it should be my decision whether to go back."

He couldn't move. Hope and joy and satisfaction froze him in place.

A hint of dismay flickered across Abigail's face. "You're happy about it, aren't you?"

He answered with action. With a quick flip he laid her flat on the couch and covered her body with his. He kissed her with a determination meant to sear any uncertainty from her mind, to inflame her with love and lust and longing. For him. Only for him.

"You're coming back with me." It was a statement this time. He nipped kisses down her neck to the swell of her breasts. "You've already bought a ticket."

"This time I didn't need any help jumping off the cliff." Her voice shook and he kissed her again.

He'd never imagined feeling this way. To be desired, to be wanted, by a woman such as Abigail...he promised himself he would never forget the wonder of this moment. Blood thundered in his ears as his mouth continued to roam.

"Are you ready for such a change?" he said. "Ready to leave everything you know behind?" He propped himself on one elbow and brushed his knuckles against her cheek.

"We only get one chance to live." She threaded her fingers through his hair, a soft smile on her lips. "My mother missed out on so much because of the choices she'd made. I don't want to look back at the end of my life and wish I'd taken more risks, dared more adventures. I have no life but this one. I want to share it with you. Wherever it takes me."

"Wherever it takes *us*," Santos stated. "Not your life and my life. It's our life. One life. Together."

LANDING

Abigail paced the concrete floor, her flip-flops snapping against her heels. "Hasn't the flight landed yet? Wasn't it supposed to be here by now?"

Santos sprawled lazily, arms stretched along the back of the wooden bench, and smiled up at her. "You just checked the announcement board for the fifth time. It says the flight is on schedule. You'll have to be patient a bit longer."

"I haven't seen Tobias for months." She caught herself nibbling on her fingernail and shoved her hands into the pockets of her skirt. "I guess I'm a bit anxious."

"You don't say."

She pulled a face at Santos' dry reply, but settled next to him on the bench, determined to relax. He draped an arm over her back and she tucked her cheek against his shoulder.

It felt so right, to be here, on São Miguel, with Santos. When they'd left Prince George together, she'd girded herself for difficulties and challenges. And while it hadn't been completely smooth sailing, the waters have never gotten rough enough to make her wish she'd decided differently.

She'd spent the first few days in a guest room at Quinta Carregado, despite Santos' offer to share his bed. He'd laughed at her self-consciousness, and she hadn't been strong enough to turn him away when he appeared at her door in the soft dark, but it hadn't felt right to stay with him in his mother's house. Shortly after, one of the many Carregados offered her a house to rent within walking distance of the farm. It was a tiny space, with a door that opened directly onto the street, a bedroom with a single, narrow window, and a kitchen/dining room/living area at the back overlooking a miniscule garden. It was cool and dim and felt like home from the moment she stepped in.

At first Santos made a show of staying at the farm with Lina and his mother, but it wasn't long before he was spending more time with Abigail than at home. Neither Lina nor Senhora Carregado seemed to mind, and Abigail soon recovered from the awkwardness she first felt.

Santos returned to his duties with Ilha Verde Aventuras, much to the dismay of Lina, who bemoaned the fact she'd be stuck with office work once again. Abigail had diffidently suggested she try her hand at the business's books, which had earned Lina's slightly reserved gratitude. With the time she now had available, Lina was able to offer different excursions to their guests. Bookings had been solid throughout the fall, and while business had dropped off now the rainy months of winter were here, the spring and summer ahead promised to be more successful than ever.

Working for Ilha Verde Aventuras took little of Abigail's time, but word soon spread that her accounting services were available. Santos' cousin who owned the restaurant hired her first, and since then a steady stream of work had come her way. It gave her a giddy sense of freedom and adventure to be an independent accountant. When she looked back on her days as part of a large firm, she could barely recognize the woman she'd been.

Passengers started streaming out of the doors leading from the baggage area and Abigail jerked upright. "It's here. He's here." She jumped up, grabbed Santos by the hand and pulled him off the bench, dragging him toward the flow of people.

She and Tobias had kept in touch with a regular use of Skype. She missed him on a daily basis, but was proud of how he was handling life on his own. When she'd hesitantly suggested he come and visit during his university's Christmas break, her heart had swelled at his exuberant response.

"Of course I'll come." His grin stretched from ear to ear. "And maybe you'll take me paragliding?"

Abigail still couldn't believe she'd not only gone paragliding again, but that she'd become a certified tandem pilot. When she had time away from her accounting business, she helped Santos and Lina with excursions, proudly introducing her adopted land to new crops of tourists.

Standing now in the stream of travellers, she strained up on tiptoe, searching for a familiar head of white-blond hair. "There!" She released her grip on Santos' hand and sped away, dodging through the crowd.

****

Santos watched as Abigail threw herself into Tobias's arms. He held her tight, rocking back and forth with her, both of them laughing like crazy people.

He was thrilled she was finally getting the chance to see her brother again. Thrilled she was so happy to be with her family.

But even more thrilled about how perfectly she was fitting in with *his* family.

He leaned his shoulder against a pillar and watched the

307

reunion with a smile. Despite his casual teasing, his relaxed movements, his chest was tight with nerves. His hand dipped into the pocket in his trousers and touched the small box, reassured by its presence.

Abigail and Tobias finally approached, Abigail clutching her brother's arm and only taking her gaze off his face for brief moments. Santos straightened and reached out a hand to shake. "Good to see you again."

"And you." Tobias studied his face, head tilted to one side, then nodded briefly. "Are you ready?"

Santos' shoulders relaxed slightly. "As I'll ever be."

"Well, then..." Tobias lifted a chin in Abigail's direction.

Her head swivelled between them, her expression bemused. "Ready for what? What are you two talking about?"

Santos took a deep breath and dropped to one knee.

Abigail froze, her eyes rounding, her mouth opening in an "O".

"I wanted to do this here, where we first saw each other." Santos swallowed, his tongue and throat dry but his heart beating steady and sure. "When I saw you that day, I had no idea how you would change my life. What joy you would bring to it.." He took Abigail's unresisting hand in his. He wasn't sure if the tremor he sensed was hers or his, but it didn't matter. They were as close as two people could be. Yet he wanted, needed, to bind her even her tighter. With his free hand he fished the jewellers' box out of his pocket and presented it to her. "I can't imagine my life without you, Abigail. Will you marry me?"

Her mouth opened and closed soundlessly, and a flush spread up her neck to her cheeks. Her eyes darted toward Tobias, who stood nearby with a proud smile. "Did you know about this?" she managed to squeak.

He nodded. "Santos and I talked."

The floor beneath Santos' knee was increasingly uncomfortable, but not nearly as painful as the tension pulsing through him.

"Answer the man," Tobias told his sister. "Or are you making him wait on purpose?"

****

A small crowd gathered around them, buzzing with anticipation and interest, but Abigail heard nothing, saw nothing, but Santos. Her hand tightened convulsively, twisting round to grip his firmly. Ignoring the ring box, she reached out with her free hand and caressed his cheek.

She wanted the next moment to be perfect, to be exactly right. She wanted to say all that was in her heart, tell him how, if she had changed his life, he had saved hers. How she had been heading for a life of boredom and misery, and he had shown her the truth about herself, had helped her discover a well of courage, an appetite for adventure, that she had only dreamed existed within her.

His eyes darkened as he waited, a small muscle twitching the corner of his mouth. She smiled, putting all her love into it, and saw the tension ease from his face, heard the air whoosh softly from his lungs. He smiled back at her, sexy and sure, and her heart thudded.

In the end there was only one word she needed to say. Only one word that was necessary to give them both the life they deserved. She said it, loud and firm, so the whole crowd would hear, so Tobias would know she had no doubts.

"*Sim.*"

Thank You!

Thanks for reading *No Life But This*. I hope you enjoyed it!

Reviews are a great way to help other readers learn about new authors. I encourage you to publish your honest review, positive or negative.

If you would like to know when my next book is available, sign up for my newsletter at www.brendamargriet.com. Just for joining, you'll receive a free copy of my short story, *The Life She Had Before*. It's a great way to keep up with new releases, promotions and contests. Or, like my Facebook page at www.facebook.com/BrendaMargriet.

Also by Brenda Margriet

Mountain Fire

A mountaintop mystery leads two conservationists to dangerous obsessions and violent passions. Natural resources student June Brandt climbs Longworth Mountain for some alone time. But when Conservation Officer Alex Weaver arrives to look into the death of a grizzly bear, June is caught up in the investigation--and fascinated by Alex. Alex is attracted by June's competence and coolness under fire-- as well as her lithe body and honey-blonde hair. Although their mutual interest in protecting the natural wonders of the area brings them together, they soon realize they view love from very different angles. He offers passion and pleasure, but June wants more. When one of Alex's colleagues is murdered, June and Alex must work together to find the poacher before other lives are lost. And Alex must look deep inside to discover if he can give June what she deserves.

Chef d'Amour

All Jemma Hedge wants to do is care for her ailing grandmother, and a job behind-the-scenes on the reality show Reservations for Two is the perfect opportunity to earn the needed money. There's one rule—no fraternizing with the cast. Easy enough, until she runs into the show's sexy bachelor, Paul Almeida, the smoldering restaurateur she's already had the displeasure of meeting. Paul risked more than money when he opened his dream restaurant. To give his fantasy a fighting chance, he accepts the role of Chef d'Amour on Reservations for Two. Flirting with the women vying for his heart should keep him too busy to worry about overstepping boundaries with the crew, until he spots Jemma. The ingredients for love are at hand. Can Jemma and Paul create the perfect recipe?

When Time Falls Still

Professor Charlotte Girardet is focused on one thing – securing tenure at a large, prestigious university. Her career is firmly on track, but her life is complicated by her attraction to rough and rugged security guard Justice Cooper. It isn't only Charlotte's heart in danger, however. Tensions blaze on campus after several students are viciously attacked. Struggling to balance her ambitions and her growing passion, Charlotte takes a leap of faith, and trusts Justice with her deepest secret. But when the assailant's attacks escalate to kidnapping, will Charlotte have the chance to decide between her long-held dreams or a new life with Justice?

The Life She Had Before

A short story – a woman is torn between the bitterness of revenge and the sweetness of a second chance.

About the Author

Brenda Margriet writes contemporary romances with heroes you'd meet at the grocery store. And by that she means real-life men – sexy, smart and looking for the love of their life. Her heroines are bold, savvy and determined to accept nothing less than the man they deserve. A voracious reader since she was old enough to hold a book, Brenda's idea of the perfect holiday involves a comfortable chair near the water (ocean, lake or pool will do), a glass of wine, and a full-loaded e-reader. She lives in Northern British Columbia with her husband, various finny and furry pets and has three grown children. Discover more about Brenda and her books at www.brendamargriet.com.